Jewish Latin America

Ilan Stavans, series editor

LOSERS AND KEEPERS

IN ARGENTINA

LOSERS *and*
KEEPERS *in*
ARGENTINA

NINA BARRAGAN

INTRODUCTION BY ILAN STAVANS

University of New Mexico Press, Albuquerque

© 2001 by the University of New Mexico Press
All rights reserved.

First edition

Library of Congress Cataloging-in-Publication Data
Losers and keepers in Argentina / Nina Barragan ; introduction
by Ilan Stavans — 1st ed.
    p. cm. — (Jewish Latin America)
Includes bibliographical references (p.).
    ISBN 0-8263-2222-0
  1. Moisés Ville (Argentina)—Fiction. 2. Jews, East
European—Fiction. 3. Jews—Argentina—Fiction.
4. Ethnic relations—Fiction. 5. Jewish women—Fiction.
6. Immigrants—Fiction. I. Title. II. Series.
    PS3552.A73189 L67 2001
    813'.54—dc21

00-011597

OTHER TITLES AVAILABLE IN THE UNIVERSITY OF NEW MEXICO PRESS
JEWISH LATIN AMERICA SERIES:

The Jewish Gauchos of the Pampas by Alberto Gerchunoff

Cláper: A Novel by Alicia Freilich

The Book of Memories by Ana María Shua

The Prophet and Other Stories by Samuel Rawet

The Fragmented Life of Don Jacobo Lerner by Isaac Goldemberg

Passion, Memory, and Identity: Twentieth-Century Latin American
    Jewish Women Writers, edited by Marjorie Agosín

King David's Harp: Autobiographical Essays by Jewish Latin American
    Writers, edited by Stephen A. Sadow

The Collected Stories of Moacyr Scliar

Sun Inventions and Perfumes of Carthage by Teresa Porzecanski

To Alan,
for his support and enthusiasm,
and for pointing out the way.
To my Argentine family,
for watching over my journey.
And to my children,
for their reassuring presence.

CONTENTS

Introduction

Ilan Stavans

Imagine a history of the Jewish people made up of chapters devoted not to individuals but to the cities they have lived in: Ur, Nineveh, Babylon, Jerusalem, Athens, Rome, Toledo, Amsterdam, Warsaw, Odessa, Berlin, New York, Buenos Aires, Johannesburg, Tel-Aviv . . . Visualize also briefer chapters of that history on utopian communes built solely by or for Jews: the Israeli kibbutz, for instance, and Birobidjan, near Siberia, envisioned by Josef Stalin as an infamous "homeland" for Soviet Jews; and Moisés Ville too, a *colonia* in Argentina sponsored by the philanthropist Baron Maurice de Hirsch in response to the Russian pogroms. Chinese sage Yi-Fu Chen once stated that human architecture is a diagram that mimics God's geometry; and Saint Augustine envisioned his *Civitas Dei* as "peaceful and in perfect equilibrium." Most urban centers have no serenity, though. Their longevity results from the surplus of energy they emanate, and Jews are a primordial factor in that emanation.

Unquestionably the lesser-known name in the not-quite-arbitrary list I've composed is Moisés Ville; therein, I trust, is the primary *raison d'être* of Nina Barragan's poignant book of fiction, here in print for the first time in any language. In it she records, in epic fashion, the rise, expansion, and decline of the *colonia* throughout the twentieth century. Moisés Ville was one of seventeen municipalities, part shtetl and part cooperative, built on the pampas by the J.C.A., an acronym for the British joint stock company, the Jewish Colonization Association. Thousands of dollars were donated to the enterprise by de Hirsch to buy real estate valued cheaply by the natives because of its desert climate. These municipalities campaigned to attract some 3.25 million poor Yiddish-speaking dwellers from the so-called Pale of Settlements, a territory in Central and Eastern Europe that encompassed Poland, Lithuania, and parts of Bessarabia and the Ukraine. The colonization plan became somewhat popular, at one point even competing with the Zionist proposal to make Uganda, on the African continent, the site for an emergent Jewish state. But it never became remotely as successful as it was hoped. In its peak, the region never attracted more than 35,000 immigrants, in large part because of the ambivalence of the Argentine government toward the project but also as a result of the poor agricultural conditions of the land.

Moisés Ville itself was founded in 1891 on 118,292 hectares in the Santa Fe province. (The Argentine province with the most *colonias* was Entre Ríos.) Each newcomer was awarded a lot with a house that included two rooms and a kitchen, a well, a wagon, plow, harrow, harness, and other tools, and a number of horses, cows, poultry, and fowl. The place was unique in several ways: for one, it was the first agricultural *colonia* of its kind, fashioned as a semiautonomous economic nucleus and half-heartedly endorsed by the government and the non-Jewish establishment to "civilize" long stretches of unpopulated land. (An intellectual and diplomat like Domingo F.

Sarmiento, in *Facundo: or, Civilization and Barbarism*, laid out the rationale to "make the national more cosmopolitan," that is, more European, by erasing the gaucho as a savage factor.)* Although Moisés Ville was founded even before de Hirsch got involved in the enterprise, he felt attached to it. Its name—in Hebrew, Kiryiat Moshe—conjures up the figure of Moses, the leader who took the Jews of out Egypt and into freedom. No other settlement had a biblical name with a French suffix, which explains de Hirsch's affection for Moisés Ville. (Another *colonia*, this one in the Buenos Aires province, was called Lucienville, after a child of his.) Like the rest of the municipalities, from Monte Fiore and Avigdor to San Antonio and El Escavel, it had its own synagogue, library, farm, dairy factory, as well as a general store, a school, a cultural building, and, obviously, a cemetery. Alberto Gerchunoff (1884–1950), the much-admired author of *The Jewish Gauchos of the Pampas*, first lived in it with his family, and in its cemetery Gerchunoff's father, killed by a drunken gaucho, lies buried. Noé Cociovitch (1862–1936), one of its many homesteaders and the informal memoirist of Moisés Ville, describes, in a book published posthumously, the way in which the environment reshaped people's lives: they took up a new diet, they found a love for the Argentine earth and the Gentiles in the surrounding areas, and Yiddish slowly began to give room to a passionate Spanish, infused with a pathos that is still alive in the lyrics of tangos and *vidalitas*.

Barragan, born in Argentina, pays tribute to Gerchunoff and Cociovitch, and beyond them, to the many *colonos* from Moisés Ville and elsewhere, such as Baruj Bendersky, Benedicto Caplán, Martín Grinstein, Samuel Eichelbaum, and Lázaro Liancho, by recounting the daily routines, the dreams and nightmares of the

* See my introduction to *Facundo*, translated by Mary Peabody Mann (Penguin Classics, 1998).

Jewish settlers. During her youth, she heard nostalgic stories about Gerchunoff and the Jewish gauchos. In return, she has drafted an unofficial popular and intellectual chronicle of the colony, infused with pathos and conviction. Rifke Schulman, the colorful and magnetic protagonist, a model immigrant, serves as Dante's Virgil in that her journey allows the reader to visit the various chambers of Moisés Ville, from hell to purgatory and onwards to heaven. With her we traverse the chessboard of financiers, thieves, pimps, idealists, wives, and Talmudic scholars that intermingled on the street. And through her eyes we witness the major upheavals of the time: the labor movement, the white slave trade, anti-Semitism, the Depression, and shortly before it, the infamous *Semana Trágica*, to this day the only full-fledged pogrom in the Americas.

On second thought, to describe Rifke Schulman as the book's protagonist might be a mistake. It is true that her journal entries are a compass, even though, interspersed, the reader comes across heartbreaking tales of common folk at the dusk of the century who attempt to reconsider Moisés Ville through the veils of memory. They are the grandchildren of the original colonists. Their assimilation to Argentine society serves as a barometer to measure the success and drawbacks of the repopulation plan. But only when the reader reaches the end of the narrative, as the smoke of a bloody and confused era begins to dissipate, does the authentic protagonist of the volume emerge: the *colonia* itself in the span of a hundred years of aplomb. At that point, as the tapestry is appreciated in full, the author's Balzacian talents come to the fore. Destiny, conceived as an inscrutable machine that moves ahead without mercy, plays a major role. It twists and turns, and, while it does, it swallows everything that appears on its path. Still, Barragan's characters retain a sense of pride and self-awareness that makes them believe they are free to choose. Argentina since independence has stumbled one too many times on its road to freedom and democracy. Baron de

Hirsch's first and favorite cooperative in the pampas, this account proves, is the perfect case study to investigate the treacherous patterns of that road. Today it is but a pale shadow of what it once was, in its heyday. A handful of Jewish families still live there, but most have migrated to the metropolis. In 1991 the *colonia* celebrated its centennial with major festivities. It paraded itself as a museum of sorts; unfortunately, its resources are limited and thus, it attracts few tourists.

Leon Edel once brilliantly announced that, should Dublin suddenly disappear from the face of the earth, it would be possible to reconstruct it with Joyce's *Ulysses*. Something similar might be said of Charles Dickens's London, Carlos Fuentes's Ciudad de Mexico, and Salman Rushdie's New Delhi. More modestly but with equal conviction, Barragan pays homage to Moisés Ville, and her homage becomes a road map by which to navigate the place in the past. If and when a history of the Jewish people scrutinized through their urban habitats is composed, her magical evocation of a doomed *colonia* shall be indispensable.

LOSERS AND KEEPERS

IN ARGENTINA

THE RIFKE CHRONICLES

THE RIFKE CHRONICLES are excerpts from Rifke Schulman's journals. Written in Yiddish and Spanish, and totaling nearly fifty volumes, they were found among her possessions in Moisés Ville, Argentina, at the time of her death. She died November 30, 1947, at the age of seventy-seven. She left no heirs and she was the last of her family line. Rifke, first child to Mendel and Divora Schulman, was born November 15, 1871, in the shtetl of the village of Tomaschpol, near Kamenets Podolsk, capital of the province of Podolia, in the Ukraine. The midwife who presided over the late-night birth declared the left leg slightly shorter than the right. Despite the deformity, Rifke was pronounced in excellent health, and indeed, a beautiful baby.

After conducting his own candlelight inspection, carefully measuring his daughter's tiny, wrinkled legs, a worried Mendel Schulman solemnly agreed with the midwife. On that night, Mendel resolved to help his child become strong. Such a handicap could surely become a continual source of grief, he realized. His wife, on the other hand, was neither serious, nor worried. Always singing, always cheerful, Divora did not consider the accident of birth a defect, but rather a positive omen, a sign that her Rifke was destined for important work.

There were many photographs among Rifke Schulman's belongings, but only one of the young Rifke, taken at age eighteen, by the well-known photographer Michal Greim. The cardboard mat is a steel gray color, the studio emblem is stamped in gold just below the oval image. On the back, in Rifke's handwriting, "Kamenets Podolsk, July 1889"—only months before her departure from Russia—as well as a note about the horrible heat wave, and the long ride from Tomaschpol, in Papa's cart. Young Rifke, with abundant black hair and a fair complexion, poses before a heavy velvet curtain. A creamy fur rug stretches across the bottom of the photograph. Rifke's left knee is bent, her foot playfully raised on a tapestry cushion, enabling her attractive, tall frame to appear erect and flawless. The hands rest on a white plaster pedestal beside her. The torso is turned slightly toward the pedestal, but the dark eyes, soulful and inquisitive, confront the camera. Despite the sweltering heat that surely permeated the Greim studio, no sign of perspiration glistens on Rifke's forehead, no hint of irritation, except perhaps, the fugitive smile. The yoke of her white linen blouse, worked with fine tucks and lace, is fitted and neat at the neck. Her skirt is simple and black. A stylish portrait, according to the conventions of the day. Yet Michal Greim reached beyond formality—studio props and clothes—beyond the physical imperfections, the lively, restless beauty of youth, inward, to that place next to the soul. On that hot July day, the camera's lens captured and recorded a sense of self and peace and passion. Fortitude and tenacity. Empathy and humor. A force to be reckoned with.

A final historical note: The concept of restricting Russian Jews to specific geographic locations began under the reign of Catherine the Great (1762–96). By Rifke Schulman's lifetime, Jews were obligated, by law, to reside in what became known as the Pale of Jewish settlement. This area included parts of Poland, Lithuania, western Ukraine, and Bessarabia. Rifke was among a group of Russian Jews who chose to leave czarist Russia, with its virulent anti-Semitism and violent pogroms. Taking their chances and hopes in hand, they journeyed to the New World, much like those who went with Columbus, four hundred years before.

October 8, 1889
Palacios, Santa Fe, Argentina

Today I begin my journal. I have not taken up my pen before because I have not wanted to write of the things that are happening to us. I can no longer wait. Today I helped bury three-year-old Sheine Gruberman. I had to watch as her poor mother was overcome with grief, as her father attempted to be brave. It made me think longingly of my own parents, and so today I begin.

My name is Rifke Schulman and I am eighteen. When I departed from Podolia, my Papa gave me the little money he could spare, and this small book, so that I might keep a journal in my new land. Papa taught me to read and write. It was two and a half months ago that I left my family, my Tomaschpol, but it already feels like years. I miss my parents, my sisters and brother.

We have been here at the Palacios train station for over a month, and fifty-five children have died since we got here. I think Sheine also died of malnutrition. What else would it be? Like the other children, Sheine was buried in a kerosene can, until the day we have our synagogue, our consecrated ground. We have no cemetery, for we have no land, we have no homes. The Grubermans grieve for their dead child. But what of the live ones? How will they feed them?

October 11

Nothing has changed, we are trying to survive. Some families have left for the nearby village of Manigotes, joining a few of our people who arrived in these parts the year before us. It seems they too came from Russia, hoping to establish themselves on the land. Others from our group have returned to Buenos Aires, thoroughly disillusioned by our circumstances here. On the steamer, I became friendly with

Leib and Esther Yosem and their five young children. They are wonderful people, and not having a family of my own, I helped look after the youngsters. Esther is a large, good-natured woman, with an incredible store of optimism. Her youngest—a sickly baby we all fear for—rides Esther's hip as she goes about her chores, often singing, despite our calamities. They have been very kind to me, insisting I travel and live with them. For the moment I am.

Those of us remaining have taken shelter in abandoned railway cars. Every morning I see the children lining up along the track, waiting for the Santa Fe Express, on its way to a place called Tucumán. The waiters from the dining car throw out crusts of bread and scraps of food. They are prepared, they know of us. People know, but no one seems to care.

I am grateful that my parents are far away from this godforsaken place. "Go," Papa said. "There is nothing here for you. Go to America, to this place they call *The Argentine*. You'll write to us, you'll let us know how it goes. Maybe we'll send your brother and sisters, maybe we'll even come ourselves." Papa, if you only knew.

Not a day goes by that I don't worry about my family, for I feel certain the pogroms must still be happening.

October 13

We are still here. Late last night, we lost the baby. Esther is inconsolable; I cannot help her. We have landed here in this new world, this new life, but I feel useless and defeated before we've even begun.

Angry and frustrated, this afternoon I walked away from our encampment toward the fields. The land is flat and open, but they say it's fertile. They call this the pampas. This is the season of wind and rain, terrible storms that sweep through this desolation with tremendous force. We have witnessed two of them already. I sat on some stones and stared at the landscape of scrub and tough grass, and I thought about how Leib has been saying that Italian immigrants have farmed this land for years, that they've made towns. He says if they can do it, we can do it. I don't know. I'm beginning to lose heart. What will become of us? More children die every day. We cannot go on much longer.

All day Esther has been crying, saying she wants to return to Podolia and her mother. The children have never witnessed such goings-on. They are terrified. Leib reprimands her, vowing they will never leave. He says that like the bones of their baby, they are here to stay. They will take their land, they will work it.

October 15

Esther is a little better. She busies herself with work, hoping not to think. I try not to think as well. But the truth is, I have great difficulty accepting that we were intended for so much grief, so many wrongdoings, and that now, our bad fortune doesn't seem to end. The land contracts we brought with us from Russia were worthless. The arrangements had been made in Paris, through a Mr. Frank, an agent who represented Argentine immigration and colonization. There is talk that this Mr. Frank, who maneuvered our transactions, was a thief. After all the arrangements, it seems we did not own land in that place called La Plata. It was a hoax, and our deeds amounted to nothing but useless paper. There were all kinds of excuses about how real estate had risen in the months since the negotiations. In the end, no one knew what to do with us, a boatload of landless Jews. How strange we must have looked to them! The immigration officer who came aboard, clearly disgusted with the lot of us, was loath to let us off the boat. Finally, after days of waiting, they put us into that Hotel for Immigrants. A terrible place, filthy and crowded. The only good thing that happened there was Julio Sandler's birth. Imagine, the first son of Russian immigrants born on this new soil!

During the time we waited in the hotel, there were endless meetings and discussions. The government wanted to send us to a place called El Chaco. But the small Jewish community of Buenos Aires suggested we not go there. Their leader, Rabbi Henry Joseph, and several representatives visited with us at the hotel. It was too isolated, they advised, the climate too harsh. Finally it was arranged we would come here, where Dr. Pedro Palacios, the landowner, would have land, shelters and food, tools and animals waiting for us. Nothing waited for us, except the empty boxcars, and more of the same hunger.

October 16

A Dr. Guillermo Lowenthal got off the train today. I saw him myself. He had a very kind face and appeared to be a refined gentleman, with his clean clothes and tidy demeanor. We watched him walk around among us, stopping to chat with us in Yiddish, asking questions. He told us he was hired by the Argentine government to conduct research on the sanitation conditions of colonization. While in Berlin, before leaving for South America, he was contacted by the city's Jewish leaders who had heard of his pending voyage. Informing him of our journey—our group had stopped briefly in Berlin, en route from Podolia—they asked him to check on our progress.

While Dr. Lowenthal knew of our existence, I do believe he was amazed when he actually found us. He was clearly not prepared to come upon a group of Russian Jews in the middle of the Argentine pampas! He told us he was Rumanian, that his father was a rabbi.

He seemed especially interested in the children. I could see from his eyes that he was pained by their hunger and our unhealthy living conditions. We are used to it, but we must appear a miserable lot to someone like Dr. Lowenthal. He spoke with Rabbi Goldman, and heard our story. He assured us he would help, that as soon as he got back to Buenos Aires, he would meet with Dr. Palacios and tend to our case. He encouraged us not to lose hope. The Jews of Berlin have us in their hearts, he said. We are a beacon for so many more like us. He was very eloquent, Dr. Lowenthal. He reminded me a little of Papa, the way he spoke. He said we have come to do important work in this new country. We will become the backbone of our people, the cradle of our culture.

I want to believe him. I do try to be cheerful; it is after all, my nature. But it's difficult. Oh, I did not expect this journey to be easy, never that. But it's time now, time for the world to acknowledge us, to remember what we left and why. We are here to work, not to hold out our hands for crusts of bread thrown from a train window! In truth, if it weren't for the Yosems, I think I might have deserted this place. I might have easily been one of those who returned to Buenos Aires. There at least, one could go out and perhaps get work.

And yet, sometimes in the evening, when I walk out in the stillness around our boxcar, I cannot believe the quiet and solitude of the night. There are great spaces here, and great silences, save for the wind's blowing, the noises of Dr. Palacios's cattle beasts, and the song of a gaucho.

Gauchos. Gauchos, gauchos! That's all I've heard since I got here! I'm not so easily impressed. Not like those Silberman girls, Malke and Golda, in car #3. Have they no shame? They're hungry, like all of us, and yet they preen themselves and then go out to lean against the rail fence behind the tracks. They wait for the gauchos. They wait to see them gallop by on their horses, their neck scarves and leather pant aprons flapping in the wind. On Sundays, the gauchos dress up all in black—boots and hats, shirt and pants, their knives and silver belt buckles shimmering through the sunlit dust, rising from the horses' hooves. In the evenings they sing around their campfires, drinking whiskey and that strange brew, *yerba maté*, sipped from a hollowed, dry gourd. I've heard it said they become wild on alcohol and can kill a man at the drop of a hat. No, I'm not so easily impressed. I guess poor Mrs. Silberman has enough to worry about, or I'd think she'd pull in those frivolous girls by their hair. Oh well, I suppose there's no harm in a little enjoyment. God knows, we could use it.

October 19

Dr. Palacios arrived to discuss plans for our future, our relocation. It was hard to communicate, as none of us speak his language yet, and he does not speak ours. He had an interpreter accompany him from Buenos Aires, a man fluent in several languages and claiming to be a Russian colonel. Most of us think he is a man of questionable morals. We did understand that Dr. Palacios wanted to place families on pieces of land that would be a kilometer apart from each other. We could not agree to this, as it would jeopardize our sense of community. After much discussion, the elders presented Dr. Palacios with a workable plan for a village, including a center square with a synagogue, town hall, and school. Family farms would surround the village.

October 25

Two neighboring Italian families—the Coniglios and the Scarafias—helped make our move possible. For eight days they worked with a hand plow to make a path from Palacios to the land that would be ours, seventeen kilometers away. Succoth is over, and today we made the move. Most of us walked, but there were some carts and horses to transport the elderly and sick. Each family was given a tent, land, and some tools. David Hurwitz was made administrator of our new colony.

November 25

We have been so busy setting up our tents and dealing with the animals, digging wells and building ovens, I have not had a minute to spare for my journal. I've never worked so hard in my life! My hands have toughened with calluses, but the amount we've accomplished is truly impressive. Today we all rested, for Dr. Palacios returned to officially name the village. We received him with bread and salt, challahs from our outdoor ovens! The aroma from those wonderful loaves filled us with peace and hope. Dr. Palacios asked Rabbi Goldman what name we would like, and the Rabbi responded with Kiriath Mosche. He said that just as Moses led our people out of Egypt to freedom, so we too have been led out of czarist Russia to a free land. We are now inhabitants of Moisés Ville.

December 1, 1889
Moisés Ville

It's hard to imagine, but at this very moment, Tomaschpol must be deep in snow, the landscape wiped clean of all color. I know the painted verandahs of our small cottages are invisible, as is the brick factory in the distance, and the wooden flour mill, which has become one with the frozen river. Only the smoke rising from the chimneys leaves a silver gray trail in the cold, still sky. My mother has surely been up for hours, stoking the fire and starting the soup, singing as she works. My mother has a beautiful voice. Outside, my father makes his milk deliveries. I can see him in his cart, the old shawl on his knees, the overcoat and fur hat. Woolen rags are tied on his hands. I know that he coaxes his ancient mare with promises of carrots and fresh straw for her bed.

Here, it has turned quite warm. It's the middle of summer and our landscape is green. We have all worked hard this month. Our wells have water and our gardens are growing. Esther has even planted the precious gooseberry seeds she brought with her from Podolia. Our fields of wheat and corn are beginning to look like something. We've started building Rabbi Goldman's house; it will be adobe with a straw roof. I help Esther with the children and Leib in the fields. Sometimes my leg aches, but I never let it bother me. I've gotten quite used to this new land. When I look out around me and see all the tents and hitched animals, I understand that Moisés Ville is my new reality.

The remaining entries in Volume One of Rifke Schulman's journals, as well as the entire Volume Two, were completely destroyed by water. Rain entered a leaking roof in the attic of her Moisés Ville home, and several boxes of writings and mementos were damaged. The following excerpts are from Volumes Three and Four.

November 15, 1894
Moisés Ville

I am twenty-three years old today. Esther made me little cakes, and the children decorated the table with wildflowers from the fields. The Yosems insisted I was not to work this afternoon, that I was to take a walk in the sun and relax. I took my journal to Leib's north field, where he has planted this new alfalfa all the colonists are talking about. He's put in a stand of paraiso trees between the field and the side road, hoping to curb the wind and dust when the season arrives.

I sat among the little trees enjoying the sun and quiet, and I read through my journal. I was amazed to find how much has changed since we got here, five years ago. The tents have been replaced with adobe houses; we have a synagogue, a school, a cemetery. Many Litvaks have come. Baron Mauricio de Hirsch and his Jewish Colonization Association have purchased the land of Moisés Ville from Dr. Palacios. We are finally independent! They've acquired more land as well, next to us, in the province of Entre Ríos. Other colonies have been established; Mauricio, Clara, Lucienville. We have survived droughts, floods, and plagues of locusts that have stripped our lands and ruined our harvests. But we have also celebrated births, weddings, and good harvests. We are still here, and growing every month. A grandfather died recently—the first—and some young men were killed at the hands of brawling gauchos. Golda Silberman left to work in Buenos Aires. Her sister, Malke, finally ran away with a gaucho. One evening at dusk, her younger brothers saw her ride off on the back of a horse, her right arm wrapped around her gaucho's waist, her left hand clutching the family's brass Chanukiah. The boys claimed they saw the menorah's gleam long after the horse disappeared into the horizon. The family has not heard from Malke in two years.

The Yosems are doing well. Esther has had two more babies. She is a very good homemaker, and the children are always fed and in clean clothes. While I have been very happy living with the Yosems—and none of us can imagine it any other way—I am feeling slightly pressured to find a husband. The neighbors are concerned about me, and Esther claims I'm too picky. She says I should go for one of the tall, educated Litvaks. I too am tall, like Papa. She thinks I'm educated because I can read and write and must wear my glasses when I do so. Leib and some of the others tease and say the Litvaks won't last long as farmers. I think they're envious because the Baron and his Jewish Colonization Association welcomed the Litvaks into Moisés Ville with real homes. Homes made of brick and zinc roofs, with ovens and kitchens and whitewashed bedrooms. A far cry from our tents. Leib says they are too citified. It's true that they came from cities—Kovno, Vilna, Grodno, Slonim—not like our villages. They arrived with books. We came with the Torah.

One of their leaders, Henoch Rosenvitch, a stately, handsome man with intense, blue eyes, is talking of starting a library. I am holding my breath for this to happen. He is a wonderful man, this Rosenvitch. They say that in Slonim he was a city merchant, that he never lived in the country. Here he has cleared his own land, planted his own crops. I understand that his wife has not made the transition well. I've noticed that for some, it takes longer to adjust. It's probably only a question of time for Mrs. Rosenvitch. Their two sons and little daughter are still young, yet Henoch is teaching them everything as he learns it. The group that arrived with him looks to him as their leader. I believe these Litvaks will prove Leib and the others wrong. I believe they will make good farmers. I have seen them work. I have seen their energy, their spirit. We need them. Perhaps the neighbors have a point about a husband. But to tell you the truth, Esther is right, I am too fussy. She tells me I'd better be careful or I'll end up an old maid!

The word from Russia is never good. When I receive a letter from Papa, it is always full of more bad things about the conditions of our people. Pogroms seem to be a constant threat, even in the small villages of Podolia. I sense that Papa wants to send me some cheerful news, but it must be hard. Since the great Jewish expulsion from Moscow in 1891, when thousands of artisan families were dragged out of their homes without warning, expulsions seems to have become a daily occurrence. Many of these families sought refuge in the Pale.

Papa says all the villages are bursting with wonderful artisans, eager for any kind of work. Revolutionary groups are forming among the young people, and emigration is on everyone's lips. The youth have become bitter and frustrated because higher education has been virtually cut off from them. Papa is worried about my brother Chaim. He has been attending Zionist meetings. I wish I could see him. Now that he is eighteen he must be so handsome! Papa says he would like to send him to me, but it is not easy to make the arrangements.

April 22, 1896
Moisés Ville

A great sadness has befallen our village. We received word that the Baron Mauricio de Hirsch died yesterday. Our colony is in mourning, as I'm sure the others are.

Happier news! The Rosenvitchs' third son was born a week ago. They have named him Julio.

May 10, 1896

The Moisés Ville library opened yesterday! Thanks to Henoch Rosenvitch, I am the librarian. It's a small adobe building that also serves as the village hall, where we keep the census records. I love working with books, and I have been able to read so much. I have never seen so many volumes! Every few days I take another book home to the Yosems and their children. In the evenings we sit around the table with the kerosene lamp, and I read. Last week I finished

Anna Karenina, by the Russian writer Tolstoy. How we all wept! Today Henoch Rosenvitch handed me a book that he says will change the world, *The Communist Manifesto*. It was written by two men, F. Engels and a fellow Jew, Karl Marx. Henoch says that everyone who cares about the fate of the working man must understand this book. I admire Henoch's knowledge, his respect for learning.

Often, while I am cataloging books, he spends many hours drawing plans for our village. He works on large pieces of paper. He draws carefully, in detail. The plaza with people strolling. The synagogue, the theater, the library with grand, white columns. Someday we will have all of this, Henoch said one evening, as he sketched a low, flat building, explaining that it will be the farmers' co-op. We must not forget the schools, he said, pointing out more buildings. He tells me that the hope of our young people lies in education. Higher education must be our next goal, once we have established ourselves on the land. If we Jews are to remain a viable community, we must be sure to produce more than farmers. We must have doctors and lawyers, engineers and writers, philosophers, we must have everything, and they must be the best.

One afternoon while we were in the library, Henoch stopped working on his plans and quickly drew a small sketch of a boot. He explained that his best friend in Slonim had a problem similar to mine, and that the solution was not difficult. The next day he gave his drawing to Eli, the cobbler, and instructed him on the design. My new shoe with the built-up heel was a miracle! I did not limp as much, and of more importance, my leg did not get as tired!

March 10, 1897

I have taken up my pen, but I can hardly move my hand . . . my family . . . they're dead! My parents, my sisters, my brother Chaim.

All of them, victims of yet another pogrom, the last for them—my loved ones—thank God. Two days ago I received a letter dictated by an old neighbor of my parents. The police came by, killed, looted, set fire to the house, and dragged my brother away. I am too emotional, I can write no more . . . another time, perhaps.

April 16, 1897
Passover, Moisés Ville

Esther says I must try harder. I can't seem to mend yet, I am still so overwhelmed by the loss of my family. She says it is good that we must prepare for Pesach, which begins tomorrow. It is good to have something else to occupy my mind.

I've had enough to think of, and now it is time to record what I have been putting off for some time. I have come to realize I must leave Moisés Ville. This has been a very difficult decision. Moisés Ville has been my home and my family for eight years. Esther and the children are very unhappy. Leib is sad, but he understands. He says he wishes me well, and that I am always welcome in his home. I will be leaving for Buenos Aires in three days, so I imagine I won't have much time for my journal for a while, at least not until I've become settled and have found work. I will stay with Golda Silberman, who has been working in an *alpargata* factory for a year now.

What has led to this decision? I am desperate for a change, and I'm hoping it will help me adjust to the loss of my family. But there's more. There is Henoch, and there is the dream, the final straw.

I will always be grateful to Henoch. Yet despite all his kindness and guidance—over and over he has shown me what I must read, always treating me with complete respect—I cannot go on another week being in the same room with him, the same town. The truth is, my feelings go beyond admiration. When we work together in that small space that serves as a library, I with the books and he with his plans, I never want the time to end. A silent bond has formed. I believe he too senses its power and dimensions; he too knows words are both impossible and unnecessary.

Esther is the only one who knows of my feelings for Henoch. It is a desperate situation and I cannot help myself, God knows I've tried. Last week when I dreamt that Mrs. Rosenvitch died, and we had to bury her in a kerosene can—as we did those first children—I knew I had to leave Moisés Ville.

April 18, 1897

I want to write of my father's last letter. I want to do this from here. I want to try and come to terms with my grief before I leave Moisés Ville.

His last correspondence was dated two months ago. The tone is anxious, nervous; he says he is holding my beautiful photograph in his hand. He asks if I remember the day he took me to Kamenets to be photographed by the famous Michal Greim, just before I left?

How could I forget Michal Greim? I found him to be such an arrogant little man, but I didn't say so to Papa. He took it on as a challenge, my short left leg. He frowned and stared at it for the longest time before beginning to fuss about. He shook that white, goat hair rug so much, the hairs got in my mouth. And that silly pedestal, I thought it would break before he propped it up just the way he wanted it. He floated about in his smock and beret, assuring me he would make me appear flawless, perfect, as he wiped the perspiration off my forehead. I wanted to tell him I did not care to be perfect, and how dare he assume I did? I know he thought I was a child. I wanted to tell him to take the photograph and be done with it. I wanted to tell him I wasn't in the least bit interested in this sitting, and that I was terribly hot. But I didn't. I bit my tongue, and I put my foot on that stupid cushion, and I posed. I did it for Papa.

In his letter, Papa asks if I remember how hot the day was, and how long the trip seemed in the cart. "Do not forget our heritage," Papa wrote. "If I weren't so old, we would already be in Argentina. Things have gotten very bad here in Podolia, and I fear for our lives. Especially for Chaim, who has become very active in a Zionist organization. One of these days," Papa wrote, "the Zionists will be banned."

I hurried to answer, encouraging him to come, that it was the only solution. I don't know if he even received my letter.

April 19, 1897
Santa Fe Express, en Route to Buenos Aires

I am writing this from the same train that brought me to these parts eight years ago. How different that journey was! We were frightened, and everything seemed so bleak. Not that I know now what my future holds for me, and there's always the possibility that I'm making a mistake in leaving Moisés Ville. I suppose one can never know such things. But I must admit, I'm excited at the prospect of change.

This morning, Leib borrowed a sulky, and they took me to the station. All of us have great difficulty when we must be in Palacios. Esther cries, so this time was no different. I know she remembers her dead baby and those first weeks, as we all do. Waiting on the platform for the train, Esther nervously jabbered about how I must be very careful in the city. She had warned me so many times already. She reminded me to write as soon as I'm settled. I'd already promised, again and again. She reminded me to eat well. Again I promised. Speaking of food, Esther suddenly jumped, remembering something. She'd left a parcel in the sulky, and she needed Leib's help.

As I watched them disappear behind the station, I turned toward the open field and sky. I realized that for the first time in years, I'd awakened and gone about my day without noticing the weather; I'd been so engrossed with the last minute packing and thoughts of my departure. There were no clouds. It would be a perfect, brilliant day for work in the fields. With my hand still shielding my eyes, and a strange, hovering expectancy, I nervously glanced across the landscape.

"Rifke Schulman!"

Startled, I turned at the anxious sound of his voice. He hurried toward me in his dark suit. Behind him, I recognized his horse tied to a post in front of the station. He learned to ride in Moisés Ville. In the old country, he was a merchant. An odd thing to think about at that moment. Esther must have seen him approaching. Clearly she was prepared, all that nonsense about the food parcel.

"You rode a horse, Henoch Rosenvitch, in your good suit?" I tried to tease, certain he intended a light farewell. But then I saw his eyes, more blue, more intense then ever. The depth of his pain overwhelmed my own.

"You promised you would not leave without saying good-bye."

The face I had known to be wise and certain and calm now struggled for control as he reached for both my hands. I looked away, not wanting to see more. I knew too much.

"Rifke," his voice was a whisper.

I was speechless.

He turned my face back to him, kissing my hair, my forehead, my tears, for all those times we had never touched.

"Rifke Schulman, I will always love you. Your mind and your soul, your eyes . . . "

I put my finger to his lips.

After turning away for a moment, squinting at the fields and breathing deeply, Henoch reached into his shirt and pulled out his drawing for my shoe. Silently he tucked it into my jacket pocket.

As the train approached, so did the Yosems, carrying the parcel Esther had prepared for me. Through tears she told me of the matzos and cheese, tea and sugar, a piece of kugel for the train, and of the small pot of her pale green gooseberry jam.

"Be sure to find a good cobbler, Rifke Schulman!" Henoch called out, smiling and waving.

I will never forget the image of my three friends standing on the platform. Esther, grown quite plump, waving her handkerchief, and Leib, balding and thin. Henoch Rosenvitch stood a few feet apart from them, tall and straight, a beacon in that landscape of pampas and perseverance.

Now, as this train carries me away from Moisés Ville and toward Buenos Aires, toward an uncertain future, I allow myself to weep. I cry for what I'm leaving—my Moisés Ville family, the Yosems. My love, Henoch. I cannot not help wondering if our paths will ever cross again.

The Assimilation
of Solomon Teper

This time, Solomon Teper flew to Argentina via Chile. As United Airlines flight 985 crossed the Andes, Sol's forehead remained pressed to the window, his eyes riveted to the mountains. How long had it been? How long forgotten, the majestic stones, the ancient stillness? The simple realization that his mind and eyes could so easily lapse, so easily forget, triggered an immediate and profound sense of loss.

Sol was shocked by his reaction. For years he had made this annual trip home to his mother, and never had he felt so emotional. Could the sight of mountains really create such confusion, pressing to expose other things forgotten? Could stone demand the taking of inventory? Bewildered, Sol turned from the window. He had never been one to dwell and mull over the details of his life, and the uncharted territories of introspection were not his terrain. His habit was full steam ahead, looking back only to see where he was coming from, and never long enough for nostalgia, or analysis.

He knew that the separation from his wife, Faith, was partially to blame for this chaos of doubt and frustration. But it wasn't just Faith. Why an inventory of his life? Sol smiled, remembering he still had his sense of humor. Why not? He could manage it.

A brilliant, so it was said, cardiovascular surgeon. Good start. Plus. Forty-five, and in somewhat of a slump. Minus?

Sol turned back to the stone landscape below him, the Andean shapes and shadows of prehistoric beasts and female figures.

A wife, two daughters, a stylish house. Plus, plus, bobkes.

The colossal stone silhouettes of hips and fecund bellies and breasts dipped and swelled in the clouds. The white, veiny roads scratching the foothills, all led to the sea.

Now the girls were teenagers, and Faith wanted a divorce. She was bored with him and tired of being the "primary parent." Without question, a shitty minus.

The deposits of iron ore, copper green and something acid yellow, stain and streak the rock. From heights and out of stagnant thoughts, he saw those colors, in beautiful, organic shapes. Strewn stems and petals.

He ran five miles three times a week. Another minus, it should be six. But his small frame was still wiry and fit. Plus.

"Dr. Teper, would you care for a drink?"

Solomon pulled away from the glass and turned toward the steward, shaking his head.

Blood pressure good, cholesterol count excellent. Plus, plus.

The flight wasn't crowded, and he was grateful no one was sitting beside him. He adjusted his seat to tilt as far back as possible.

He'd become an American. Plus. More than that really, an Iowan. It was love at first sight of her shape on the map. Iowa, planted so solidly in the middle of the country, so cer- tain of her straight Minnesota and Missouri borders, more al- lowing to Nebraska, gentle to the curves of the Mississippi River. Her farms and campuses, her bankers and library vol- unteers, she became his America. On her part, love took longer, not like his impetuousness. A slow respect developed, steady and committed, until he felt himself taken to her heart and core, claimed forever. He hadn't intended such a love af- fair, nor had he ever imagined that love would change him so. That part was sad. Except for his accent, there was little else remaining that reminded him of his village in Santa Fe.

There was little that made him different from his col- leagues at the hospital. They wore the same clothes and built the same kinds of houses, with whirlpools and Italian tile floors. They had the same kinds of wooded lots, the same cars, even the same friends, and memberships in the same athletic clubs. Plus? Minus? Who knows. Those were the things he had never cared about.

How many other beautiful things, like the mountains, had he forgotten in his life time?

Inventory complete, so soon? No, his mother. She was old and lived in Argentina. Plus. She could be old and living with him in Iowa. Minus. She still thought he was a genius, and gorgeous. Plus.

One more thing. Sol sat up straight.

He wasn't balding, like so many of his American colleagues. His thick, curly dark hair was rapidly turning gray, but he wasn't losing it. Plus.

Now it was done. Surely, Faith, surely these are all the makings of a desirable, contemporary, North American male?

Sol felt the tightness in his chest again, tense and swift, burning. He knew he shouldn't think about her, he knew he should let her go. But why, Faith, why?

"Your sarcasm, for starters."

He could hear her voice, he could see her long, slim body leaning against the stone wall beside the fireplace. She had just showered. Underneath her loose, white sweats, he knew her shoulders were tan and lean, fit from the months of tennis. Despite her usual calm, her body had tightened nervously as divorce crossed her lips; the high, cool forehead and fine nose on the cutting edge of concentration. She had pulled her blond hair up, away from her face, still so incredibly beautiful. Years ago, when Faith had met the deparment's legendary, retired surgeon at a cardiology cocktail party, she'd blown him away with her slim physique, her cool, Norwegian looks. Although teetering at the brink of senility, crackers and cheese crumbling down his tie, the old surgeon was still preoccupied with ancestry, physical delineation, and of course, racial characteristics. He was not at all surprised to learn that Faith was from Decorah. Carefully he explained to Sol that the Scandinavian immigrants had gone north in Iowa, while the others, the Italians, the East Europeans, had remained in the south. For in Decorah, he added—this stalwart of surgical innovation, this pillar of scientific knowledge—in Decorah, the streets are wider and the people are taller and fairer.

It had been a rainy, damp evening. Sol could still smell the spring earth outside the living room windows, the scent of Faith's shower as she pulled away from the fireplace wall and walked past him toward the piano. He knew there had been stress, now and then. But never before had she mentioned divorce.

"Seriously Sol, we've grown apart. What more can I say?" She ran her fingers along the keys.

He had watched her face in silence, not taking in her stupid words. Even the new freckles seemed intense. She had spent the weekend at the cottage with the girls, closing up for the season. He would do anything for her, absolutely anything.

"You know it as well as I do. Surely I don't have to stand here and make a list!"

"Faith, you're asking me for a divorce. I want to know why."

"For God's sake!" She walked over to the window. "I'm tired of this marriage, Sol, tired and lonely. I'm sick of being the primary parent. I'm sick of competing with the hospital for your attention." She stood with her back to him, looking out at the wet hostas clustered along the walk. "Then, when I get your attention, I'm bored," she said quietly. "You bore me. Do you understand?" After a few seconds of silence, her shoulders drooped, she turned around. "Sol?" her face had softened. "I didn't mean it to come out that way . . . but surely you've known? Surely you've felt it?"

She'd never put it quite that plainly, that he bored her. But she would not wound him, he would not permit it. "Do you think I'll just give you a divorce? The way I've given you other things you've wanted, with love and affection, and no questions asked?" At that moment, he'd felt like a surgeon gearing up for the operation. The cool determination, the energy, the control. "You really are a spoiled bitch, Faith."

"Really?" Her voice became crisp, mocking.

"Yes, really. And I'm fed up hearing about your primary parenting!"

"Don't make me lose it, Sol!"

"My darling, you knew I wasn't going to stay home and change diapers and make peanut butter sandwiches. You knew I was a surgeon when you married me."

"What about me!" Her face suddenly contorted, her clenched fists pressed into her chest. "ME!" She moved quickly around the room, window to fireplace, fireplace to couch, couch to piano. Her body was taut, like a fine, pacing lioness. Finally she dropped down onto the piano bench. "I just want out, Sol," she'd said quietly.

"And what if I don't?"

A sudden blanket of clouds obstructed his view, but it didn't matter, Sol decided, because they'd passed over the Andes. Exhaustion caught up with him. He wasn't looking forward to attending the centennial celebrations of his village, but he had promised his mother. He leaned his head against the back of the seat and closed his eyes. His flights had generally been Chicago–Buenos Aires direct; it was peculiar that his agent routed him through Santiago. As usual, Flo, his secretary, had made the arrangements. She had even seen to the airport limousine that met him at the hospital door. Flo had worked in cardiology all her life, but she would be retiring soon, wanting to travel before it was too late. Her varicose veins, she said, were not getting any younger. Last week, in

her steady, upbeat, American manner, she threatened to check out
this village he kept returning to, this place she'd heard so much
about.

*"Moisés Ville, the village of Moses, founded as a haven for
Jews escaping czarist Russia."*

He'd brought her the articles and brochures his mother had sent
him on the centennial preparations. Over the years, Flo had learned
to read and translate Spanish. She was slow and methodical, but
enthusiastic.

"The Jerusalem of South America!"

It had taken on mythical proportions for her, she confessed, shyly,
like Shangri-La, or Camelot. Sol had been touched. He realized,
with resigned sadness, that he had spoken about his village more to
Flo than to his own daughters.

He would miss his chats with Flo. The rare, quiet moments over
a cup of coffee and dictation, sometimes dressed in his green surgical
garb, sometimes standing at the window of his office, staring down
at the new construction. His life was consummated in that ever-
expanding edifice of steel and glass and cement. Surgeries were
performed, consultations conducted—colleagues, patients, the
families of patients. Staffings and meetings, research in the labs that
flew with him in paper and spirit to conferences in the Hague, Paris,
Tokyo, the endless other cities. The patients, pushing their intrave-
nous racks in the mirrored lounge with the art displays, waited and
hoped. The birth of babies, the wasteland of cancer, the triumph of
life. Those who would die and those who would live. Despite his
desires for the contrary, his life had a way of beginning and ending
at the hospital door.

How could he fight? He loved her. She could have the house, if he could keep his sanity. She could have the cottage, if he could remain a good surgeon. She could have the Volvo, if he could continue to send his mother money. She already had it all anyway, because she had the kids. The "things" were *bobkes*.

They had been "Faith's girls" from the beginning. She had made them in her image, and it was no one's fault but his own. He had permitted it because he loved it, and them. Perhaps he should have listened to his mother and occasionally brought them to Argentina. She'd always said it would be good to bring them, to teach them Spanish. But clearly he had not cared enough, more than that really, he had not wanted it. Yes, he had not wanted it, and it had been through choice. His past had been his past and his present was his life. When the girls were young, the excuse was the long trip. He'd convinced himself he was doing the right thing by sparing his little, blond daughters. And Faith had supported him, saying, "All that way, to spend a dusty week in Moisés Ville?" Faith had been to Moisés Ville only once, and once had been enough. In the early years, he'd sent his parents tickets, so they could visit their grandchildren in Iowa. His own visits to Argentina had been sporadic events, when guilt suddenly weighed on his shoulders. But since his father had died five years ago, he had returned, conscientiously, every year.

The plane arrived in Buenos Aires on time, and Solomon made his connection to Rosario without problem. An hour later, a driver was waiting at the Rosario airport, and they began their journey around noon. The air was unusually hot for the end of October. As the car crossed the soft, rolling pampas, Sol was comforted that the landscape between Rosario and Moisés Ville never changed, year after year. The occasional cluster of paradise trees or a farmer's small ranch made him think of his grandfather's beautiful homestead. How clearly he remembered the five eucalypti, the house with the verandah, the animals grazing on stretches of uninterrupted pampas. Sol had been very close to his mother's father. He was looking forward to being back, to finding the calm that always seemed to fortify him during his visits home.

He knew the centennial events would disrupt his peace, and he was resentful that he had to be present. He was coming to please his mother. He had proposed to her that he come in December—his usual month for visiting—after the fact, when everyone had gone away, when it was quiet again. She would not hear of it. He tried to muster some enthusiasm by talking with the driver about the celebrations. But talk of the numbers they were expecting and the general preparations for the event deepened his melancholia. He was depressed enough without thinking about the thousands of returning descendants, swarming the streets of Moisés Ville. At least he would see his cousin Beatriz, and that was a consolation.

As the car approached Moisés Ville, Sol noticed that the department of highways had provided the village with an "Urban Zone" sign. Across from it, in his landscape of empty field and sky, the recently constructed allegorical monument. This was what his mother had written him about. This would commemorate one hundred years of existence, with its menorah and immigrant ship twisted into an abomination of cement and steel. It awaited its centennial dedication in the ephemeral spirit of an American billboard. Sol felt embarrassed. He concentrated on the fields, the animals. He knew there was still a quarter of a mile before they would pass the creamery, and what they had called as children the "suburbs" of Moisés Ville, the poor dwellings of the landless farmers. Sol waved to a woman washing clothes in a front yard. Her barefoot children played in the dirt, while two dogs slept under a tree. He felt the familiar burst of adrenaline as the cab entered the village.

Sol Teper awoke in his old bed, rested and peaceful. Sunlight and the distant sound of children's laughter entered his window. From his bed he could see the long narrow leaves and peeling beige trunk of the eucalyptus in his mother's front garden. Earlier, he had heard the neighbor's rooster. He looked slowly around his room, relishing the familiar calm. As he knew every leaf of the garden, he knew every inch of the small, stucco home. His mother had recently repainted the white walls. Everything looked fresh and simple. He could hear voices downstairs in the kitchen. He knew his mother and her hired girl were busy with plans and arrangements for the centennial and the next few days of guests.

Peace. Would he find his peace? It would be difficult with the commotion of visiting relatives. He resented that he would have to share his mother and her house, but he could not spoil her happiness. Last night she had joyfully told him that every bed would be in use, and that Uncle David, his father's brother, head of the clan, would also have a full house. It would be like the old days, she'd said—her face animated, her eyes bright—when families were families, when Jews were Jews, and when Moisés Ville was something. Really something! She promised to walk with him early in the morning before it got too hot, before she got too busy with her day. He wanted to tell her about Faith while he had her alone.

This white house of his childhood, of his adult dreamscapes—white Moisés Ville sand, and white Iowa snow—was on one of the outer streets of Moisés Ville, where the asphalt ended, where the fields began. As a kid, he used to begin at his doorstep and walk his way slowly around the village, finally ending in the center, in the plaza. When Sol and his mother started out for their walk, he noticed that her stride was slower, but she was still energetic and enthusiastic, refusing to allow his father's death to end her life too. When they passed the children's park beside the school, she asked if they could sit a while.

That was when he told her. She did not make a scene, but took the news quietly, shaking her head, slowly closing her eyes. She was not surprised. Clearly, all along, she'd known something he hadn't. Then she made some soft, quiet noises about the children, saying that for them, it would be painful. Finally, in a very gentle, wistful voice, his mother asked if maybe Faith wouldn't change her mind. He hated that Faith's hold could cross continents.

In the afternoon, after lunch, Sol walked to the café facing the Plaza San Martín. He sat out at one of the three tables on the sidewalk. This was his favorite time. The streets were quiet, the storefronts shuttered, and people were home resting after their meal. It was almost guaranteed that he would have the café to himself for at least an hour. The centennial events were not scheduled to begin until the following evening. They had spiffed up the Kadima Theater, he realized, looking across the plaza at the building's façade of Corinthian pilasters. They had fixed the cement work. The iron grillwork on the balconies had been cleaned and painted. In the center of the plaza, flowers had been planted around the monument. Except for a few children playing around the statue and two workmen adjusting the stones along the walks, the plaza was empty. He sipped his coffee slowly, enjoying the peace and sun.

His life in Iowa seemed very far away at that moment. It always did when he visited his mother. He thought of the house they had built in the beautiful wooded bluff, overlooking the river. He thought of waking up with Faith in the dawn stillness of their room. Half asleep, they'd pull on sweat clothes and tiptoe out into the morning cool. They ran along paths in the woods, down by the river, and then back along the asphalt residential roads with the clusters of mail boxes. She had an incredible body; she never stopped, she could outrun anyone and never tire. Like a fine motor, it was tuned and taut. It had to be heredity because no matter how hard he tried, he could never match her physical prowess. He missed her, he wanted her. And his girls, he needed to see his girls every day. He had moved out three months ago when she asked him to, and it was still as horrible as the first day. He might well be a forty-five-year-old heart surgeon, but he felt like a loser. He stood to eat at the kitchen counter of a dismal, furnished apartment; he crashed to sleep in a strange bedroom. He still couldn't believe it was happening.

Sol paid for his coffee and then crossed the plaza and headed up the street. They had painted the Baron Hirsch Library. He stood in front of the Greek Revival building with its large, white columns, feeling empty and awful. What next? Clearly this visit was going to be difficult. He would have to get through it as quickly and painlessly as possible. He always came looking for his library, but this time he did not care to enter. He didn't even want to find Clara, his old librarian, who had guided him through his childhood with books. Hovering, supervising, she had made sure everything important landed in his hands. Maybe tomorrow he would look her up. Tomorrow he could come with his cousin, Beatriz, soulmate of his youth. It would be wonderful to be together again.

Later that afternoon, the relatives began arriving. Sol's uncle, Chaim, his mother's brother from Salta, came with his daughter, Mina, and four grandchildren. An hour later, two of Sol's spinster aunts, retired schoolteachers from Santa Fe. Sol hadn't seen them in years. Finally, Beatriz and her daughter. The drive from Cordoba had taken only four hours in her new car.

After the excitement of the meal, the older women took the children to stroll in the plaza, and Chaim walked up to Uncle David's house. Sol and Bea retired to the back patio. At sunset, they heard the familiar neighborhood noises—basins of dish water splashed out against back fences, dogs fed and silenced, tired children rounded up for bedtime. They talked for hours, beyond day into night, when finally, quiet and dark prevailed, and the only light left was the small bulb on the back kitchen porch.

"What do you mean, what more can I tell you? She's bored and she wants a divorce." Sol tried to sound matter-of-fact. "That's all I know."

"That's all?" Bea's voice prodded.

Sol watched his cousin as she drew slowly on her cigarette, the beady eyes lively, the cropped, dark hair fresh, careless. The family had always worried about her almost midget-like stature. But Bea's eager personality had never allowed her small size to hinder her. She had climbed trees, squeezed through fences, and avoided housework. After receiving a degree in child psychology, she married, had a child, and pursued her career as a clinical psychologist. Sol's mother had told him that Bea had recently left her husband for a lover.

"You had no hint this was going to happen, none at all? This came as a shock?"

"Beatriz, listen to me. I leave my home at 6:30 in the morning, and I spend my entire day at the hospital. I get back between 6:00 and 7:00 in the evening, when I'm not away in Europe giving talks or attending conferences. When was I supposed to get hints? On the weekends?"

"Sol, what's happened to you? You used to be such a smart kid. Has this Iowa place hurt you so much?"

"Don't blame Iowa for Faith's nonsense."

"Still such loyalty!" Bea clucked her tongue.

"And please don't tell me I should have 'made time' to get hints from my wife! That's what some of my colleagues tell me." Sol stood up and walked over to the waist-high stone wall surrounding his mother's back patio. "I broke my back as a kid working on these farms!" He leaned against the stones, staring out at the dark fields beyond the last village street. Sol's voice stopped, the pain was back in his chest. He held very still, breathing slowly, feeling the perspiration break on his forehead.

"What is it, Sol?"

Even in the dark Bea had noticed. She was still Bea. "Nothing, not to worry." He straightened up cautiously. "Just a little tension." He remained silent for a few moments, aware of his rigidity. "I worked for years saving money for medical school." He felt the cool air bathe his clammy face. "Do you think I'm going to take time from my work to sit around waiting for hints?"

"Sol, it's me, Beatriz. Remember?"

Sol stared hard into the darkness. "Sorry, Bea . . . I'm so angry. I can't believe she's done this!" The pain had passed. "Thank God my father is dead. Do you know what he'd say if he knew that my wife asked me to move out of my house?! Shit." Sol turned away, remaining silent for a few moments as he stared at his mother's potted geraniums, the tomato plants. "On the plane, I tried to do an inventory of my life. I've never done anything like that." Sol smiled. "I remembered a patient I once had who needed a job but didn't have a resume or credentials. Her prospective boss told her to write down all her positive assets."

"Did it work?"

"For me it went nowhere. All I learned is that Faith has my children, and that it has taken years of work to pay for the house, the cars, the cottage."

"But that's not why you worked."

"No, but I've given Faith everything she wanted, for herself, for the girls. Now everyone tells me I shouldn't have worked so hard. I should have taken it easy, so I could have spent more time at home. Bea, what am I going to do? I'm still crazy about her. I need her!"

"That's the best thing I've heard you say all night."

"So now what?"

"Is there any chance Faith would reconsider?"

Sol shook his head. "I call her every few days. She assures me we're finished, and that her lawyer will be contacting my lawyer about the divorce. She says she wants to begin again. She wants to go back to school." Sol grimaced.

"What does she want to study?" Bea asked.

"Does it matter?" Sol asked bitterly.

Bea smiled patiently.

"She wants to get a master's degree in film!"

"Set new goals for yourself, Sol."

"Did you hear? She's leaving me because she wants to study film!"

"That's not why she's leaving you. Listen to me, Sol, you need new goals."

"New goals! Bea, I'm not interested in new goals. All I ever wanted was to be a heart surgeon, and Faith. I wanted Faith. And don't tell me she was always a bitch, and that you and my mother knew it from the beginning."

"It hardly matters now what I or your mother knew. You've lost Faith. But you have your daughters, and you're still a surgeon, and you still have half a lifetime to want something, or someone else."

For the next two days, Sol felt himself caught up in a blur of movement centered around meals, the comings and goings to attend the centennial events, and the brief encounters with old friends. He couldn't seem to focus or get himself together. Relatives and neighbors trailed in the front door, sat down in the kitchen long enough to chat and have a drink, and then were off. He watched them disappear out the back door, across the patio, and through the gate to someone else's house.

Like a zombie he accompanied his mother and Bea to the dedication of the monument, the discussion groups on immigration and emigration, the theatrical performance at the Kadima Theater, and even the Friday evening service at the main synagogue, something he hadn't done in years. It was impossible to walk down the street without being jostled and pushed, called to, slapped on the back, or kissed. People continually threw themselves at each other. Reaching back into their mutual past, they reminisced, they laughed, they wept because their village, once the cradle of

Argentine Judaism and a thriving agricultural community, had entered the land of memories. Sol knew that when the centennial celebrations were over, people would leave, and Moisés Ville would slip back into its shadowy existence; a few old people would wander its streets, a few children would cluster around modern comics in the Baron Hirsch Library. Even its famous farmland no longer remained in Jewish hands.

Finally, on Saturday afternoon, wanting to escape the noise and commotion of his mother's house, Sol walked over to the old Brener Shul where he had attended cheder. It was cool and quiet inside. Someone had cleaned and repaired, painted. Sol sat down on a bench in the front row. Nothing had changed, he realized, looking at the simple green walls and the wooden railings of the women's balcony. He saw the same trees through the two large windows flanking the carved wooden ark. It was still there, the ark, with its painted lions and cornucopias of fruit, still as he remembered it.

Sol suddenly stood up and quickly left the synagogue. He did not need to sit there and confront his ghosts and the ghosts of his town. He did not need to hear the old voices. It was enough that his village was dissolving. It was enough that he had not given to his children—never mind his heritage, his language, his culture—but he had not even permitted them a piece of his own clear, ringing childhood, peaceful and nurturing. Had it been through good intentions? Or neglect? Or perhaps fear, fear that his two blond daughters might stake their claims, and that his past would no longer be his? It was enough that he'd been so self-involved, that he hadn't known, honestly hadn't known that Faith was tired of him. It was enough that it took his mother to make him realize that the divorce would affect his children too. And were they all better off for it? He, the girls, Faith, his mother? Were they better off because for whatever reasons, he had not shared? Sol walked slowly home, hoping to find Bea.

The final event, after the parade, was the Sunday luncheon for over four thousand people. Bea had prepared him, knowing his phobia of crowds, knowing he hadn't come to Moisés Ville to be with 4,000 people. The circus-size tent had been erected in a field at the edge of town. Everyone walked. Reluctantly, Sol accompanied his family, his Uncle David's entourage. He was shaken to find the tent in that place, only a stone's throw from his grandfather's old homestead.

Families were seated by tables; loud speakers called out names as people crowded into the noisy, stifling interior. Fleisman, number 8. Grubers, number 24. Goldman and Pollock, number 89. Sol and his family were designated a table on the north side. The heat was unbearable and still, penetrating the tent roof, spilling in through the separations in the canvas. Eighty sweating waiters ran up and down beside the long, paper-covered tables, carrying the swords of grilled chicken, bowls of salty salads, bread and wine and water. Seated at the table, Sol calculated the distance to the nearest opening—where the tent flaps were tied back—and how much time it would take to reach it. Fire engines, ambulances, and police vehicles were parked at every exit. The head table was in the center, crowded with town dignitaries. Throughout the meal, there was constant noise. Microphoned announcements, testimonials and songs that became garbled garbage because of the faulty loudspeakers, and the incessant drone of 4,000 talking, laughing voices. It was so hot, sweat ran off the waiters' hands as they served. People fainted. Bottled water was used to cool down children. After the chicken course, Sol could take no more. He leaned toward his mother, who was clearly holding her own, and asked her if she intended to stay for the dessert.

"Certainly. At the last celebration, the anniversary fifty years ago, your father insisted on staying home to finish taking off a field of alfalfa. I missed the ice cream, the speeches, everything."

After consulting with Bea, who assured him she would escort his mother home after the luncheon, Sol stood up, said his good-byes, and as quickly as possible, made his way out of the enormous tent.

He walked around the outside. He passed the temporary toilets, the countless refrigerated catering trucks, the temporary barbecue grills, and the waiters, resting, smoking. He crossed into the eucalyptus forest at the edge of the open field. It was cool under the long, shaggy branches. He didn't sit, as he often had in childhood, stopping to rest on one of the large, felled trunks, punky from ground rot. Instead, he hurried across the next field, and then down the narrow side road.

He found himself running the last stretch toward his grandfather's homestead. His heart pounding from the exertion and heat. He thought of Faith. Her body would love it; it would simply pull itself into gear and proceed, smoothly, like a race horse. She would reach his grandfather's five eucalypti before him. She wouldn't even be panting, just a few beads of moisture above her upper lip, her skin damp, her eyes clear from the effort.

Sol stopped running. He expected the trees, the house, even Faith. There was nothing, only five stumps in a row. Glancing around, he saw that the old yucca was still there, the one beside the well that he used to cover with rags when the locusts attacked. But clusters of pampas grass grew in place of his grandfather's house. The landscape was slightly unfamiliar without its landmarks. What had happened, and when? He had come to see the homestead on his last visit. His mother had written him nothing. Clearly she had not wanted him to know of this, anymore than he had wanted her to know about the divorce.

Sol dropped to the ground in exhaustion. Pain racked his chest. He buried his face in the grass. Running had left him dehydrated. He could taste the earth, the dryness of his tension.

"Faith . . ."

Her name rolled gently from his lips.

He raised his head, tilting it backwards.

"Faith! . . . Faith! . . . Faith . . . !"

Stilled by the shocking depth of his own voice, Solomon Teper heard his echo, rattling through the empty pampas, heaving through his chest.

THE RIFKE CHRONICLES

In 1904, the year of these journal entries, incidents of class struggle have become commonplace in Buenos Aires. In other cities, labor activity germinates. In Rosario, a general strike. In Tucumán, sugar plantation workers strike for the first time.

Russia and Japan: war! A colored race defeats a white people. Never before has this happened in modern history. The United States: Theodore Roosevelt is re-elected president, and the New York City subway opens for traffic. There is no record of Rifke Schulman's initial years in the capital. The first Buenos Aires journals, Volumes Five and Six, dating from her Moisés Ville departure in April of 1897, were among those destroyed by the leaky Moisés Ville attic. The following entries are from Volume Seven, part of which is still legible.

May 10, 1904
Buenos Aires

I have time to write tonight, because the Union did not meet this evening, and I was able to come straight home from the factory. The winter has begun with the usual cold winds that blow in off the port. I travel to and from work in the dark of dawn, in the dark of evening. My leg aches terribly in this dampness that chills to the bone. First I must walk east on Lavalle, then over to Plaza de Mayo where I can catch a trolley on Defensa, which will take me the thirty blocks to the factory. In moments of frustration I have fantasized that some dark night the massive stone Fabrica Argentina de Alpargatas will be blown apart by an anarchist bomb. This event would bring the end to an oppressive, dismal world, an end to the power and grip of one family's empire. In my fantasies, no one dies in such an act, and somehow, I don't need to worry about all the girls and where they subsequently find work. I am not an anarchist, but I have my weaknesses, my evenings of total exhaustion. Tonight is one.

I've washed my hair and a few clothes and I'm soaking my feet as I write. Besides this entry in my journal, I must also begin a letter to my friends Esther and Leib Yosem in Moisés Ville. It's been so long since I've written. As the years pass, I find I tell them less and less about my life. Of course they know that when I arrived in Buenos Aires I lived with Golda Silberman for four years until she got married, the same Golda from Moisés Ville who used to lean on the rail fence and watch the gauchos.

After she left, I remained alone, not wanting to room with other girls from the factory. I know the Yosems did not understand this, but there have been many things they wouldn't understand, many things I haven't shared with them, thank God. They don't know about my work with the Union of Jewish Workers. Why should I give them more to worry about? They don't know about David

Kaminski, the painter. Only recently, I finally decided not to marry him. What would Esther say if she knew this? I can imagine Esther fretting that I'm thirty-three and still unmarried!

I suppose I never wrote about David because I knew it would end as it did. We were not a strong enough union, David and I, despite the fact that we courted for so many months, propelled by the assumption of marriage. I came to understand David, to admire his commitment, to believe I could be his wife. But we had our differences, and in truth, the past with Henoch still looms over me, refusing to loosen its grip, refusing to recede. The Yosems know only that Henoch Rosenvitch and I parted company at the Palacios train station on that fateful day seven years ago. I have spared them the complicated reality that ensued. Six months ago, I moved into a single tenement room on Calle Lavalle, number 1454.

My block on Lavalle is damp and crowded, with a variety of old buildings that have been turned into multiple dwellings. Stone and wood, large and small, one, two, and three story, these structures shelter and encourage the street's confusion of horses and carts, shoppers, and the shouting of fruit vendors and junk dealers, established in every possible nook and cranny. David and his painter friends talk about "the pulse of life," the "vitality," the "raw beauty," as they wander the streets of the eleventh district, easels on their backs and paint cases under their arms. I see immigrant neighborhoods with the accompanying squalor and joy, despair and hope. I see buildings rising from the chaos of the street to create chaos in the sky; billowing clotheslines and crowded cast-iron balconies where housewives shake mops, mattresses air, and invalids sit next to geraniums, waiting to catch a few rays of sun.

I see sensitive, intelligent young painters spending hours discussing beauty and art, yet feeling no urgency about the plight of the common worker. David made a few half-hearted attempts to explain that he and his companions are dealing with reality the best way they can, through art. I remain convinced they're escapists. These painters are immigrants; like all of us, they know how much their help is needed. I'm impatient and hurt that they've chosen to focus their attention elsewhere, and I'm angry that David never approved of my Union work.

Of course it's dangerous! Who ever said it wasn't? After the police brutalities of ten days ago, workers are still nervous, and the city is extremely tense. A mounted squadron attacked a workers' rally celebrating the first of May, Labor Day. Wielding sabers and revolvers, they charged the crowd of men, women, and children, leaving one dead and many wounded. They were anarchist workers. But fear spread quickly to the Socialist groups, even to our little Union, which is apolitical. Hoping to relieve David's fears, I've oftentimes tried to explain that our concerns are not political, even if we do call ourselves a "union." I've tried to explain that we were founded as a relief organization for immigrants. Not that any of this matters in the face of violence and panic.

So how did it end, our ill-fated match? Two months ago, on a Sunday afternoon, David and I went to visit the new zoo near Palermo Park. We were resting in the grass, watching children with balloons in front of the elephants' compound. The sun was out, and young, happy voices hung in the air. I was telling David about the new printing press at the Union. But as usual, David was elsewhere, busy taking in the scene, busy floating in his imagination. Anxious to engage him, anxious once again to make him understand my commitment, I told him he was right, it is dangerous to belong to any workers' group. He was right, but I must continue to support what I believe in.

David turned to me, finally, reached over, and gently smoothed the hair out of my eyes. "Moorish," he said calmly, as though revealing a secret that would explain all, and he pointed to the brick-red decorations on the elephants' house. "Moorish motifs at the Buenos Aires zoo, in the year 1904." Then he looked out beyond the elephants and the zoo, beyond the city, west to where he'd heard the mountains of Cordoba were. "When you become my wife," he said softly, addressing that invisible mountain range, "your union concerns will seem very unimportant."

I was speechless, crushed. Was this the man I was preparing to marry? After all those Sunday afternoons, did he still not know me? Could he truly believe such a thing? At that moment, I knew our obsessions would always be at odds.

The quality of light, the moisture in the air, the tone of the sky? Is the grass green from a recent rain, or dry? These are David's passions, the visual world. Needing further distraction after the Moorish motifs—for I believe he too suddenly understood the futility of our situation—David became absorbed with the brilliant, brief journey of a sunbeam streaming down through space and trees, down to a small boy's sailor cap, with the two ribbons hanging. David did not blink as he watched the sunbeam's landing and metamorphosis, the taking on of shape and shadow of the very leaves that had fractured its intensity. The boy sat on the ground, playing with a spade. Not until the sunlight shimmered and pooled on the cap's whiteness did David turn away to the motions of the child's mother.

How naive of me to think immigrant workers' needs could ever compete, could ever capture his imagination. His eyes stilled the elegant woman into a tranquil pose as she bent over her baby in the carriage. Did her clothes, the yards of fine fabric, yield to the movements of her body? He saw the constrained waist; did he wonder how it would look without corsets? Or was that irrelevant? Was the lace at the neck uncomfortable? She wore a braided straw hat. The stylish wide brim was trimmed with ribbons and violets and leaves. Surely one swift movement of the head could make the invisible tortoiseshell combs slip away from the hair. Would that face change perceptibly in the haze of an evening stroll, or in the soft light from a parlor hearth? Did she spend hours in worry and sadness, perhaps because her husband had taken a mistress? Did David think these concerns—like mine—would become unimportant, with the passing of time?

David is convinced this place called Cordoba is his destiny. There he could live and paint in peace. The mountains, the air, they had to be better than the crowded city. How could I possibly run away with him, abandoning everything I'd worked for? He needs a woman who will be devoted to him and his work, to his children. This is a normal expectation on his part, for it is thus that the world turns. But I am not such a woman. Sitting in front of the elephants' house, I found myself grieving. How could he spend so much energy on that privileged, elegant woman in the straw hat and be so oblivious to the volatile state of the working class, to the voices calling for change and justice? How so eager to remain uninvolved? I could never abandon the Union, not for David, not for mountains, not for the children I haven't had. Despite the sun and the happy voices, we were left weakened and estranged, finally, by the very realities that made us separately strong and whole.

Those are the reasons I never wrote the Yosems about David Kaminski . . . once again I've digressed, and the basin of water at my feet is cold.

Where was I? My neighborhood, the eleventh district. Walking toward the waterfront, east on Lavalle, you meet Calle Libertad, at the corner of Plaza Lavalle. The plaza has long been a marketplace and point of congregation for new immigrants. There they buy, sell, and look for work, taking shelter from the sun under the branches of the huge ombu trees. From morning to sundown the plaza hums with activity. Calle Libertad, which runs alongside the plaza, is a wide street, airy and sunny. It's on Libertad that they built the synagogue of the Congregation Israelita of the Republic of Argentina. It was inaugurated in 1897, the same year I arrived in

Buenos Aires from Moisés Ville. Perhaps that explains my affection toward it, for though I often pass it, I've never entered its doors.

I am not observant; I take after my father in that respect. Papa entered the shul only for Rosh Hashanah and Yom Kippur. In contrast, his father, my grandfather, was very learned in Torah. He spent his life in our shtetl's little shul. When he returned home in the evenings, he studied his tomes late into the night, a glass of tea, a crust of bread, and a small tallow candle at his elbow. The certain presence of this synagogue on Calle Libertad, with the star of David on its cupola, and the Ten Commandments carved in its stone façade, fills me with hope for our people.

Directly across from it, also facing the Plaza Lavalle, construction continues on a big theater. In this, I take more interest. I inherited my love for theater from Mama. I understand this will be the new Colón, taking its name from the old theater on Plaza de Mayo. Whenever I pass by, I see the stone masons laboring on imported Italian marble and granite columns for the interior. They've been working for years. I've heard rumors of a golden hall with a painted dome and crystal chandeliers. They say the stage will hold 600, and 2,500 people will sit in red velvet seats on tiers of gilded balconies. There will be standing room for another 1,000 people. It promises to be spectacular!

In the meantime, the tenement I call home is crowded, noisy, and dirty. It's a three-ring circus, but I've become accustomed to it, just as I have to the city, and I'm grateful to have my privacy. In the center of the patio an iron staircase rises to separate into two walkways leading to the left and to the right of the open, second floor. I live in the left wing. To my right is a family with eight children, the Milekofskys—whose dream is to buy a small grocery—and to my left, four rabbinical students share rooms. When I climb up or down the staircase, I must fight the lines of laundry strung in every direction. Downstairs, I have to be careful not to trip over one of Mrs. Gorzky's chickens running wild in the patio. She claims her neighbors' children let them out of their cage, just to make her crazy, from morning to night.

Though I am at the factory all day, my neighbor Peshke Milekofsky keeps me informed of the goings on in our tenement. Peshke watches over me. In the six months since I've lived at number 1454, we've become very good friends. She is like an older sister to me; she's only six years older than I am, but she makes sure I eat well and that I'm not always alone. I disappoint her, however, because I do not drink *maté*. Like so many immigrants, she quickly took to the custom and cannot live without it. In the evenings, when she sees I've returned home, she hurries over with her *maté*. While I make myself a cup of tea, she brings me up on the events of the day. Besides her daily chores of cooking and cleaning and supervising children, Peshke takes in piece-work sewing, as many women do. Her figure has become matronly since the births of her children, but she is still very pretty with her light hair and her clear, blue eyes. I've encountered so many fair Polish Jews in Buenos Aires. Like her husband, Peshke is a hard worker and kind-hearted, but she likes her gossip. She lets me know who fought with whom, who hogged the water faucet, which child was discovered with head lice, and whether any vendors came around.

There is rarely a day that a vendor or two doesn't appear in the patio to sell his wares. Occasionally I leave an order with Peshke— a hank of elastic or perhaps a new comb—and she acquires the items for me. When the vendor arrives, the women and children gather around to see his display of soaps and ribbons, pots and pans, corsets, trinkets, and anything else he can fit in those huge wicker baskets. The baskets are attached to both ends of a pole that he balances across his toughened shoulders, day in and day out.

With the exception of a few old grandfathers, the only man who remains in our tenement during the day is the anarchist cobbler,

Pincus, who has set up shop in the front passageway of the patio. In the years I've been in Buenos Aires, Pincus has made me several pairs of shoes, following Henoch's drawing. The city's cobblestones are hard, and I seem to wear through my soles far too quickly. In Moisés Ville, we had only dirt roads. Pincus keeps my heel in good repair, and he has been very kind and generous. Once, when I was very low on funds, he told me to wait and pay him when I could. He is fascinated by Henoch's drawing, and he carefully returns it to me after every new shoe. Pincus and his adolescent son work hard. Every day they mend and repair, and on occasion, they even make a new pair of shoes. Whenever I walk by, I hear him speaking softly to the boy, instructing him with another lesson from history. One day he tells him about the czar and the pogroms, and the next about Nikolai Lenin, and how only last year the Bolshevik Party of Russia adopted his thesis on party organization. Pincus says that Lenin will help change the course of Russia. He reminds his son that in 1887, seventeen-year-old Lenin saw his brother, Alexander, hanged to death for attempting to kill the czar. He insists that we have yet to see what this Lenin will do. I have heard Pincus speak of Plato, of Homer, and of the American President Abraham Lincoln. I know of these names from my years in Moisés Ville, when I helped Henoch Rosenvitch with the library.

That time seems so long ago now, and Henoch is from another life. Since that evening nearly a year ago, on June 11, 1903, to be exact, when we vowed never to see each other again—but I won't go into detail, I can't; there has been enough said of Henoch Rosenvitch in these journals, enough joy, enough pain. Since that evening, I've thrown myself into my Union work. I've forced myself not to think about him, and I've tried to make a new life, with new interests, new friends, like David Kaminski. But the temptation of memories is always only steps behind me, jumping at the chance to seize me, to catch me off guard, to meddle with the present.

My neighbors at the tenement wonder why a woman of my age is not married, or at the very least why I don't share quarters. I don't bother telling them about my old roommate, Golda, nor do I tell them that I too have known passion. I don't reveal my history. I don't explain that it's easier being alone because I prefer not having to account to anyone about love or work, and thus, why I arrive home so late. In front of the other women, Peshke pretends to nag me about my spinsterhood and finding a husband, a serious man, not like that artist, Kaminski, I wasted so much time with. Peshke always called him "The Dreamer." She warns me to hurry. She says I am still young, still attractive, but I will not be so slim and tall forever, my hair will not remain black forever, nor will my eyes burn brightly forever. And someday, she adds, someday my leg will bother a man. The neighbors nod in agreement, clucking their tongues. I know Peshke doesn't mean it; she knows me too well. But Peshke will continue to tease me. Somehow it eases her own resignation to the reality we both understand now, the certainty that I will probably never marry.

Peshke's idea of a good man is her quiet, handsome brother-in-law, Aaron Milekofsky, who has recently arrived in Buenos Aires from the Russian-Japanese War. It's merely a joke that I should consider Aaron for a husband. Peshke and I both know that a fiancée waits in Vilna. Besides, he is in his early twenties, a child. Aaron Milekofsky has high cheekbones, small, dark eyes and a fine, straight nose, which is certainly his most striking feature. There is a sadness about his face. He is a baker by trade, a printer by choice, and he's already deeply involved and committed to the Union. Peshke knows more than she lets on. She knows I'm dedicated to the work, and secretly she approves. When we're alone and she sips her *maté*, she tells me that since I'm a woman who can read and write, I should make good use of it, and it shouldn't be wasted on one man alone. Peshke's humor has seen me through some long days!

When Aaron and I run into each other at Peshke's house, we never discuss our work at the printing press. I've grown fond of Aaron. He reminds me of my brother Chaim, who disappeared in the same pogrom that killed my parents and sisters. Aaron works hard; the bakery by day, the printing press by night. Sometimes on Sundays, I hear him playing his trumpet on the rooftops of our tenement. It's the only possession he brought with him from Russia. The few times I've heard Aaron speak at the headquarters, his voice has always been quiet and his manner serious. His discussions have focused on other unions, the government, the problems faced by the masses of new immigrants. He has never mentioned that he shot himself in the toe to get out of further fighting during the Russian-Japanese War, nor has he ever mentioned his betrothed.

He, like so many other young men, will work for years before he earns the passage to bring over the girl. Everything I know, including her name, Sonia, is from Peshke. Peshke claims she doesn't like Sonia's looks, despite the fact that she has never met her. Once, when Aaron wasn't home, Peshke showed me the photograph he keeps beside his bed. I saw an attractive girl with willful gray eyes and a formidable presence, uninhibited by the stillness of photography.

The Union is what gives me hope and keeps me going. I work in the library, I teach Spanish to new immigrants, and I assist with the press. The printing work has become totally engrossing, and every free moment I spend at the headquarters. I learned the trade by helping printers, and now others learn from me. Printers are in great demand, and the truth is, there are not many who are women. They tell me I am one of the few! I feel this is an honor, and I take my work very seriously; there is much to do. My hands are permanently stained and I always smell of ink. Because of our small press, others read and hear and know that they do not have to put up with their miserable lots.

If Papa were still alive, and if he knew of my activities, what would he think? What would he think of his Rifke, the daughter he sent off to the Argentine, the New World, so that she might be away and free to make a new life? I believe he would approve, for he is the one who taught me to read and write. I know Papa was an unusual man, wanting his daughters to be educated. Even today, it is a rare woman who is allowed to pursue learning. I am one of the few literate women at the factory. I hear the girls continually complain about their parents, how old-fashioned they are, how they cannot adjust to this new country, the new ways. I tell them over and over they are lucky to have parents. When Papa was a very young man, before he married Mama, he worked at the government printing house in Kamenets. Sometimes I am certain that he must have known—because of that early work and his love for books— he must have known that printer's ink can become a source of nourishment.

For the last year or so, the Union's headquarters have taken a permanent address—an empty warehouse next to Soltansky's Tailor Shop. Marcus Soltansky was one of the original founders of our Union. Sometimes, when I get out of the factory in the evening, I don't go back to my room but straight to the warehouse. I take a package of bread and cheese, and I eat there. It's drafty and cold, but we boil water, so there is always *maté* and tea and crackers, sometimes even dried fruit. That of course is a delicacy.

More often than not, Marcus is there, preparing the press for the evening's work and the arrival of the others. I chat with him while I eat and he works. I love to listen to his stories about the old days in Kovno. With this permanent address, we are now able to have a real library space, with newspapers, a few books, and blackboards, to teach the immigrants their new language. The printing press is set up in another corner, and meetings are generally held in the large, center space. Before this building, the Union's address changed frequently. I used to be relayed a message at the factory if I was to appear at a different location that evening.

We began in 1896, innocently enough as the Union of Jewish Workers, a mutual aid society established to help new immigrants find jobs. But membership has become increasingly more dangerous, especially now with all the new leftist groups that are forming. Everything is risky—the meetings, being out at night with the bundles of printing, and not being caught by the factory bosses during the next day's distribution of flyers. Certainly there is danger. But we all feel it is work that must get done.

Although we advocate no political solutions, we are still considered part of the leftist movement. Leftist speakers continue to come to Argentina to address the masses, a steady stream of them. This is exciting and frightening. In 1901 and 1902, Pietro Gori, an important member of the European anarchist movement, addressed a congress of twenty-seven different organizations in Argentina. He urged the anarchist workers to unite their forces and organize into syndicates. The anarchists, the Socialists, the Bundists, even the unionists, they're all gathering strength. The Socialists! How can they insist upon complete and total assimilation? Surely there is a more humane way to emigrate, to immigrate? I cannot align myself with these ideas!

The general strikes have become widespread. It was because of the one in 1902, uniting dock workers with other unskilled laborers, that congress convened and passed the terrifying Residence Law, designed to discriminate against the foreign born. Now immigration officials have the power to throw out anyone they consider a threat to peace.

We are only the Union of Jewish Workers, but now the police are watching us because they think we're one and the same, all Russian troublemakers. "Rusitos," as we Jews are commonly called. They are constantly looking for "foreign revolutionaries," as they call us.

There has been talk within our ranks that eventually our Union will take on a new face and deal with the health needs of immigrants. So far, no organization does that. So much is to be done.

I've written enough about this subject tonight. I am always preoccupied with these ideas; they both worry and stimulate me. Tonight I sat down to soak my feet and write about something else. How I stray! I've written about David and the Milekofskys, the Colón and the laborers of Buenos Aires! Now it's late and I must stop. What I wanted to write about will have to wait until the next time.

THE RIFKE CHRONICLES

May 12, 1904
Buenos Aires

The other night, my intention was to write about Bela Palatnik, a most remarkable young woman. Bela is struggling with a shocking reality that most of us cannot begin to comprehend.

On the evening of May 9th, when we arrived at headquarters for our usual printing work and union meeting, we were told that Moses Soltansky, Marcus's son, would be bringing a visitor to speak to us. I assumed it would be yet another representative from one of the anarchist cells or some other group wanting to convince us to join forces with them. They come around so often now, and they're so exhausting with their commitment and almost violent zeal. At about half past nine, while we were busy cleaning the press and assembling the flyers, our work was interrupted by the code knock at the back door. I unlocked and opened the door. Moses stood smiling shyly in the doorway; beside him, a pale, young woman with determined eyes shivered in the dim light of the alley. She seemed too frail to be an anarchist. Moses is a tall, burly man of twenty with a head of thick, curly red hair. His friends call him Big Moses. He did not follow his father into the tailoring profession. His large, rough hands could never hold a needle. Moses is a metalworker. On the evening of May 9th, he seemed as meek as a lamb beside this strange, young woman.

After Moses gently led her in and introduced her to all of us, he announced that Bela had come to tell us about the white slave trade and the misfortunes she encountered when she arrived in this country. Bela's slight figure was wrapped in a dark woolen shawl. Her attire was drab, devoid of any indication of the life she had been forced to lead for nine months.

Bela began speaking in a quiet, subdued voice. Slowly it took on more volume as her story progressed. She was anxious for us to know there were more girls like her, trapped in a nightmare existence with nowhere to turn and little hope for escape. She is determined to help the others. She kept repeating that she was one of the lucky ones, she got away. Bela's dark eyes and small, pretty face displayed a commitment that overwhelmed us all, and her tale held us transfixed for the duration of the evening. She spoke eloquently; her voice and story softened hearts in our drafty warehouse full of toughened young revolutionaries.

Bela Palatnik landed at the port of Buenos Aires a year ago. She arrived on a ship from Germany, destined for the Clara Colony in Entre Ríos where she had an aunt and uncle. I was struck by how similar her story was to mine, even though I was older and had arrived earlier. She too left her parents and family behind, she in Vilna, I in Tomaschpol. She too traveled alone, except for the friend she made on ship, another young woman also headed for a colony.

"We were met at the pier by a well-dressed, well-mannered couple. The woman, stout and friendly, announced that she too had come from Vilna. In a soft-spoken voice, the man explained that he represented a hotel for newly arrived young women, a haven where we might stay for a few nights before proceeding with our journeys. Exhausted by the voyage and frightened by the strangeness of our new surroundings, we eagerly accepted the couple's invitation to lead us to the hotel. Not until we arrived at the 'hotel' was the true nature of the situation revealed to us. The man was paid by the owner of the establishment—a Mrs. Guttman—for delivering us. It was horrible. In all my days in Vilna I had no idea such things happened. I had no idea that it was possible for a woman to be 'sold' for her body. Until I arrived here, I did not even know the word 'brothel.'

"I see from the look on some of your faces that you are wondering how my friend and I could have been so innocent, so naive as to follow strange people across Buenos Aires. You are right, we were naive. But the important and frightening thing is we were no different from so many of the young women who arrive here alone. It happens everyday. More and more Jewish women are being forced into prostitution and most often by Jewish perpetrators."

At that point, Bela Palatnik dropped her head. "My parents in Vilna know nothing, nor my aunt and uncle in Colony Clara. I have never written them." Bela remained silent for a few moments. "I prefer to have them think I am dead."

I and another woman in the audience both moved to sit beside Bela, to be near her, to offer support. She continued with her story.

"If you had known me a year ago upon my arrival, you would understand. I was a pleasant enough looking girl, but young and with no great reserve of nerve, and certainly no sense of commitment to anything in particular. I was journeying to the Colony Clara to live with my aunt and uncle in this new country. Like most young girls, my greatest concern was finding a husband and having a beautiful dress for my wedding. It all seems a lifetime ago. I can hardly believe I was ever that girl." Bela closed her eyes for a few moments, clearly drawing on inner strength. "I intend to dedicate myself to helping girls in distress, and to fighting this horrible evil that is plaguing our women."

There was quiet clapping in the room. Bela smiled briefly. She no longer looked quite as frail as she had shivering at our back door. As she spoke, she became energized with dignity and strength.

"If it hadn't been for Moses Soltansky, I might still be in that awful place. It was Moses who helped me escape." Bela looked in Moses's direction. He acknowledged with a shy nod.

"How did you manage to get away?" Someone asked curiously from the audience.

"Moses happened to be walking beside Mrs. Guttman's 'hotel' when I threw a small rock out the window. I had tied a note to the stone, explaining the situation and the nature of the place, asking for help. The timing was luck," Bela said softly. "Moses promptly returned the next day with several large companions." Bela grinned for the first time. "After some discussion, I was permitted to leave the establishment without much problem, although Mrs. Guttman stood in the doorway jeering at us as we departed."

"As for my friend," Bela's smile disappeared, "I don't know where she is. We were separated only days after our arrival at the brothel. I heard people whispering that she was taken to another establishment in another city."

"Maybe the owners of the place should be forced to reveal where they sent your friend!" An angry voice called out from the back of the room. "There are plenty of us who wouldn't mind marching over to that address this very evening!" Cheering began in the warehouse.

"No!" Moses Soltansky jumped up. "That's not the way!" He took a few moments to collect himself.

I've always known Moses to be a shy young man, a reticent speaker. But that evening, he became an orator. Driven by his obvious feelings for Bela and his disgust for white slavery, he quickly overcame his shyness.

"We must be systematic, organized," he continued. "It's the only way. Violence will only attract the police, and the police are involved in this terrible ring of prostitution. The white slavers are referred to as the *tmeyim*, the unclean ones, and they've become a powerful organization. They have enormous control and they're steadily gaining. Politics, law enforcement, the business world, the theater."

Here Bela interrupted. "They've even formed their own synagogue and benevolent society. Last Yom Kippur, I actually saw a Madame taking her 'girls' in for services!"

"My father can tell you," Moses said, glancing at Marcus, "he can tell you of how they have not been allowed to bury their dead in our cemetery, although they've certainly tried."

Marcus Soltansky spoke slowly and articulately. "As many of you know, I am on the board of the Congregation Israelita's burial society. A few years ago, in 1899, the *tmeyim* wanted to donate an enormous sum of money to the synagogue—to insure their people proper Jewish burials—but they were turned away, thank God. I understand they have finally bought their own cemetery, and that the Moroccans have bought a piece from them with a meter strip of land separating the 'pure' from the 'impure.'"

Moses raised his arm. "Perhaps some of you don't know of these things because you do not frequent their establishments. But I tell you, they are a pestilence. We must work to rid our community of them."

Applause broke out.

"What's to be done?" Aaron Milekofsky asked quietly from the shadows of the headquarters.

"Many things," Moses said, "many things. We can write home to family and friends in Europe, warning them of the dangers to their daughters, sisters, and yes, even wives. Many girls are brought under false pretenses. Dealers go to small towns in Europe, collecting girls by promising to bring them to Buenos Aires where jobs and husbands await them. The girls are usually violated during the voyage by the dealers themselves. By the time they arrive in Argentina, they have no choice but to enter a brothel.

Bela stood up. "We can patrol the port when ships arrive," she said eagerly. "We can make sure girls are not led away in the manner that I was, and my friend. At times the girls are lured with offers of candies and perfumes. We can send women onto the ships to warn the girls and to encourage them to be very cautious. The Jewish Association for the Protection of Girls and Women has been working with Scotland Yard, helping to track down missing women who traveled to Argentina by way of England. Posting warning signs in the port buildings is a good idea, but I'm afraid that won't help much because so many girls can't read. Then, of course, you men can actually rescue women from brothels, the way I was. By pretending to frequent these establishments and keeping your eyes open, you can help many escape. Then there's the problem of where these girls go after. They are no longer considered respectable for marriage," Bela's voice quavered, but she continued, "and many cannot return to their families, or continue on to the families they were joining." Bela turned to Moses.

He nodded and began speaking again. "As for how you deal with men who knowingly sell their wives and daughters into prostitution, I don't know." Moses stared out across his audience. His large figure with the shock of red hair was an enormous presence in our suddenly hushed warehouse. It was as though everyone had stopped breathing. "I've heard," Moses began again, "I've heard of this happening with a family that was bound for the Colony of Moisés

Ville. Once they arrived at the colony, things seemed so very bleak, the husband—to his wife's horror—turned around and sold their eldest daughter to the white slave 'trader' who had pursued them all the way from Buenos Aires. That 'trader,' that disgusting piece of garbage, was a Jew."

When Moses and Bela had no more to say, the atmosphere in the warehouse was heavy and still. I felt as though I might choke. We were left speechless and shocked by this story. I, like everyone else in the room, felt only grief. One never likes to hear of the existence of evil among your own, and in the place you call home.

So, Who Was Pietro Gori?

In Buenos Aires, in the barrio of Urquiza, there is a small neighborhood bar called *La Torre de Babel*. It's been there for decades, and it still has its original mirrors and marble counter, brass fixtures and bentwood chairs. Andrés, the present owner and bartender, looks after it with pride. He keeps the mirror and brass polished, the chairs waxed, the tile floor swept and clean. After a long day, it's a pleasure to drop into La Torre, especially when the weather has taken a chilly turn, or if it has been raining all afternoon, as it has today. Several students at one of the small, round tables are examining a laptop computer. One of them, a young woman with a red beret and red lipstick, is demonstrating while the others watch with interest, drinking and commenting quietly. Two elderly men, wearing fine vicuña scarves over their suit jackets, are playing chess at another table. A young couple sits near the front windows, both reading the newspaper, steam still rising from their coffees.

At the counter, a stocky, middle-aged man named Marconi stands talking to Andrés. He wears a business suit, he's balding, and he has a mustache. There is nothing remarkable looking about Marconi. In fact, he's quite ordinary in every way, except perhaps for his unusually large eyes. Dark and deeply set, they are, at the moment, even more striking for their bewilderment and exhaustion. In his state of confusion and hurt, Marconi has been speaking anxiously, gently slapping the counter for emphasis. Suddenly speechless, his frustrated gaze settles on the television's silent screen, as though waiting for a miracle.

"That's it. Exactly as I heard it." His eyes turn back to the bartender. "Can you believe it? Can you believe my wife, Ida, would tell me such a thing? Imagine, the year is not 1998, but 1898, and she is the reincarnation of Pietro Gori's mistress, a tragic Jewish feminist and beautiful besides!" Marconi shakes his head in disbelief, unbuttoning his collar, loosening his tie. "And you, my friend, wonder why I haven't been in this week for my glass of wine!"

Andrés smiles. "So, who was Pietro Gori?" He asks calmly, polishing the glass in his hand.

"Who, indeed!" Marconi says. "Until last week, I'd never even heard the name! Listen," he leans across the counter, tugging on one of Andrés's white sleeves. "Last Monday morning when Ida woke up and told me about it, how it all came to her in a dream, I asked about this Gori fellow," Marconi shakes his hands in a questioning motion, "and she called me a capitalist pig! Just like that!" Marconi pulls back away from the counter, as though surprised by his own words.

"Only a capitalist pig wouldn't know one of the great leaders of the Argentine anarchist movement!" She screamed at me. Have you ever heard such a thing?" He asks, stepping closer, his eyes opened wide. "I don't know what's come over Ida. She's never been interested in politics. Does she even know what an anarchist is? Ida has always minded her business, tended her own affairs—the home, the children, the usual things. Now, suddenly, she's telling me it's not today, but a hundred years ago. She's the anarchist feminist, and I'm the capitalist pig! Right! I'm supposed to go along with this?! Oh yes, I shouldn't expect dinner that evening because she has a lecture to attend at the university!"

"A lecture?" Andrés looks surprised. Yes, he knows Marconi's wife, he's known her since she was Ida Gerstein. Often, early in the mornings, when Andrés washes down the sidewalk in front of the bar, Ida shuffles by on her way home from the market, carrot tops and turnips hanging out of her bags. Short and heavy set, her face is flushed and mottled, like spoiling peaches. He can hear her heavy breathing as she passes, as they exchange familiar greetings. The last time Andrés saw her, it crossed his mind that the years have not been kind to Ida, once so slim, so fair, so pretty. They grew up together on the same block of Corrientes. His Spanish parents ran a corner grocery, her Jewish family operated a small furniture factory. Then she married Marconi, the candy maker, and for years now, Ida has been puffing past Andrés's wet sidewalk with her carrots and turnips. A lecture was hard to imagine.

"On penal reform, no less! I swear to God." Marconi slaps the counter again. "A lecture on penal reform! She made my coffee that morning, she even heated a roll, but she had no time to sit with me because she had to hurry to her cell meeting."

Andrés blinks, reaching for another glass to polish.

"One week ago, everything was normal. My life was as it should be!" Marconi says with anguish, pressing his small, tight fist into his chest. "I was an ordinary fellow, the contented owner of my candy factory. My candy, those nougats and bonbons, marzipan. I bring your wife a box every New Year's Eve. For two years running, Evita Perón asked my father to send 2,000 free boxes of Marconi Confections for the poor. Of course he sent. What else could he do?

Only a fool wouldn't send. You think he wanted to be closed down? Ida still talks about that. We were only seventeen at the time, but she still talks about it! She never understood. She said it was persecution, anti-Semitism, that they knew my mother was a Jew. But my mother wasn't the owner of the candy factory, my father was! And he wasn't a Jew! Sometimes I go crazy trying to understand Ida's logic! She said my father shouldn't have given in so easily; he should have held his ground, the way the Groismans did. The Groismans! The whole Groisman thing happened because the family refused to donate money to Evita's favorite causes. Every businessman around them was donating, but not them! Oh no, not them! As if there wasn't enough friction."

Andrés looks confused.

"Oh, you didn't know?" Marconi lowers his voice. "One of the Groisman brothers was a Socialist leader, an active anti-Peronist!" He sighs. "Well, in any case, Evita knew how to deal with them. She placed an enormous order for candy. For the poor, of course. You know the rest of the story?"

"No," Andrés says.

"After the factory shipped out the candy, she was sent a bill. Can you imagine?! Those Groismans were a nervy bunch. Naturally, Evita was furious, so she had the factory closed down. We're not talking about a small operation, like Marconi Confections. There were four Groisman brothers, and the Mu-Mu Candy Factory employed 700 people. Government 'inspectors' simply appeared on the premise, reported that the factory was crawling with rats, and that the chocolate being sold to Argentine children was poisonous. All those people lost their jobs, and the Groismans were ruined!"

"So, we all know what would have happened if my father had 'held his ground.' Ida still insists it was a matter of principle! Who cares about principles if your livelihood has been taken away? If Marconi Confections had been closed, God knows what I'd be doing, and your wife wouldn't get her box of bonbons on New Year's Eve."

Andrés nods in agreement.

"What does Ida understand about politics?" Marconi asks. "When the military was in power, she could never accept that it was important to be on good terms with them. Remember, I used to be friendly with that Colonel Jimenez, the one I would bring around to the bar? His wife liked my chocolates, and I liked his clout. Of course for Ida, again it was a matter of principle." Marconi closes his eyes and massages his temples. "One week ago, my days were ordered and simple. My wife was devoted to me, perhaps not a lot to look at, as you know, but devoted. A good woman who tended to me and our house with the same pride and care she took with our children. That was one week ago. Today I'm a capitalist pig whose wife has not only deserted him, but has been reincarnated as an anarchist!" Marconi reaches for his glass of wine. "I haven't had the nerve to tell the children yet." He says softly. "Thank God they don't live in the city. What do I say to them?" For a few seconds, Marconi stares blankly at the young people with the computer. He turns back to Andrés. "That was only the first day. You want to hear about the second?"

Andrés is called over to one of the round tables for more drinks. While he tends to his other customers, Marconi finishes his wine and lights a cigarette. He can't accept this is happening. He can't believe Ida really thinks he will fall for this nonsense.

"So, what happened next?" Andrés asks, refilling Marconi's wine glass.

"On Tuesday, Ida did not make the bed." Marconi blows smoke up toward the television screen. "I don't ever remember Ida not making the bed. In all the years we've been married, every morning, she made the bed. When I said something about it, she retorted that if it bothered me so much, I could make it. She was too busy. She was meeting Pietro for lunch before his lecture. Then I got this speech about how important he was, how he'd been on a lecture tour of the United States, speaking in every major city between the East Coast and San Francisco. While she was combing her hair, she told me I would appreciate Gori's ideas on penal reform. In his opinion, mental disease is responsible for at least 50 percent of Argentina's criminal population! Do I care about what happened a hundred years ago?!" Marconi angrily stubs out his cigarette in the ashtray beside his wine glass. "She assured me I would like Gori because he's my countryman. I told her that just because he's Italian, this is not enough reason to like him. Especially since he's been dead for so long. I hate corpses, I told her. I couldn't resist that. I thought I'd be able to get through to her, get her to admit that all this is some crazy game!"

"And?"

"It didn't work," Marconi says quietly. "She just ignored me and left for her luncheon date anyway." Marconi clutches his head. "What am I saying?! How could Ida have a date with a dead man? She probably went off to the park to feed the pigeons. Wherever she went, she didn't come home until 11:30 that night. I had gone to bed, exhausted from waiting. I'd been to the little restaurant around the corner for dinner. There was nothing to eat in the house. As she climbed into bed, she told me Gori believes in free love. As if I don't have enough problems!"

Marconi finishes off his second glass of wine. Andrés refills the glass and then pours himself one. He was still having trouble visualizing Ida in this new role.

"Remember, Andrés, we're talking about a hundred years ago!"

"I'm trying to, I'm trying to."

"Well, on Wednesday, Ida woke up and told me that since Gori has taken up residency in Buenos Aires—he left Italy because of his politics, of course—since he's taken up residency here, he's been invited to lecture at the university. He recruits the women in his courses to become active in trade unions. He encourages them to become involved in social reform, ending the exploitation of women in factories, and the home. *The home!* Ida repeated to me, as though I hadn't been listening." Marconi takes out his cigarettes and lights another. "Then she told me women find him inspiring. They come to his lectures in droves." Marconi draws deeply on his cigarette. "They fall madly in love with him! Ah, but Gori does not believe in marriage. He feels the legal union is contrary to love! Now, Andrés, I ask you, you know my wife, Ida; can you make any sense of all this?"

"I can't, Marconi. Did she say anything else on Wednesday?"

"No, she simply left without lifting a finger around the house. Thursday, I had to wash the bathtub myself. It had gotten impossible. On Friday morning, I was ironing my shirt when she came in and announced, happily, that it's now 1901, and that Pietro has returned from a trip. She even told me she missed him terribly and that he's such a passionate lover! That very day, Gori would be addressing a congress of twenty-seven different Argentine labor organizations. Ida told me he wants to encourage the workers to unite and organize into syndicates." Marconi's eyes are large and desperate. "I'm worried, Andrés. This may be nonsense, but where will it end? I tell you, with every passing day she becomes more committed, more verbal, more passionate about this Gori fellow and what he stands for!"

"*Stood* for, Marconi, *stood* for." Andrés says firmly, but kindly. "Now, let's be reasonable." Andrés reaches over to pat his friend's shoulder. "First, this is some kind of temporary aberration, it will pass. Second, have you any idea where she actually goes during the day? Maybe she really is feeding the pigeons? You should find out. And where have these notions come from? Has she been talking to someone, or perhaps reading about this Gori fellow?"

"Ida, read?" Marconi looks at Andrés in disbelief.

"Well," Andrés the bartender scratches his head, "I thought perhaps she'd taken it up again. You know, the way she used to when she was young." He smiles, recalling that Ida Gerstein read, and that Ida Gerstein attended lectures. Suddenly he's embarrassed that only a few minutes ago it came as such a surprise to him that Ida Marconi would attend a lecture. He's chagrined to realize his surprise is because she's gotten heavy, and her face is mottled, and because he's used to seeing her with carrots and turnips. "I never saw a girl read as much as she did." Andrés nods at Marconi. "She'd sit inside her old man's shop, keeping an eye out for customers, while her face was deep in a book."

Marconi blinks. "No, Ida doesn't read, as far as I know." He puts out his second cigarette. "Never has, since we've been married." He tightens his tie, straightens his collar. "The children, the house, they kept her busy enough. She never had the time, you see. I can't imagine that she has any more time now."

Andrés shrugs. "Well anyway, Marconi, perhaps you should keep an eye on her, see where she goes."

"You're right. Maybe tomorrow. I won't go in to the factory, I'll follow her. Did I tell you about Saturday?"

"No."

"Our daughter phoned to say she and the children would come for Sunday dinner. Ida wasn't even home when she called. I lied, I said she was marketing. I didn't know what to say to her, how to put her off. You can imagine, by that point, the house was a disaster. I really didn't know where to begin with it. It took me an hour just to find where Ida keeps the broom and rags. I'm embarrassed to admit it. I cleaned up as well as I could, and when Ida came back, she didn't even notice the house, or that I was still wearing an apron. She breezed in, changed her clothes, and left again. Where the hell do you think she goes?" Marconi asks anxiously.

Andrés shrugs. "I guess there are any number of possibilities.

What happened Sunday? Who cooked dinner, and what did your daughter say? She must have been very surprised?"

"Fortunately, they didn't come. One of the children got sick. I worried all Saturday evening about how I was going to tell her. Now I have another week to worry about it. Surely they will want to come next Sunday." Marconi looks at his watch. "It's late, I'd better go. I'm going to cook for myself tonight, Andrés. I'll get a piece of steak, I'll boil potatoes." He slaps the counter with determination. "I've never done it, but I guess I have to start. Maybe she'll be home early, for a change."

"Good luck!" Andrés calls, as his friend disappears out the door.

Marconi is in better spirits when he leaves the bar. The wine did him good. He walks slowly under his umbrella, stopping first at the butcher. As he waits in line, he looks around at all the men out shopping for the evening meal—some young, some old, some more or less his age. They all seem to take it in their stride, and none appear bothered by shopping for food. Clearly it isn't such a humiliating act for a man. Times have changed. But when? Marconi suddenly wonders, stepping up to the counter.

He enjoys selecting his meat, and later, at the grocer's, he picks his potatoes with great care and even buys a head of lettuce, which looks very fresh indeed. As he walks home, he realizes he will have to grill the meat out on the patio, the way Ida does. He can manage; God knows, he's watched her often enough. Perhaps he can fry some onions too. By the time he reaches the bakery, Marconi is so excited at the prospect of preparing his dinner, he feels like a nervous schoolboy. "I'll take two of those little tarts," he tells the baker, who is surprised to see him and not his wife. "Two tarts, and half a dozen of those buns."

"Mrs. Marconi doesn't eat lemon tarts, and she never buys the buns," the baker says perfunctorily. "She always gets the loaf."

"I'll have the buns, thank you."

Marconi is actually singing when he unlocks the front door and picks up the evening newspaper.

An hour later, the potatoes have burnt on the stove, and Marconi cannot start the grill. He doesn't know what the problem is. It's started to rain again, and he's gotten quite soaked standing out in the patio with the briquettes that won't light. The contraption is so ancient, no wonder it doesn't function. Marconi suddenly realizes how many times Ida has told him they need a new grill, the kind that comes with its own gas tank. Finally he gives up, takes the meat back into the kitchen, and fries it on the stove. He doesn't eat the potatoes. He washes the lettuce, but shakes it so hard, it's completely bruised. The buns are good, and he finds the lemon tarts delicious, realizing he's never had them before. Next time, Marconi decides, next time he will do better with the meat and potatoes.

When Ida arrives home, Marconi has fallen asleep on his chair with the newspaper. She is careful not to wake him as she picks up after him and cleans in the kitchen. She laughs gently as she washes the pot of burnt potatoes. At least he ate some meat, she smiles, cleaning the frying pan. She dries her hands on the dishcloth and walks into the living room. Ida looks at her sleeping husband and wonders if he's had enough? Is he ready to talk?

She's been ready for years. But Marconi never wanted to talk, never wanted to deal with their lives and routines. If it were up to him, he would never want anything to change. His life, his wife, the world. Ida doesn't want a lot, not really. She just wants a little independence. Should she call it freedom? Occasionally she would like to attend a concert or a lecture or go for a walk without always having to explain herself, without always feeling that everything she does is out of duty or responsibility.

Ida sits in the chair across from Marconi. She's as much to blame as he is. She assumed a role as eagerly as he expected her to. Motherhood and housekeeping, all those things. But years have passed and the children are gone and times have changed. She's often lonely, and the days seem long. Women do all kinds of things now without their husbands. Why can't she? Why can't she indulge her other interests? Why should she continue to pretend she doesn't read? Why should she feel he will ridicule her, commenting that he doesn't know how she can possibly have the time?

She glances at Marconi snoring into the newspaper. He really is a terrible boor, but she loves him. He looks exhausted. She is sorry about the whole Gori thing; she never intended to let it go so far. But it was fun while it lasted! It was fun to leave the house early in the morning, skip the marketing, and go straight to the library for a few hours. In the afternoon, she enjoyed the long walks in the botanical gardens and San Telmo, the long bus rides to Tigre and Olivos. She missed cooking for Marconi, and she felt awful leaving the bed undone. But she needed to upset him. She needed to have him wake up and look around, see things for what they are.

None of this might have happened if she hadn't been reading that biography. There was something sparkling, almost magical about Pietro Gori—the way women flocked to hear him speak, the way he didn't believe in marriage. He wanted women to feel liberated, free to become active members of society. He showed them they could be more than just daughters and wives and mothers. Perhaps the time is ripe for another Gori, Ida realizes, smiling. She could do with a mentor right now.

The reincarnation plan came to her in minutes, seconds really. Ida didn't know if Gori had a mistress, let alone if she was beautiful or Jewish or a feminist. But it was a nice thought. The idea occurred to her one morning while she was reading. Looking up from her book, glancing out the bedroom window at her neighbor's tile terrace and the rows of laundry, in that moment when the sheets looked so white, and the tiles so red in the clear morning light, in that moment, she was certain she would have known Pietro Gori had she lived in his time. Absolutely certain. The whole plan rolled from there.

Ida stands and moves gently toward her husband. Now she will wake him and do the best she can to explain away Pietro Gori. Perhaps she and Marconi can set a new course together.

THE RIFKE CHRONICLES

In the year 1907, factory stoppages and strikes continue in Buenos Aires. One of the big labor events is a national strike organized by the railway engineers.

By this same year, American meat-packing companies have established plants in Argentina. The meat is exported to Europe. This is the first important investment tie between the United States and Argentina.

LONDON: women gather to bring attention to the female suffrage bill.

FINLAND: nineteen women are elected to the legislative assembly. They are the first female representatives to any national legislature.

NORWAY: the parliament votes to grant suffrage to 300,000 women.

HOLLAND: the second Hague peace conference meets to establish rules for civilized warfare.

For several years, Rifke Schulman has been working at the *alpargata* factory by day, and the Union of Jewish Workers at night. Her work at the Union continues to consume her energy and time.

The following entries are from Volume Nine.

February 15, 1907
Buenos Aires

Good news! The Jewish Colonization Association, the organization that purchased the land for Moisés Ville and later for many
other colonies in Entre Ríos, has now given my Union of Jewish
Workers a budget to work with! The stipulation is that those who
benefit must leave the capital. We are to find them jobs in the
interior. We have placed people in Santa Fe building railways, and
in the northern forests they are learning to be lumberjacks. This is
the kind of work the government and investors are offering—heavy
manual labor that is often temporary. But at least it's a start! While
there have been some willing to take on such work, I know this is
not really a solution for our people. Their hope lies in crafts and
industries—tailors, watchmakers, carpenters, and the like. I've
heard rumors that a disillusioned Russian colonist from Entre Ríos is
attempting to start a furniture factory in Rosario. He will certainly
employ Jewish laborers. That is what we need, and that is the
direction we want to head in.

I know it sounds good, that the Union has been able to place
more and more workers in jobs, but the system is faulty. The truth is
we need an organization that would truly be in charge of immigrant
affairs. I understand that unlike our "proletariat" class, the
"bourgeoisie" is making great strides in uniting the existent middle-
class Jewish organizations. Rabbi S. Halfon of the Congregation
Israelita on Libertad Street is working hard in this direction. The
Chevrah burial society, the schools, and a welfare society
established by Buenos Aires Jews will soon be under one communal
organization. I notice, however, that there is no mention made of
the poor new arrivals in their grand plans.

Our Union works hard, but we are only one small organization,
and from the look of things, our direction and purpose are on the

verge of change. We have added a new department to provide medical aid to those in need, and this is becoming the main focus of the organization. In the next few years, we will no longer be the Union of Jewish Workers but rather the Bikur Holim. I'm not exactly sure what my role will be in the future. What will become of the library and the teaching of Spanish, I don't know. I feel frustrated that I cannot do more for the Union, but my work time is limited to evenings and Sundays. By day, I must continue to work at the *alpargata* factory. It's not a pleasant job, but I cannot complain. I have work, unlike so many. At the factory, I'm able to advise other workers about coming to the Union for help. At least I feel I'm doing something useful there.

I am still boarding at number 1454 Lavalle. Peshke has helped me fix up my rooms. She has made me a curtain for the window and a cloth for my small table. We've grown very close, Peshke and I. She insists that I eat with them every Shabbat if I don't have better plans. I always enjoy being at Peshke's. When I can, I bring them a treat of a few oranges. The whole family enjoys them. The Milekofsky children are healthy and hard working, like their parents. Abraham, the eldest, and the next two boys, Jorge and Juan, all work full time in factories, along with their father. Of the eight children, only two are girls, so they are kept busy working at their mother's side, maintaining as clean and organized a home as possible. Peshke's rooms are immaculate. The beds are always neat, and somehow, without fail, she manages a large pot of soup or stew.

If someone is in need, Peshke can always feed an extra hungry mouth or squeeze another tired body into a bed. If not, she sends over one of her girls to sleep on my cot for a few nights, so a bed is available. Usually it's fifteen-year-old Deborah who comes, a shy, beautiful girl with blond hair and blue eyes like her Mama. She has my mother's name, so I am especially fond of her. Peshke's husband is a quiet, serious man, much like his brother, Aaron, in temperament. Wisely, he leaves Peshke in charge of the home and good deeds.

Aaron, who has been living with the Milekofskys, helps them out with part of his weekly salary and puts away the rest. Finally, he has saved enough and he has brought over his fiancee, Sonia, and her younger brother. Peshke told me that it was made quite clear to Aaron that if he wanted Sonia, he was to bring her little brother as well. In Vilna, they left a married sister with many children. Sonia and her brother are inseparable. I admire her for that. I still wish I'd been able to bring my younger brother with me. For the moment, Sonia and her brother are living with an older cousin and her family on Talcahuano Street, not far from our apartment building. Sonia helps the household by doing piece-work embroidery.

I've met Sonia once. She is indeed as striking and formidable as her photograph promised. The evening we met, she was wearing a deep amber velvet dress she'd brought with her from Vilna. The bodice was pleated brocade and strips of lace in the same rich color, and more lace at the collar and cuffs. I haven't seen such wonderful fabrics in years; I'd almost forgotten they existed! We've gotten so used to our dark functional cottons, our simple blouses and skirts. We wear poor versions of the "Gibson Girl" attire. Sometimes Peshke's girls bring home fashion magazines, hoping their Mama might produce a clever reproduction on the next occasion for a new dress! Peshke is clever with her hands, and her girls are never disappointed.

Sonia's dress looked so incongruous in our tenement but so beautiful. It enhanced her figure, with the full sleeves and tight waist, and made her look positively regal. Her pearly skin and shiny, chestnut hair make it quite clear why Aaron is so smitten. She has a smooth manner and is quite articulate, but she makes me nervous, and I can't explain why. Despite her great beauty, there is something calculating, almost cold, about her steel gray eyes. Peshke is not pleased, and she does not look forward to being Sonia's sister-in-law. A wedding is planned for a few months hence.

March 28, 1907
Buenos Aires

The immigrant situation has gotten extremely serious, and I know it will only get worse. Every month, boatloads arrive at the docks. Besides the agents of the white slave trade, there is no one to meet them and look after their needs, financial or otherwise. Only a small percentage go off to the colonies in the interior; the rest stay in the capital, trying to carve out an existence for themselves, all needing work and accommodations. The huge buildings in the eleventh district are continually being subdivided into one-room flats, housing whole families. Rents are outrageously expensive, but the tenements, referred to as *conventillos*, fill up in no time.

This month our tenement and many others were involved in a serious rent strike, not that it did much good. The police were called in, and the men lined up in front of the building across the street from us. Serious and determined, they waited in the drizzle, prepared to intervene with their helmets and bats.

The exterior of our troublesome stone establishment has always had a fine appearance, once the elegant home of an élite Buenos Aires family. But the yellow fever epidemic of 1871 sent the upper class rushing away from the downtown area, away to higher ground, to the outer limits of the city. When I was first looking for a room, it was our building's ornate façade and bulging ornamental stone and iron balconies that attracted my attention. Outside we're respectable enough, but inside, as you know, it's constant chaos.

On that specific day, the tenants all crowded into the patio—the healthy, the sick in their pajamas, old and young, employed and unemployed. Many of us with jobs made a point of staying home that day. We women linked arms and held brooms, demanding lower rents. You can be sure that Peshke Milekofsky's voice was one of the loudest. She told me later that night that it was the women who were instrumental in bringing about the strike. She spoke of Juana Ruoco Buela, the deeply committed eighteen-year-old Spanish anarchist who was chiefly responsible for leading the women. We heard the next week that she was deported to Spain for her involvement. They organized according to buildings and blocks, communicated through the children, and held meetings in preparation. The women in our tenement all look up to Peshke. She has a good head and is not afraid to say what she thinks, with her steel strength and heart of gold. Without her, we would all be diminished.

The owners of the building put in a token appearance, two smartly dressed gentlemen who were nervous and uncomfortable, but they did negotiate. Trouble did not break out, thank God. I had an image of the police rushing in and beating down the old people with their bats. But this is Argentina, not Russia, and such things do not occur here. The rents were lowered a bit, but it will take more than a few rent strikes to improve the living conditions of the poor in this country. With the population growth that Buenos Aires has undergone in the last year or so, the problems of sanitation in these tenements have increased dramatically. We are lucky in our building. We have running water and a sewage system—a common faucet in the center of the patio and latrines at the back. But these necessities do not exist in more than half of the housing in Buenos Aires. Disease has become rampant. The children suffer continually from all kinds of gastrointestinal problems, and tuberculosis is the greatest killer.

Because of these problems and all the others, the working class of Buenos Aires has stepped up its protest. One can be guaranteed of rallies and demonstrations every May 1st, and last year, for the first time, Jewish workers joined the demonstrations. Carrying Yiddish placards and red banners, they were clearly visible. At this point, however, Jewish workers are not a serious component of the proletariat movement. With time, their involvement is inevitable, I have no doubt of that. Only two months ago a Jewish Socialist Party was formed, the Avangard. Its aim is to spread socialist principles in the Jewish communities. I worry about the almost certain bloodshed, and I worry that once again Jews will become victims, as they always have.

Peshke tells me I worry too much about too many things. She told me the other day that my life is the factory, the Union, and the worrying. Sometimes I have to agree with Peshke. Sometimes I wish I had more, but I don't.

The fight against white slavery continues, but it is an overwhelming battle. Bela Palatnik and Moses Soltansky have become key figures in the last couple of years; her unfailing strength and devotion to the cause are an inspiration. They have made great strides. Big Moses is always at her side, supportive, totally devoted. I would love nothing more than to hear they've become lovers, those two. But Bela is not, and never will be, capable of that, poor thing. She once confessed to me that if a man were to ever touch her again, she would simply go to the pier and throw herself into the water. I know Moses remains hopeful that one day she will consent to marry him and find peace from her torment.

I've seen a lot of Bela, and we've become close friends. In the last couple of months I've been very concerned about her; she doesn't look well, and she's always exhausted. She has worked very hard rehabilitating girls rescued from brothels. She has found them work and places to live, giving them a glimmer of hope for the future. Happily, a few have even found understanding husbands. Many have joined her passionate campaign. When we can, the Union has helped her find jobs for her girls, and she has helped us. As often as time permits, I accompany her to the docks when the steamers arrive. As much as possible, we try to warn the young single women traveling alone.

Sometimes I wish I could do more, at least as much as Bela does. Bela works ceaselessly. Regardless of the time of day or night, regardless of the weather, Bela goes to the docks. On a few occasions, she has agreed to a Sunday afternoon outing. Once, Moses accompanied us to see the new Palace of Justice. But Bela is resistant to leisure, and she has only a half-hearted interest in excursions. Her mind is always with the girls.

She has grown tiny, and her eyes have become sunken. She coughs continually now. I know she's ill, but she refuses to get medical attention. She says she doesn't have the time; there is too much to do, and others need more attention than she does. I have pleaded with her not to go out when it is so cold. I have seen her shivering under her shawls, unable to control her shaking and hacking. I have no doubt that Bela knows she is consumptive. Moses is distraught over her condition. He pleads with her to stay in on cold nights, to leave the docks to someone else. She listens to no one.

As the weeks pass, Bela is physically diminished by this dreadful disease. What her body loses, she gains in spirit. Her words ring clearer, sharper, carrying the ever-deepening strength and conviction of her commitment. From looking at her, I wonder how many can guess her secret pain. She has confided to me that she still suffers nightmares every night, nightmares from "her time of hell," as she describes her months of captive prostitution. Bela says she is still a prisoner in her heart and soul, though her body is free. I told Peshke this last week when I stood in her kitchen peeling potatoes. Peshke sighed, saying Bela will not be among us for long.

THE RIFKE CHRONICLES

Partial entries from the water-damaged volumes, numbers Five and Six, the first Buenos Aires years, have recently been salvaged. Regretfully, the timing of their discovery would not permit their chronological placement in the text. They are presented here, as found, four fragments, the first written when Rifke was twenty-six.

Fragment #1, written sometime in the summer of 1897,
the year Rifke arrives in Buenos Aires.

. . . how I wish Mr. Kahan would leave us in peace. His clothes smell rank and surely his teeth are rotting in his head. When he leans over our sewing machines, cackling to us in that voice like gravel, faster! faster! faster! we swoon in the heat and his stinking presence. Black collars, cuffs. Brown collars, cuffs. Black collars, cuffs. That's all I do from morning to night. Every day, for seven months, since I arrived in Buenos Aires. At nights, when I go home to the rooms I share with Golda Silberman, she encourages me to quit, suggesting that perhaps I can get a job in the *alpargata* factory where she works. I'm scared to quit at Kahan's. There are so many people without work.

I do not complain when I write to Esther and Leib in Moisés Ville, but I can't imagine any other job being quite so awful. Sometimes I wish I'd never left our adobe home, the crisp air, and the wide open fields of Moisés Ville. This Mr. Kahan is a man who surely has no respect for humanity. Two days ago, when one of the young girls passed out from the heat and hunger, he simply fired her. He pays us next to nothing, yet he does no work for he is the boss, he reminds us as he struts about. We work in one of the small, crowded rooms of his family's apartment. There is only one window and ten of us crowded into the room like sardines. The place is disgustingly filthy. There are rats and rotting garbage in the hallways, messy heaps of fabric scraps, dirty clothes, unclean dishes, and now, at the peak of summer, this unrelenting, suffocating heat.

The pace of the work plus the noise of his children running around keep me in a constant state of tension. Mrs. Kahan, no less distressing than her husband, periodically makes an appearance in the door. She wipes her hands on her dirty apron, her body taking up the entire doorway. She's convinced he's fooling around with the youngest seamstress, a young girl of seventeen. All the women in his sweatshop know to keep the top snaps of their blouses done up, regardless of the heat. Mr. Kahan tries to see more than our seams when he leans over our sewing . . .

. . . I regret nothing. It would be against human nature to regret love. I am alone now; he has returned to Moisés Ville, to his wife and family, to his work. We have played our cards, Henoch and I. Our fate is sealed.

It began some months ago. One drizzly, cold evening as Golda and I left the factory, I stopped to take a flyer that was handed me by a serious young lad, lurking in the shadows of the colonnade across the street from the factory entrance. Before this, I had listened to Golda and never accepted those pieces of thin paper I was offered. Although Golda could not read, she insisted they would lead to trouble. The factory bosses were continually warning their workers not to take or read the flyers. I don't know why I chose to reach for one of those pieces of paper on that specific evening. Perhaps it was the nervous determination in that young boy's face as he worked the crowd with his flyers. Perhaps it was just curiosity getting the better of me. I quickly looked over the printing in the half-light of a street lamp. It was something about a union meeting for workers. Folding it away into my pocket so it wouldn't get wet—I knew I could read it later that night when I went to bed—I felt Golda nudging me silently with her elbow. I assumed she was trying to warn me, trying to prevent me from taking the flyer. I ignored her until the paper was safely tucked away. But she kept nudging me, and finally I looked up.

There, standing no more that ten feet away from us, was Henoch Rosenvitch from Moisés Ville. Tall, in his black suit with the gold watch and chain, he held a suitcase in his hand, and the sight of him, of those blue eyes, took my breath away. Everything around him fell away. It could have been snowing instead of drizzling, it could have been daytime instead of night, we could have been standing in a Moisés Ville field instead of a city street. Nothing mattered, time stopped, I saw only him. We had neither corresponded nor seen each other since the Palacios train station when we said good-bye three years before.

Golda, delighted to see someone from home, rushed up and threw herself in his arms. Henoch gently embraced her, smiling, telling Golda her parents sent her their love. When it was my turn to greet him, we merely shook hands as he mumbled some words about Esther and Leib Yosem. He asked shyly how my shoe was, his eyes settling on my feet. Golda was too busy weeping happily to notice the reserve with which we greeted each other. We stood in the drizzle for a few moments as Henoch explained that it was a trip back to Russia that brought him to Buenos Aires. He would be leaving by boat the next day. When Golda heard this, she insisted he return with us to our dwelling. I was shocked. She insisted we could eat, and he could tell us more about the trip, and of course, he would spend the night on our cot by the stove. He agreed. What could I say or do?

Later, Henoch brought us up to date on Moisés Ville. Golda and I had, on occasion, received news. In the last few months, it had mostly come in the form of complaints from disillusioned colonists leaving Moisés Ville, passing through the city on their way to other places. Each time, much to our dismay, they had made it sound like a steady stream was leaving the colony. Good news seemed to come more slowly, more hesitantly. For like Golda, her parents could neither read nor write, so they never corresponded.

Occasionally I received a painstakingly written letter from Leib, but mostly, I wrote to them. So Henoch was a godsend, the first happy colonist to bring us news of our village! The first bit of good news was about Golda's sister, Malke, who years before had run off with a gaucho by the name of Hernán. The Silbermans had recently received a letter from Mendoza, where Malke and her husband had settled. They owned a small farm and had a first son, born two months before the letter had been written. Golda wept at the news. Henoch gave her Malke's address in Mendoza, and I promised to help her write a letter to the Hernáns.

So much had happened. Henoch told us that due to a fall in Moisés Ville's population, the colony's social and spiritual life was being diminished. The elders believed that the recent modest economic prosperity—owing to the planting and harvesting of alfalfa and the introduction of cattle grazing—could be a positive reason for enlarging the colony. An influx of new colonists from Russia, especially if they were related to Moisés Ville's existing families, might just be the answer. It was this incentive that resulted in Henoch's recruiting trip to Russia.

He was in high spirits about the trip, and our evening together was wonderfully pleasant. We took out bread and cheese, and Golda found some biscuits and jam we had been saving. We ate and we had tea, and we listened to Henoch tell us about his plans for our village. He still dreams of creating an agricultural co-op, so the colonists can feel more self-sufficient, more independent from the Jewish Colonization Association. He wants a bank, good schools, and a hospital. I know Henoch Rosenvitch will accomplish these things for Moisés Ville; if anyone can, he is the one.

And so it was thus that Henoch Rosenvitch landed again in my life, some months ago, on his way to Russia.

This Sunday afternoon he returned, once again finding his way to our rooms. I received him alone, for Golda had gone off on a country outing with her boyfriend. A gentle spring rain fell outside my window and onto the patio as I listened to Henoch's sad accounts of the miserable pogroms throughout the Pale. We had tea and talked more, feeling grateful to be in the Argentine and not Russia. Then, as naturally as the rain, we became lovers, he and I, and we sealed our mutual fate . . .

Fragment #3, written in April 1903
Buenos Aires

. . . and so we await further news from Russia. We know only that
the pogroms are occurring at a frightening rate. On April 19th,
there was a massacre of Jews in Kishinev. There is nothing we can
do from here except pray, and I've never been very good at that.

Did I mention that Golda is married now? She has moved many
blocks away, and I don't see her often. I miss her. Golda knew about
Henoch, of course. After she moved out, I remained alone, not
wanting to room with other girls, not wanting to explain my life.

My bliss with Henoch has been my salvation. Since that rainy day
in October of 1900, we have been indescribably happy. How I look
forward to his visits! Naturally we do not correspond, and I never
know when I'll see him next. Sometimes I come home, and there he
is, waiting on the doorstep, smiling, suitcase in hand. For three years
he has managed to find reasons to visit the city. Another trip to
Russia in 1901. Sessions with the ever-changing J.C.A. administration. Meetings with other colony leaders.

When we're together, we go for long walks along the piers in La
Boca, or into the old part, San Telmo. There is so much to talk
about. Workers and unions, the future of Moisés Ville, with its
tensions and stress, Russia. But we never discuss our private past or
our future. We live for the moment . . .

Fragment #4, June 11, 1903
Buenos Aires

. . . I am writing this in grief and confusion. It is dark and late,
and Henoch has left. It's over. It came to an end as quickly as it
began. He arrived this evening, unexpectedly, tired and visibly

shaken. When I saw him empty-handed, with no suitcase, when I saw his eyes, I knew. He confessed that he can no longer live with his guilt and shame. His wife is a sickly woman. He fears that she is aware of his involvement in Buenos Aires and that it is making her worse, with frequent attacks of nerves leading to depressions. He has resolved that we must give each other up.

What could I say? I know he is right. What could I do but agree with him? I've always known that someday this moment would arrive.

Henoch's stay was brief, and after he left, I sat in the dark and wept. I lost track of time. When I finally forced myself to stand and light the lamp, I saw the small paper parcel on the table, and I realized I'd forgotten to give Henoch his gift. Earlier, on my way home from work, I stopped to browse at my favorite bookstall in Plaza Lavalle. I often stop there, but I rarely buy anything. Tonight was different. On a crazy impulse, I paid the vendor for a book of Anton Chekhov's two new plays, *The Three Sisters* and *The Cherry Orchard*. Henoch so admires his stories. I rushed home, excited about my purchase. I would present it to him on his next visit. There will be no next visit.

We parted bravely, vowing never to see each other again. I'm sick that I don't even know where he went, so late, so dark. On this night, June 11, 1903, I struggle with my loss and fear that I will not be able to continue without him. I cannot think about tomorrow . . .

THE PHOTOGRAPHER, HER
LOVER, AND HER DREAM

"Rent a child? How could we rent a child? What are you saying, Jess?" Victor Levin sounds irritable and threatened as he looks out across the hot summer fields. They are deep in the Argentine pampas near Rosario and the endless land stretching before him does not comfort his urban soul. The bus, La Flecha de Santa Fe, has stopped suddenly for yet another break. He should never have left New York, Victor realizes glumly. This is the third time the bus has stalled, choking and spluttering, the third time the smiling driver slides under the vehicle, assuring them that they mustn't worry, that they will get to Moisés Ville in time for the celebrations.

Half an hour has passed. The dubious passengers wait about in the heat. Some sit, some pace, some appear to enjoy the scenery. Victor glances at the crippled Flecha. He knows the driver isn't telling the whole story, and his sidekick, an overweight Indian girl, reveals even less. She wears a short blue skirt and white blouse with a Flecha Tours hostess pin that says Marisol. Marisol's still eyes and vapid face register nothing.

"I told you," Jess smiles, "through an agency. We rented a little boy through an agency."

Her voice eases his tension. "Like rent-a-car?" Victor asks, turning back to Jess. She's setting up her tripod, happily engaged, as usual. Her tall frame moves with grace and confidence in her loose cotton clothes, and the bags of cameras and lenses and film never seem to hinder. On the contrary, they hang from her like friendly appendages. There's a joyful generosity about Jess. Long ago, Victor decided it must have something to do with her height and that constant perspective, and with her belief that when human failings accumulate too greatly in any one person, he or she simply becomes "magical."

She's looking incredibly attractive in Argentina, he has to say that for the country. Her red hair has grown long and she's wearing it pulled back into a thick, curly braid. At that moment, there's a slight breeze, and the heat and brilliant light warm and soften her angular face. Her blue eyes are intense with concentration as she attaches the camera. He feels almost inspired, though they've lost ground during the time they've been apart—she here in Argentina, he in New York. Not that things were exactly terrific for the few months before her departure. He doesn't know why. Last week before he left New York, his sister, Masha, warned him. "You're going to have to give a little, if you intend on keeping Jess. Tell her, Victor, it's time you tell her about Robin."

But he can't. He can hardly bring himself to think about his daughter, about her death. After all these years, that pain is still his constant companion.

"I suppose it was like renting a car," Jess laughs lightly. "The agency was in Mendoza. I don't know why Mendoza. We went in and asked to rent a child." Jess checks the focus. "You know where the idea comes from?"

Victor doesn't answer.

Jess looks up from the camera. Now what, she wonders? He's miserably unhappy, and he won't talk. Struggling to maintain her equilibrium, refusing to become unbalanced yet again by their relationship, Jess sets her attention and camera on the group of passengers directly behind Victor. They're laughing and complaining bitterly about the bus. Their name tags connect them to a Jewish Lions Club from Buenos Aires.

Earlier that day, while they'd all waited to board the buses in the dark hours of the Buenos Aires dawn, Jess listened to their annoying chatter. One of the Lions, he'd introduced himself as Judah and was clearly leader of the pack, explained the situation to some of the other passengers. "The members of my party are not descendants of your beloved and renowned village, Moisés Ville, the Jerusalem of South America!" He spoke in a loud, confident voice, wagging his impressive head of wavy white hair. "Nevertheless, we've decided on this excursion because it has all the makings of a good time!" He wore white shoes, a white belt, and baby blue pants. "We're all Jews!" Judah announced commandingly into that gray Buenos Aires stillness, "and we're going to help you celebrate Moisés Ville's centennial!" His wife, a short, plump woman with dyed black hair—high and puffy—clung to his arm. Her pasty face looked bewildered as she moved silently to his energetic body language. She wore many rings and her tiny feet were perched in spindly, transparent, plastic mules. "Moisés Ville, the cradle of Argentine Judaism!" Judah shouted out. Cheers and laughter followed among his companions while the other Moisés Ville passengers watched in silence.

Too much light, Jess realizes, adjusting the aperture. Hours ago, in that chilly dawn, she was embarrassed by the Lions, especially by Judah's aggressiveness. They were in sharp contrast to the other passengers, the ones for whom this pilgrimage would be a serious confirmation of their own lives, of all that existed before them, all that will after. Once again Jess focuses on Judah's wife—the uncertain face, the ringed fingers reaching tentatively for her hair.

Victor is still speechless. He reaches for the handkerchief in his pant pocket and wipes his face. He hates being so uncommunicative, but he cannot help himself. Jess dreams about renting a child, and she expects him to know where the idea came from? What does it matter? People are jabbering, he's hot and tired, his head throbs. Thoughts of Robin haven't helped. He feels drained. Of course it's always worse when he isn't in his lab. At least when he's working, his defenses are up. But when he's not involved in his research, a passivity settles over him, and he withdraws into an inactive state— a form of retreat—a condition which makes self-defense virtually impossible.

An hour ago on the bus, Jess spoke enthusiastically about the final photographs she still needed for the book on Moisés Ville. She explained about illusive light, cast shadows, and silhouettes. She told him about the unusually small bricks used in construction, about the century-old painted storefronts, now faded by time and circumstances. Farmacia Juan Levisman, Panadería Portnoy. He listened, all the time wondering how she could be so committed to a village that began and ended on a remote, godforsaken field? He listened, all the time wondering how he could be jealous of an idea, a place he's never seen, an event that happened one hundred years ago?

Last winter while she researched, Moisés Ville and the Baron Maurice de Hirsch were all she thought of—when she ate, when she slept, when she brushed her teeth. Victor grew tired of hearing about the Baron's philanthropy, his commitment to the cause, to his people.

"He got them out of czarist Russia!" She called out from the kitchen one evening as she prepared vegetables for their stir fry dinner. Victor pretended he didn't hear, sitting in the living room of their apartment, reading the newspaper. He knew she was standing over the stove still in her work clothes, herringbone blazer, leather boots, distractedly pouring oil into the wok.

"They were from the same cities in the Pale as your grandparents, as mine, and Hirsch resettled them as farmers on the virgin soil of the Argentine pampas. Their new homeland!" It made him crazy that she never measured the oil, that she never wore an apron. She probably did it intentionally. He never helped in the kitchen. Masha was always warning him about that too.

Her link to the famous Moisés Ville? Simply that one of her grandmothers passed through, staying in the colony for a year before emigrating to the United States. Nothing more. It seems a ridiculously thin thread connecting Jess to this incredibly aggravating country, Victor decides. He glances at the dead bus. He thinks of the freeways and the reckless driving, how they pass on the right side, at whim. Why does she want a connection? He thinks of the miserable economy and the near daily fluctuation of restaurant prices. Why does she always say "there, but for the grace of God, go I"? He wouldn't be surprised to learn that Argentineans don't pay their taxes. Jess has no stake in Argentina, yet her passion leaves him feeling miserably empty, angry because he can't understand.

So, an hour ago, the bus traveled on. Through the landscape of Rosario, through the landscape of Jess's obsessions. Field after field of ochre wheat rolled up to the bus windows, meeting her voice in a gentle union of magic realism. Then, the crash landing into Jess's dream. The crazy child-renting dream that synchronized with that peculiar noise coming from under the bus. Jess didn't notice until she saw the dramatic trail of black smoke, until she heard the driver quickly announce another short stop.

Victor's eyes are riveted to the bus.

"Victor?"

He turns. Jess is asking him something.

"The idea of renting a child, Victor?" Jess repeats. "Know where it comes from?"

The heat is overwhelming. He feels as though an eternity has passed in the moments since she asked. He shakes his head. "Can't imagine."

"Really?"

He realizes that Jess is going to attack again, with that energy and swiftness that is hers. She's going to attack their long-standing commitment to no marriage, no children. She's approaching forty. Despite her career—the freelancing, the numerous books of photographs, and now this grant to pursue her Moisés Ville project—none of it will matter. She wants a child.

Wants, with the same intensity she wields her focused camera. In the end, women always do, Victor concludes somberly, as though he's lost a battle. He has his work at Columbia, his research and teaching. She has hers. They share lives. But none of this will matter. She wants a child. His sister warned him.

"Don't you remember, Victor, really?" Jess is amused by his distractibility. She loves that about him. Yet she knows it to be a sign that he isn't coping well, and she wishes she could help. But if he refuses to talk, how can she help? How many times has she thought this? Silence is nothing new with Victor, it's the game he plays best. She had high hopes for this visit, but they haven't reconnected smoothly; in fact, they haven't connected at all.

She watches as he stands with his hands in his pockets. His eyes turn from the fields, to her, to his feet kicking at pebbles, and up to her again. She wonders in which cavern he has been detained. She knows his scientific mind works best in the compressed, intense spaces his imagination creates, one grotto leading to another. There, he gropes and struggles with the unheard of, the incomprehensible. Phenomenal ideas that grow out of those airless, lightless tunnels, like stalactites. She knows he spends his days in that lab methodically cutting up leeches and shrimp. He studies those veiny bits of greenish gray flesh—she's often thought they're the only real colors for him—charting their tiny nervous systems. Somehow, as she understands it, they are the closest animal life to the human brain. For Victor, these pampas and this talk of old Russian Jews must be like making a salad.

"Remember? In Buenos Aires," Jess continues, "we were told that it's not uncommon for professional beggars to rent small children from poor people. Business is better if they sit on a street corner with a baby in their arms, or if they have a small, hungry child standing at their side."

"I didn't remember," Victor says quietly. "That's unbelievable."

"I know. It's pretty shocking. Anyway, I'm sure that's where the idea of our renting a child came from."

A welcome breeze sweeps around them. Jess bends to blow dust off the lens.

"Babe," he looks at her, "why would we rent a child, if we've decided not to have any? It doesn't make sense."

He calls her Babe when he's nervous. "Vic, how can you say a dream doesn't make sense!" Does he catch the humor in her voice?

Jess watches as a group of fellow passengers make their way into the wheatfield, heading for the only tree in sight, and shade. The ombu's branches and thick foliage reach in all directions, creating a natural awning. Perhaps, Jess realizes, the time has come for her to deal with Victor's refusal to discuss children. She focuses her camera. Their children. A woman, slightly hunchbacked and wearing a blue dress, more midnight than royal, with a pattern of large rust chrysanthemums, hesitates in the field for a moment's rest.

The woman begins to move in the direction of the tree, and Jess shoots quickly, easily. She finishes the roll. The vociferous Lions hurry to the shade and seat themselves on a log under the far reaches of the branches. Other passengers find places to sit around the ombu's base, where the magnificent trunk divides into a bulky network of exaggerated, root-like protrusions. Surely nature intended these roots to provide companionship for the branches, in the desolation of the pampas.

"I wonder what's wrong, and how long it will take him to figure it out?" Victor is irritable.

Jess looks up.

Victor nods toward the driver who is still lying under the bus. Only his feet are visible. Two male passengers are squatting beside him. Marisol stands hugging her sides, staring down at the driver's feet. She looks bored, as though she's waiting in line at a government office.

Jess shrugs and returns to her camera. "You'll love Moisés Ville, Victor." She knows he misses New York, and she knows he's angry about the bus. She wishes he could enjoy where he is, when he is. "Do you want to hear the rest of my dream?" She asks, hoping to distract him.

"Sure," Victor says. "We went to an agency to rent a child. I can't wait to hear what happened next."

"Well, the agency said they didn't have a child at the moment, but that they could put together a package for us."

"A package?" Victor asks. "Like a travel agent's package? Hotel, excursions, two tickets to a show, all for the low price of—" Victor's laugh is dry, tired.

"I guess so." She knows the dream threatens him, but she perseveres. "They said they had the 'alma', the soul, of a beautiful, unusual child, yet unborn, and they could put it into a vacant body."

"My God, Jess! Do you realize most people don't dream?" Victor takes out his handkerchief again and wipes the palms of his hands.

Jess ignores Victor's comment. "The only hitch was we had to have the child back to them by the end of the month, because the unborn baby would be ready for birth and would need its soul."

"But of course! We can't have a baby without a soul! Jess, I don't believe this!" He turns away, angrily. "Between your dream and the damn bus breaking down, all we need is a watch. It would melt by itself in this heat. Who needs Dali!"

"Look, Victor!" Jess points to some burros approaching the passengers under the ombu.

"Don't worry about the bus. This kind of thing happens all the time in Argentina." She unwraps another roll of film and loads the camera. She takes a series of shots directed toward the animals. "Can you imagine what those first colonists felt like when they laid eyes on the land? Moisés Ville is very much like this. Of course they had nothing, and there was nothing waiting for them, only flat, uncultivated fields."

"Like fools," Victor says. Jess has been trying to get him to relate to those colonists since he'd arrived in Argentina. He can't. He can hardly acknowledge any connection at all, except perhaps his having been born a Jew. Even that was an accidental fact of birth, irrelevant to his life.

"Victor, your grandparents went through Ellis Island, but they could have as easily ended up in Argentina, heading out to one of these first colonies," Jess says, looking across the landscape.

"Not mine. Never. I do not come from a line of people who would have placed themselves in such ridiculous circumstances. Your grandmother had the right idea, leaving this place for New York." He watches her adjust the focus. "How much farther is it to the village? And remind me again why we're doing this?" Victor laughs anxiously. Now there are six men squatting beside the driver's feet.

"I told you," Jess says, breathing deeply and wiping her hands on her skirt before peering into the camera. Victor is being negative, and the heat is beginning to distress her. "I need to interview a few more people, and there are still photos to take. I thought you might enjoy seeing the village, Victor. Besides," she looks up, trying not to sound hurt, "a centennial happens once every hundred years." Why is she apologizing, Jess wonders? "And it's nice to be away from the city, the pollution."

They both remain silent for a few moments.

"So, Babe, did we rent the child?" Victor asks quietly, sensing Jess's attempt to ease the strain.

"Yes, it was all arranged. We traveled for a month with him, from Jujuy down to the Patagonia. It was a wonderful time, and he was indeed as beautiful and unusual as one could hope for." Jess's voice becomes quiet and soft. "You became very attached to him, Victor."

"Dream on, my darling!"

"At the end of the month," Jess continues, calmly, "we returned him to the agency, as planned. Two days later, we were contacted and informed of the birth of the expected child, the one who was supposed to receive that soul. Remember?"

"How could I forget?"

"We were told we could visit him at the hospital."

"For God's sake, surely we didn't go, Jess!" Victor is disturbed.

"You wouldn't." Jess quickly swings her camera around and focuses on Victor, snapping, snapping. "The light's perfect, and the horizon behind you is beautiful," she explains. Snapping, snapping. What she doesn't explain is the sadness in his face.

"You know something? I don't know why I'm here," Victor suddenly complains, dejected. "Seriously, Jess, what am I doing in Argentina? I don't even speak the language. I should be in my lab in New York."

"For me. You came to visit, remember? I'm here for a few months, and you . . ."

"I'm sorry. I didn't mean it to sound that way, Jess. Of course. I came to see you." He attempts a smile. "I guess I just can't relate to all this," he waves his hand out over the landscape. "This is so disorganized, so unpredictable. Look at that damn bus! I don't do well without a sense of order."

"I know. What can I say?" Jess speaks quietly. "Everything you say about Argentina is true. I guess to be a survivor here, you have to roll with the punches, relax, expect nothing, and you'll probably find what you're looking for. It's such a beautiful country, Victor, and, I don't know, I guess I've become kind of attached."

"Attached? No!" The sarcasm has returned to Victor's voice. "Listen, Jess," he steps toward her, puts his hands on her shoulders. "I want you to hurry with this project and return to New York, where you belong. O.K.?" His eyes are nervous, his mouth anxious.

In the last few seconds, he's made a stab at two smiles. The first time all afternoon, Jess realizes. She knows all this Moisés Ville talk means nothing to him. For her, it's only the beginning. She still hasn't told him she's planning to extend her stay in Argentina, and that it will be another three months before she returns to New York.

A heavy silence settles between them. Victor turns to watch the driver pull himself out from under the bus. He stands talking to the other men about a short length of pipe he is examining. After a brief discussion, he walks off down the highway, the pipe dangling from his greasy hands.

"We're in for a bit of a wait," Victor says, nodding toward the figure moving away from the bus.

"Where's he going?" Jess asks, watching.

"Who knows. To get help, I hope. It could be hours."

Jess notices that most of the passengers remain very calm about the stalled bus and the disappearing driver. Perhaps it's the heat, or the late afternoon hour, but a trance-like mood settles over the lethargic group. A few of them stretch out along the grassy bank beside the bus, closing their eyes or pulling down their caps. Others remain at the tree. Some young people cluster around a transistor radio. Only the Lions Club group complains, unsuccessfully trying to stir up excitement among the other passengers.

At that moment, Marisol, the young hostess, approaches. She

explains something in a monotone voice, waving one hand at the bus, while inspecting the chewed nails of her other hand. Victor doesn't understand a word. She isn't big on eye contact, he decides, staring at the offensive pencil lines she has drawn in place of her plucked out brows. He can hardly concentrate on what she is saying. Jess engages her in conversation, pointing to her camera and equipment. Marisol unlocks the storage compartment on the side of the bus. Without smiling she points down the highway, mumbles something, then moves on to another group of passengers.

"She says there's a café where we can wait about fifteen minutes down the highway. Some of the passengers are walking down to it."

"What's wrong with the bus?" Victor asks.

Jess shrugs. "No one seems to know. She says the driver will pick up any passengers at the café, once it's fixed. Do you feel like a walk, Victor?" Jess puts away her camera and folds up her tripod. She packs them into the storage area and closes the door.

Jess and Victor start down the hot highway, the trail of passengers moving slowly ahead of them. "So, I suppose you went to the hospital to see the baby?" Victor turns to her.

"Of course." Jess smiles. "I arrived to find the mother and grandmother holding the infant in the light of a window. They had placed him on the ledge, proud of the dark Indian baby. I was taken aback by how wonderful he was, and I spoke admiringly of his beauty. When the infant heard my voice, he turned to me in recognition, crying and holding out his arms as though I was his mother."

"Jess, that's impossible! Newborns don't hold out their arms," Victor says seriously.

"I know, Victor, but he did. He wept, and he would not stop. It was not a baby's cry, rather that of an older child. I realized this was indeed our child—wiser through his travels—but trapped in the body of an infant, and I could do nothing for him. I felt horrible."

They walk in silence the rest of the way to the café. Victor knows the dream is some kind of turning point for Jess, but he isn't sure how, or about what. He feels depressed, alienated. He's sorry not to be more of a conversationalist. He's sorry he hasn't been able to explain about his daughter, Robin, and why, after her death, children can never again be part of his life.

As they approach the café, a small, sad place with a beaded curtain, Jess is stopped by a lone young girl about ten years old. She's dressed in old, faded clothes, but there is an attempted tidiness in her tucked-in blouse and the ribbons in her braids. A nagging cough accompanies her thin voice. She's selling something from a cigar box. The other passengers ignore the child, brushing rudely past her as they enter the modest establishment. Victor watches as Jess peers into the small box, asking the child what she has. He notices that the girl has fine, white dust in the crevices of her skin—her toes, her fingers, even around her mouth. It's just dirt, Victor assures himself, the fine, white clay that she would have kicked up as she walked barefoot along a path. But there is something eerie about the whiteness, as though the child can't rid herself of a nagging premonition of her own death.

Jess speaks in gentle, quiet tones, smiling as she examines the articles in her box. A sudden ache of emotion strikes at Victor's stomach, as he watches Jess's tall frame virtually melt with kindness toward the child. Somehow, this wonderful woman has the ability to make her own incredible presence seem less, so as not to overwhelm with her radiant health and good fortune at having been born in the Northern, rather than the Southern Hemisphere of neighboring continents. He sees Jess reach into her purse, withdraw some money, and hand it to the child. The girl smiles meekly as she wraps the items in a scrap of wrinkled paper. Oddly, it is at that moment that Victor knows something is terribly wrong.

They are sitting at a small round table inside the café. Jess realizes an hour has passed before they talk about it. It comes up rather casually, not the usual tense, compressed way that she knows fights and separations begin. They order more bottled water, and then she starts looking through her cigar box purchases. They are small, knitted things—a hot pad, a covering for a clay flowerpot, a long multicolored band, perhaps a belt. She examines them silently, upset. She throws her head back, her eyes closing for a few seconds. Finally she opens them and stares at the rotating ceiling fan.

"It's not going to work anymore, is it, Victor?" Jess says, still concentrating on the fan.

At first he pretends not to know what she means.

"Hmm?"

"Us. You and me. It's over, isn't it?"

"Jess?"

"You know want I mean. I want a child. I can't help myself. I think about it all the time, everything I do, everywhere I go." Jess's eyes close again.

"You're upset, Babe. It was probably that dusty girl." He tries to sound reassuring.

"No, it wasn't the dusty girl," Jess says, looking down at the knitted things spread over her lap.

"I want my own baby, and you don't want one."

"Jess," Victor's voice is low. "Do we have to talk about this now?" he asks uncomfortably.

"Yes, now. Right now."

"Come on Jess, relax, have something to drink. Let's get you something cold." Victor turns quickly in his chair, signaling to get the waiter's attention. With his arm still raised, he looks back at her. "We're on our way to Moisés Ville, right, Babe?" He can hear the mild desperation in his silly, upbeat voice, but he continues anyway. "You have work to do, and I'll help you! Would you like me to pose? I could lean against one of the old synagogues . . ."

"Please, don't."

He says nothing.

"Victor, if you won't have a baby with me, I'm going to leave you."

Victor remains silent for a few minutes and then nods toward the bus hostess entering the café door.

"I think we may have other things to worry about at the moment."

Marisol stands near the door, looking slightly uncomfortable. She speaks quietly, without emotion. It's obvious she's talking about the bus, but Victor can't follow what she's saying.

"It's hopeless, they can't repair it," Jess says, her eyes on Marisol. "They've already contacted their Rosario office to send out another bus. Unfortunately it will be several hours."

Groans are heard around the café. Marisol's face shows no involvement as she stares at her fingernails and then at the far wall, as though waiting for her next cue. Her voice continues in its low drone. Silence falls over the café.

"For those passengers who do not wish to continue their journey, a bus will be passing through from Santa Fe in half an hour, destined for the capital." Jess continues translating, without looking at Victor. "Anyone who wishes can return immediately. Naturally tickets can be presented at the central office of La Flecha de Santa Fe for refunds."

"Refunds, my ass," Victor complains. "The way this country functions, I'd be surprised if the bus company admits this vehicle ever existed! As a matter of fact, I'll bet they'd even try to erase this route from the map!"

Jess has turned away from Marisol.

Victor knows she isn't listening to him. He watches as she pours more water into her glass, plays with her napkin, and finally looks at him.

"We're headed in different directions, aren't we, Victor?"

Victor shrugs.

"We are. I know it and you know it."

"What am I supposed to say?" Victor asks.

"Admit this isn't in my head."

Victor turns away from her. He watches the other passengers talking and complaining among themselves. They're probably trying to decide what to do—return to Buenos Aires, or take their chances with the new bus to Moisés Ville. These are the things that happen to him when he goes on vacation. He should simply never leave his lab.

"And all because of a baby," he finally says.

"Not all."

"I suppose you're going to talk about 'sharing', the way my sister does?"

"No, I'm not going to talk about anything, anymore."

Victor is overcome with frustration and anger. "So! Does this mean I'm to go back to Buenos Aires, pack my bag, and return to New York? Am I correct, this relationship is over?! And what about you? Are you planning to come back to the apartment?"

"Of course. I'll be back in a couple of months and I can move my stuff out. If it's in the way before I get back, I can arrange to have someone . . ."

"No!" Victor turns from her, staring bitterly at the waiter who is wiping glasses. "I can't tell you how cheated I feel. Three years together, and where did they lead?"

"I know," Jess whispers. "I hoped they'd lead to a family."

"This is useless," Victor manages.

"Yes, it's been hopeless for a while, hasn't it?" Jess's voice is soft, gentle.

There are a few moments of silence, and finally Victor speaks quietly. "What will you do?" He sounds bewildered, lost.

Jess feels Victor is really asking her what he is to do. But she answers anyway.

"After I complete this project," Jess finishes off her drink, "I guess I'll probably look into renting a child." She tries to smile.

He doesn't respond.

"What about you?" Jess puts down her glass. "Victor?" she waits. "Don't you ever dream, Victor?" Her words are close, pressed with frustration and sadness. "Dream?"

Victor can't bring himself to tell her that for many years now, his dreams have been indistinguishable from his reality.

THE RIFKE CHRONICLES

The last entry—four fragments—was a chronological interruption. We are now back in Volume Nine.

May 18, 1907
Buenos Aires

Bela is gone. I am still numb. Peshke has tried to console me, telling me it was destined to happen, that it was beyond my control. But her words do not help, and I blame myself.

Two nights ago, Bela sent me a message that a steamer from Liverpool was expected in the early hours of the morning. She asked that I meet her at the waterfront when I could, so we would be there before the "agents," as she referred to the white slavers. I sent back word that she should spend the night at home, out of the cold. If we were there by dawn, it would be plenty of time. I got word to Moses Soltansky as well, telling him of our plan to meet in the morning. With that, I retired for the night, confident that she would heed my advice, since the steamer wasn't scheduled to dock until early morning.

When I reached the pier it was still dark, and I was horrified to find that Bela had spend the night outdoors, waiting. The steamer had arrived early. Bela said she had a premonition that it would, so she had come the evening before, shortly after she had sent me word. Consequently, she had not been in to receive my message, asking her to wait at home. Not that she would have anyway. The winter wind blowing in off the water was horribly cold, and Bela's clothes were soaked through from the dampness. She mumbled, laughingly, that she couldn't feel her feet, they were so cold. Other than that, she seemed in good spirits, although feverish, and trembling with nervous excitement.

Activity picked up in the cloudy daylight. Heavy carts drawn by obedient horses began making deliveries and pick-ups along the port. Docked ships that had looked dormant an hour before were now awake. The sky was a circus-like confusion; steam and smoke poured from the factory chimneys along the waterfront, cranes and pulleys and posts slanted in all directions through the fog, and the masts and flags of ships stood straight and tall. On our pier, the misty dampness bathed the crowd that was beginning to congregate around the iron grill gates. They'd come to wait for friends and relatives. Everything took on the steel grayness of a Buenos Aires winter morning. Wood and metal, cloth, wicker hampers, and even flesh. Soon, the "agents" began arriving in carriages, dressed in their fancy clothes and spats, carrying flowers and boxes of candy.

Finally, at around nine in the morning, the passengers began descending the gangplank. As was her habit, Bela clung to the fence, watching like a hawk, searching the crowds for single girls.

When she spotted some, usually they came through the gate in pairs, she hurried toward them. Clutching at their elbows, she began whispering in a frenzy, pointing toward the fancy men working the crowd. Lately, she had become so obsessed with her mission, she would dispense with all formalities, and even forget to introduce herself.

I approached matters more calmly. I spoke with the young women quietly, in Yiddish, for they would not understand our Spanish, but I refrained from touching them.

I merely explained the situation, warning of the dangers. I gave them the addresses of several reputable hotels. Sometimes the girls responded with resentment, disbelief, but more often than not, they listened seriously, their eyes frightened. I had managed to speak to several girls when I realized something unusual was happening at the other end of the pier. Instinct told me Bela was involved.

By the time I worked my way through the crowd, she was standing in the middle of a circle of people, trying to get their attention. She was coughing so hard, it was difficult to understand her, and her subject—white slave traders—was soliciting more laughter than serious attention. One of the major problems with this cause is that so many people refuse to believe such things are happening. At that moment, Bela looked far worse than most of the immigrants in her wet, bedraggled clothes. It wasn't hard to understand why people were laughing and turning away from her.

Two young British women, rather smartly dressed in hats and heavy woolen coats, were staring at Bela in disbelief. Their features were not pretty, I noticed, but their healthy, pink complexions stood out in the surrounding grayness. I wondered, briefly, how they had managed to keep themselves looking so nice, after their trip across the ocean. They must have traveled first class, I decided. I had heard rumors that it was very different from steerage. As I turned away from them and back to Bela, I spotted two agents. One was the notorious Noé Traumann, who actually sold girls to an auction house. The other I didn't know by name. As these two men rapidly approached the circle of people, they smiled and smoothed their mustaches. I saw them wink at each other before approaching the English women, just as I hurried to Bela's side.

I caught her as she slumped to the wooden dock. I knelt, holding her head in my lap. She was shivering and her teeth chattered as she whispered frantically that they wouldn't listen to her. I tried to soothe her, patting her head, dabbing her face with my handkerchief, telling her not to speak, to save her energy. A kindly old man with sidelocks put down his ancient suitcase and got down beside us, offering the dark shawl off his back. I thanked him, accepting the shawl, and wrapped her up as best I could. I didn't know what else to do. I could feel the cold from the dock entering my knees. After a few minutes, Bela's shaking subsided, her face relaxed, and she became unusually calm. I looked up. We were alone with the old man. He had pulled a worn book from his pocket and was reciting a prayer. The apathetic crowd had lost interest and dispersed—the English girls, the agents, all those who had smiled or laughed while Bela tried to alert them, ranting, even yelling. It was no longer amusing. What could be new or exciting about a poor, sick woman, dying in the arms of another, with an old man as their sole companion.

Minutes later, it began to drizzle again, and Bela was gone.

"Sh'ma Yisra'el, Adonai Eloheinu, Adonai Ekhad."

His voice was quick and gentle, and I was grateful for his presence. I straightened Bela's hair and her clothes; I tied up one black boot that had become undone. When I looked up, I saw a tall, large man hurrying toward us. Big Moses Soltansky. His red hair stood out around his head in a frenzied halo, his face frozen in grief.

I walked behind him as he cradled her tiny body, maneuvering the streets. Disoriented, and not knowing exactly what to do with her, Moses carried Bela to his father's tailor shop. From there, I was able to get word to Peshke of what had happened, asking her to send one of the children to the factory to explain my absence. Marcus managed to convince his son that he ought to take Bela back to her own dwelling, assuring him that he would look after the arrangements. As we left the shop, Marcus pulled the blinds, locked the door behind himself, and headed immediately for the burial society.

I stayed with Moses all day. After they came for her body, I pleaded with him to come to my place, or to Peshke's, to eat something, but it was as though he did not hear me. I was able to make him tea in Bela's room, but he refused even that.

Finally, at night, after I could do no more, I left him, stumbling home to Lavalle. Never had I felt so depleted. It had been a long and bitter day, and the walk home from the waterfront had never seemed so miserable. I wanted nothing more than to fall in my bed. Despite my grief, as I approached number 1454, I sensed a strange, quickening bit of hope. Confused, I hurriedly entered the patio and climbed the metal staircase to my room.

Henoch Rosenvitch sat reading at my table. He had lit the kerosene lamp and made himself tea. My exhaustion and the wrenching shock of seeing him were overwhelming. Fast tears, and for a fleeting moment I wondered weakly how he'd found me. He must have gone to my old address; someone must have told him where I'd moved. I realized Peshke had let him in. Although she had never met Henoch, Peshke knew everything. She probably recognized him immediately. In a moment of weakness, I had once shown her the photograph I kept wrapped in a piece of flannel, tucked away in the corner of my suitcase.

I am certain that in her mind, Peshke had somehow justified it—because of Bela's death, or because of my leg, or because life is fleeting, or because love is love. I could smell bread toasting on the stove, and I saw he had brought me a pot of gooseberry jam. From

Esther Yosem, I wondered? Was she party to this, as she had been that day at the Palacios train station? As I stepped in the room, he looked up over his reading glasses, smiling. He put down his cup, he pushed his chair away from the table, he stood. It had been almost four years since we had last seen each other, since I had purchased the copy of Chekhov's plays. On the night of June 11, 1903, we made that promise, never to be together again. Now, nothing could be a more welcome sight than his wise and patient blue eyes.

In those silent, eternal moments before we reached out to each other, I realized there existed no power that could ever force such promises again.

THE RIFKE CHRONICLES

While Rifke Schulman is busy with the Russian Jewish library in Buenos Aires, and Henoch Rosenvitch forms La Mutua Agricola in Moisés Ville, Santa Fe, the years 1908–1909 are witness to other remarkable events.

PARIS: Nijinski and the Ballets Russes give their first performance in the West, under the direction of Diaghilev. Picasso and his fellow artists begin to collect the art of Africa. In a large, drafty studio Auguste Rodin continues his struggle with sculpture. It has been ten years since he split with his sculptress muse, Camille Claudel.

SALZBURG: Freud's work is publicly recognized at the first Congress of Freudian Psychology.

RUSSIA: the photographer Gorski, experimenting with color separations, photographs Tolstoy seated outdoors at Natanya Polyana. Because of that photograph, Czar Nicholas will commission Gorski to document Mother Russia in full color and provide a train for Gorski's travels. At the same time, the czar's government issues a decree that Russian university professors must renounce membership in political parties not recognized by the authorities.

GERMANY: Albert Einstein continues his work on the theory of relativity.

SPRINGFIELD, ILLINOIS: race riots and Negro lynchings.

THE NORTH POLE: the Peary expedition.

VENICE: the painter Monet, of whom Cézanne said, "He's only an eye, but what an eye," pays a final visit to his favorite Venetian sites, his vision desperately blurred and failing.

PERSIA: a diplomatic representative is sent to Athens for the first time in 2,399 years.

The following entries are from Volume Ten.

May 30, 1908
Buenos Aires

Saturday, and it's been a beautiful day! The air was crisp, but the sun was strong and bright. This morning I did my laundry, and in the afternoon I spent a few hours at the Union office assisting with paperwork, registration, and records. The Union has officially become the Bikur Holim, the Institution for Assistance to the Ill. I mentioned before that this was imminent. Now that we are a relief organization, a great deal has changed. There are many working who take a keen interest in the health and sanitation needs of new immigrants. It's not the kind of work I prefer doing, but when I'm needed, like today, I'm glad to do my share.

The exciting news is that I'm also helping out at the Russian Library, which has certainly the best collection of Russian and Yiddish books in Buenos Aires, 5,000 volumes! It was formed in 1905 and has become an important Jewish workers' cultural organization. Aside from the frequent evenings of speakers and discussions on world social problems, the library sponsors Russian and Yiddish theatrical events and raises money for Jewish victims of Russian pogroms. It feels wonderful to be in a real library again!

I work at nights, and often stay quite late. When it's time to close up, there are usually one or two others still working or reading who live in my area. We always return home together. The streets of Buenos Aires are certainly no place to be at night, alone. Crime has increased, and the business of the *tmeyim* has grown to a disgusting level. I heard the other day that young women are being abducted leaving their places of work, sometimes in broad daylight! Peshke still worries about me, and I know she waits up until she sees the light go on in my rooms. I've gotten into the habit of tapping on her window so she knows I'm back and can go to sleep.

My wonderful Henoch was very impressed with the library on his last visit a few months ago! He said he wished he had access to many of the books for the Moisés Ville library, and wouldn't it be wonderful if libraries could share books, sending them from one institution to another, as needed. Henoch came to represent Moisés Ville at a meeting of the Jewish Colonization Association here in Buenos Aires. In truth, I don't know how he manages to remain so optimistic about his colony. It seems to me Moisés Ville has undergone one catastrophe after another. In the years since I left, they've been plagued by locusts; they've endured floods, droughts, disillusionment, and abandonment. Now, the sad news is that this year, forty-one families have left the colony because of a contract dispute with the J.C.A. I don't know what fate has in mind for Moisés Ville. I can only hope for the best, as I leave the village in Henoch's capable hands.

While he was here, Henoch found the emerging profile of Jewish workers extremely worrisome. In recent months, they have certainly become a visible element of the protest movement. Only last week I saw nearly an entire page in the anarchist newspaper, *The Protest,* expressing dissatisfaction with working conditions. This of course is not unusual for *The Protest*. But the fact that it was written in Yiddish was remarkable! This article in a Spanish-language newspaper might be one of the first times Jewish workers have gone public with their complaints. It demonstrates Jewish workers' support of the anarchists, and the anarchists support of the various language groups present in the country.

Henoch frets about this. He says it will surely lead to trouble, perhaps even bloodshed. I try to keep away from the politics, the endless conflict between Socialists and anarchists. I disagree with the Socialists' insistence upon complete assimilation, and I'm certainly not an anarchist. I detest violence. I prefer my libraries.

I tell Henoch that when he is in Buenos Aires, he must try to relax and learn not to worry so much. His time in the city should be a change for him. I realize that relaxation does not come easily to Henoch. When we are not discussing Moisés Ville or politics, Henoch tells me about the books he is reading, or of some new discovery published in a periodical. Sometimes he draws diagrams for me of equipment he has designed for the farm or the interior spaces of a future building for Moisés Ville. And always, he speaks of his children. He is terribly proud of them. The oldest boy is almost nineteen, and Henoch says he has become his right-hand man on the farm. His beautiful, eighteen-year-old daughter is devoted to her mother. She is being courted by several young men, including a pharmacist from Rosario. The second son is scientifically inclined, and the youngest, Julio, who is only twelve, says he will study medicine. Occasionally I am successful in convincing Henoch to go out for a walk, or perhaps even to a performance at one of the Yiddish theaters. The truth is, he is reluctant to be out in public with me. I understand. We have learned to live with our guilt because we cannot live without each other.

The new Colón Theater was officially inaugurated the other

night! I knew I would have a good view from Plaza Lavalle, so I went to watch the proceedings. I tried to get Peshke to come with me, but she said even a new theater wouldn't catch her out in what was sure to be a very cold evening. I wore my winter coat, realizing that Peshke was probably right, because the evenings had become quite nippy in the last few weeks. Many people had already congregated directly across from the main doors of the Colón, but they were waiting patiently and speaking quietly. It wasn't long, however, before the plaza turned into a thick, noisy crowd, and there was considerable excitement and activity. People were shoving and pushing around me when I felt someone tap my shoulder. It was Aaron Milekofsky. He told me he'd been on his way home from the bakery, when he'd stopped to see what the commotion was about. He said that by the time he arrived, the crowd had already been waiting for hours.

From where we stood, we could see the elaborately dressed Grenadier Guards on horseback, flanking the front entrance. As beautiful ladies and elegant men began arriving, I heard great sighs of amazement rise around me. The excitement mounted as the hour approached, culminating in the arrival of the President of the Republic, accompanied by his entire cabinet and various foreign ambassadors.

I could imagine how the glorious marble Hall of Honor must look! Against the backdrop of marble columns, gilt, crystal chandeliers and maroon velvet drapes, there was the pomp of military and diplomatic uniforms with their medals and ribbons, the brilliant white vests, the contrasting black tails. Exquisite, elaborate gowns, shimmering jewels, combs, and fans. I knew the orchestra would play the national hymn. I heard rumors in the crowd that there were spectacular potted plants on every step and bouquets of beautiful flowers tied to each balcony. It had to be sheer brilliance and splendor! I had read that an opera called *Aïda* had been selected for this opening performance, but I knew nothing about it.

Aaron watched in silence. I asked him if he knew the opera, for I was aware of his keen interest in music. I wondered if he still played his trumpet on Sunday afternoons. He told me, shyly, that a man called Verdi composed it. He hadn't heard it, but he knew it was about an Ethiopian slave, Aïda, the part to be sung that night by the famed soprano Lucia Crestani, and a high priest, Ramfis, to be sung by the bass, Arimondi. He told me that someday he would like to see an opera, perhaps there, in the Colón.

Aaron seemed unusually quiet. I hadn't seen much of him lately. After his marriage, he'd moved out of number 1454. Since I'd been helping out at the Russian Library, I didn't often go to the old Union headquarters. Now that our old Union had become the Bikur Holim, I wondered if Aaron was still as involved. I suspected not. I'd heard from Peshke that Aaron was working double shifts at the bakery to pay for all the pretty things his Sonia wanted, and to save for the fares to bring over more relatives. Peshke told me that Aaron, Sonia, and her brother had taken rooms in a boardinghouse on Talcahuano, close to Sonia's cousin. He'd only been married six months, but I didn't like the way his shoulders drooped. I asked him how things were going.

He said nothing about Sonia. Instead, he told me that his co-workers are discouraged and angered by the miserable conditions they must work in. I know that most of the bakeries in the eleventh district are stuck deep in subcellars, with no windows. The newly arrived immigrant bakers must sleep in shifts on straw mats. Straw does not protect them from the dampness, and they are constantly plagued by rats attracted to the bags of flour. Winters are damp, and summers are impossible because of the intense heat created by the huge, primitive ovens. Aaron said two of his friends have become consumptive, and one has died from an infection and fever brought on from a rat bite.

I commiserated with him and asked if he thought the bakers would unionize soon. Aaron said it was likely. I told him I missed seeing him at Peshke's, that he didn't seem to come around much anymore. He merely shrugged, saying that he was very busy now that he was married. We said good-bye, and I watched him disappear across the plaza toward Talcahuano Street.

October 10, 1908
Buenos Aires

On the way home from the factory the other night, I ran into Moses Soltansky on Defensa, just as I got off the trolley. He looks well, Big Moses, and he always brings a smile to my face. He walked me home, on the excuse that he wanted to drop by Peshke's to speak with her eldest son, Abe. They are close friends, Moses and Peshke's boy; they work together at the Pedro Vasena Metal Works factory. Moses told me he'd recently attended a performance of the play *Miriam* by P. Hirschbaum. It's become a "much talked about" production in the Jewish community. It deals with white slavery, and Miriam, the heroine, finds herself in a brothel. Because of the popularity of theater in recent years, everyone wants to attend, including the *tmeyim*, the unclean ones. Moses said that perform-ance was attended by several "dealers" and their women. It seems the women were so embarrassed by the brothel scenes, they left the theater. Outside, they were confronted by a group of angry young men, and a ruckus started. Moses, of course, was among them. He has continued to work closely with the movement against this scourge, and I understand he has become an important leader. He's only twenty-four. He has never again spoken of Bela's death, and Peshke tells me that he seems to have no interest in finding a wife.

At number 1454 Lavalle, life goes on as usual. Peshke and her husband have saved almost enough to start a modest grocery. In a few more years she will realize her dream. She says she expects me to move along with them when they leave. In the meantime, their eldest daughter, Deborah, had confided to me that she has a boyfriend, and that he is Italian. She is still very young, seventeen, but she insists she is in love. She is worried about what her parents will say when they find out. She is certain her father will forbid her to see him because he is Italian and Catholic, Deborah says. I have seen them together on occasion, when I come and go from the building. They linger on the street corner, when Deborah has been sent out on errands. He too is young, but Deborah tells me he works very hard in his father's restaurant.

I got a letter from Henoch yesterday. It seems Moisés Ville has begun the agricultural co-op, La Mutua Agricola. Henoch, of course, was responsible for its formation. He sounds very excited about how it will become the "central nervous system" of the colony. It will provide the farmers with seeds, tools, and machinery for the fields, and one of its main functions will be to intercede between the colonists and the J.C.A. I remember those early years in Moisés Ville, and Henoch's drawings of Moisés Ville's layout. He took special pride in that low, flat building he said would be the co-op. His letter also mentions that his wife has not been well again. Although he doesn't say it, I know it has to do with nerves.

Peshke respects Henoch very much. She says he is an admirable man to stay with his wife; most men wouldn't. At the first sign of trouble, they're off and running. The only thing Peshke has against Henoch is that, like me, he prefers tea to *maté*.

LEAH UBERMAN AND
THE PHOTOGRAPHER

Leah Uberman arrives with plenty of time, walking slowly, carrying her light, overnight bag. At almost six in the afternoon it is still unbearably hot. Leah knows her back must appear very exaggerated; it always does when she is fatigued and in pain. La Flecha de Santa Fe and the other tour buses are parked at the entrance to Moisés Ville's eucalyptus forest. Soon they will reload and begin the journey back to Buenos Aires. The weekend is over, and many local residents have accompanied their visiting relatives back to the buses. Leah insisted, on account of the heat, that her two elderly cousins not come. The area is crowded and noisy with people milling about, looking hot and exhausted. "What are the buses waiting for?" That is the question in every conversation. The centennial celebration was wonderful, but now people are tired, ready for home.

Standing patiently near the bus, Leah has intentionally not sat down. She knows how long the ride will be, what it will do to her back. But the exhaust from starting motors is making her nauseous, and she has to find a place to rest. There are no park benches; people sit on their suitcases and parcels or on the ground. They drink bottled water and snack on fruit while they wait. Leah starts toward the trees, where it isn't so crowded, where she might find a cool place to sit. The buses were to leave at four. The hour has come and gone, and then five, and now it is nearing six. Who is to know how much longer? But she refuses to get anxious, certainly not now at the end of the trip.

During the last three days, she managed to avoid worries about Nojke, her husband of forty years. It was still dark when she left her Buenos Aires home early Thursday morning. She was to be at the park beside the university law complex by 5:30; the buses would depart shortly after. She called for a cab the night before, but no amount of talking convinced Nojke that she could manage her departure alone, that he need not get out of bed. At 4:45 in the morning, Nojke stood at the living room window in his bathrobe, his hair mussed at the back. He'd pulled aside the long drapes just an inch, and he waited, spying out at the dark and empty Buenos Aires street. She hated seeing him like that. He spent hours of his day at that window, spying through that inch. He sold his practice, retired from the hospital, and they were robbed twice, all in the last year. The thieves took only small, stupid things, but the events turned Nojke into a paranoid. He refused to leave the house unattended. He refused to go out at night. He didn't even attend their son's evening wedding reception three months ago. He took to bundling up and wearing a wool scarf in the house, swearing he could feel drafts. Before the paranoia, he would have insisted drafts were an impossibility in his house. When they built, five years ago, he worked closely with the architect, calculating, checking and rechecking, making certain every detail was as it should be. But now there were drafts. For weeks he was certain the thieves were the two drunken laborers working on the house across the street. They took their breaks sitting on the curb directly in front of Nojke's spying spot. He was convinced they flaunted their wine bottles at him. When the cab finally pulled up, Nojke turned and called to her anxiously, those huge, dark bags under his nervous eyes. Stepping out into the street and the waiting cab, Leah felt guilty thinking how refreshing the cool air was, after the stuffiness of her own home.

As Leah approaches a large eucalyptus, the din of bus motors and voices almost disappears. Unsettling thoughts about Nojke surfaced over the weekend, but she allowed them to dissipate into the warm Moisés Ville air, the cloudless blue skies. Throughout her life, Leah prided herself on being an optimist. So, instead of Nojke, she thought about their daughter's beautiful baby, Letitia, named after her other grandmother. The recently deceased Doña Letitia, a tall, aloof, devout Catholic, was a magnificently handsome woman of Spanish descent. Leah always felt physically awkward in her presence, and the Catholicism made her nervous. But baby Letitia was a gift, a joy.

Leah carefully steps around some branches. It was a beautiful few days. She will not spoil her contentment with a case of nerves because of a delayed bus. Only a few feet into the forest, and she is delightfully alone. Nerves, in such a wonderful place? During her childhood summers, when she left her parents' home in Rosario to visit her mother's Moisés Ville family, the Rosenvitchs—her grandfather, her uncles, aunts, and cousins—she used to walk home from the village through these woods. Under the protective trees, her hunchback did not exist. Leah stands still for a few moments, taking in the woods' opened and closed spaces. There is much to be grateful for, she realizes, watching the sun's rays through the branches. Her loving, gentle parents, Nojke, her children. Nojke's devotion made it possible for her to live normally, to bear their son and daughter. She wasn't young when she became pregnant, and the doctors were worried about her spine, worried that it would not take the stress. Nojke made her stay in bed for the last few months of her pregnancies. He hired a nurse and a housekeeper; he did not want her to worry.

Focusing on the ground again, temporarily blinded by the sun and a few happy tears, Leah is startled to see the familiar nylon camera bags lying in the eucalyptus bark. Jess, the American photographer, sits on a felled log, elbow on her knee and chin in her hand. The long, soft cotton skirt is everywhere. The thick, red braid. Absorbed, Jess stares out at the fields and horizon beyond the woods. Leah realizes she nearly forgot about the girl in the excitement of the weekend. How could that have happened? The dreadful trip out from Buenos Aires last Thursday, with all the ensuing bus problems and the endless stops, seemed so long ago.

When the bus from Buenos Aires broke down completely, they all spent the next few hours in that little café. Having sat for quite some time at a small, round table, Leah finally got up. Standing for a few seconds, holding on to the back of her chair, she glanced again across the café at the American. The poor girl was despondent; her male companion had left twenty minutes before. Perhaps she could keep her company, Leah thought. But first she must exercise her back, she must walk around, just in the café. Sitting on the bus since early in the morning had not been good. Of course, Nojke had warned her.

"With your back? A bus ride like that? You're courting danger, Leah! Believe me!"

Oh, she believed him. He had been a surgeon most of his life. But the curvature of her spine wasn't the real issue. The real issue was that he didn't want her to go to Moisés Ville. He didn't want her to leave him, not even for a few days. What hurt her the most was that he tried to make her feel guilty, as though she was uncaring. From the day she'd come home with the brochure information on the excursions to the centennial celebrations, he tried to make it seem a mere whim on her part, an excuse to leave him. When she asked him to go with her, he became angry. They both knew she hadn't been back to her mother's village since 1939, when she was twenty-three years old. That was before they were married.

The children promised to be attentive during her absence. He was to go to lunch at one house and have his dinners at the other, and yet he pouted. Granted, this had been a very bad year for him, suddenly idle and depressed after so many years of such hard work. She hadn't really expected him to be sympathetic and encouraging about her returning to Moisés Ville, for he had never felt a positive attachment to his own past. On the contrary, he was always running from the misery of it all. But still, she hadn't expected he would make her feel guilty. Oh, she knew that deep down he loved her, as she had always loved him, good times and bad. But he had become very difficult. This was the first time in a year she'd left him alone, except for her rushed trips to the market, or on other errands.

At the far wall of the café, Leah stopped to inspect a few pictures before heading toward the American girl's table. She moved cautiously, knowing that any quick movement could immobilize her for days. It wasn't often that she thought about her spine. But when it gave her pain, she inevitably remembered her wonderful mother fussing over her, making her clothes that would camouflage the back, accentuate the small waist, always assuring her that the hump wasn't very big. Her mother-in-law, on the other hand, had always made it quite clear that the unfortunate disfigurement was very obvious. After Leah ordered two coffees from the waiter, who was still talking to Marisol, the bus hostess, she crossed the floor.

This was clearly a crisis of separation. It hardly seemed right that a relationship should end, then and there, in that sad café in the middle of the pampas. Leah knew that the girl was Jess, the man Victor. On the bus, something had compelled her to watch and listen. It wasn't only the question of language, that Leah loved English, that she'd studied it all her life. It was more. Leah was profoundly moved by this tall woman's compassion, by her enthusiasm as she spoke to her companion about Moisés Ville.

After the bus broke down, for the final time, Leah wandered into that waist-high wheat field, attracted by the shade of the ombu. It was a struggle making her way through the wheat, and several times she paused to catch her breath. But she was aware of Jess's camera turned in her direction, drawing her in. It was an odd, significant moment, a brief connection with Jess, with the landscape. Leah felt certain that her dress, a deep blue, with large, rust chrysanthemums, had collaged with the ochre field.

After, she followed behind Jess and Victor from the stalled bus toward the café. She hung back, listening, while Jess spoke in her gentle, awkward Spanish to the small Indian girl selling things from her cigar box. In the cafe, Jess and Victor talked and argued tensely before he stood up and left, boarding the bus that came through from Santa Fe.

Standing beside Jess's table, Leah pulled out the empty chair and sat down. Gingerly she leaned across the table, tapping the girl's arm. "Perhaps a little coffee might help?" she said in English.

Jess turned, startled.

Leah felt the girl's bewildered stare, as though she'd been disturbed in sleep. Her eyes were red. "Coffee?" Leah repeated.

"Yes, thank you," Jess said, straightening up.

"My name is Leah Uberman." She stopped talking, allowing the waiter to place the cups on the table. "And I could not help noticing," she shrugged apologetically, "your distress. I hope you're all right, and that you don't mind my asking?" Again she patted Jess's arm.

"I'm fine. Thank you." Jess shuddered as she reached for the coffee.

"Sugar?" Leah held out the dish of sugar packets.

Jess shook her head.

Leah carefully tore one open and poured it into her cup. She stirred the coffee slowly, looking around the café. "The replacement bus should be here soon. We won't be getting in to Moisés Ville until very, very late. Do you have a place to stay? It will be quite crowded."

"The Pension. I always stay there."

Relieved, Leah sat back.

Some time later, when the bus finally came, Leah and Jess walked out of the café together. Leah was amused to think what an unlikely pair they must seem—a stout, middle-aged lady with a hump, and a tall, straight young woman, so recently, so deeply wounded. It was an odd thing, the way they connected, in their combination of Spanish and English. They sat together on the bus and stayed awake straight through the night. At first Leah spoke. Mostly memories of her childhood summers in Moisés Ville, and her grandfather, Henoch Rosenvitch, one of the early founders of the village. Jess had taken interest, so Leah had nattered on, hoping to keep Jess distracted, hoping to cheer her. Finally Jess talked. First about a strange dream, and then about Victor, and how it was over. Leah realized they'd joined forces in that fast way that only strangers can.

The sun, filtering through the eucalyptus forest, is still in Leah's face. She shields her eyes with one hand, as she moves slowly around the camera bags, the bark and ferns. "Jess!" Leah calls out approaching the felled log.

Jess turns.

"How was your weekend? No more dreams about renting babies, or Victor, I hope?" Leah's voice is cheery, upbeat. "Isn't this heat unbelievable?" She pulls a handkerchief out of her pocket.

"No more Victor." Jess agrees, moving over, beckoning Leah to sit. It was not easy getting through the weekend, Jess realizes for the first time. It took all her strength and perseverance. More than once she wondered if she hadn't made a terrible mistake with her ultimatum to Victor about having a baby. More than once she wanted to hire the first cab she could find to drive her straight back to the Buenos Aires airport so she could fly home to their New York apartment, forgetting everything about Moisés Ville and Argentina. But a stubborn common sense prevailed, and self-respect finally kicked in. She moved through the weekend and the centennial events slowly, cautiously. Every day will be better. Every day she will gain ground, she knows that too, because this isn't the first time. She's been through it before.

Leah looks wonderful, Jess realizes, as she watches her friend dab her face and neck with a handkerchief. Her delicate complexion is flushed from the heat, her blue eyes are relaxed. She's wearing the chrysanthemums again. They looked so perfectly harmonious in that landscape with the ombu, as though those blossoms could defy nature by jumping off the blue dress, joining the wheat field. When she focused her lens on those flowers, it was a rare moment of unity and peace.

"And the photographs, the interviews? Were you able to get your interviews?" Leah asks, carefully sitting on the log.

"Yes, but it wasn't easy. Everyone was very busy with the centennial events. How about you, Leah? Did you do everything you wanted?" Jess lifts a strand of hair out of her face. Yes, she will gain ground, slowly, but it's depressing to be going through a separation again. Again she feels as though she has lost, as though she has less than when she began. Once, she told Victor about this feeling that accompanied the end of a relationship, the realization that with every time, a bit more of her inner core is absorbed by her body, for reinforcement. He didn't want to discuss her feelings, or even the idea. So, in his scientific manner, he told her that the bone of a leper's finger is ultimately absorbed by the flesh around it.

"I think I did it all," Leah smiles. Jess looks tired, she realizes, but at least she seems better than when they arrived in Moisés Ville. There were moments on the bus ride up when Leah was quite concerned about how Jess would manage the next few days. She knew the pension where Jess was staying, and she had fully intended to check up on her during the days of celebrations, but she didn't get to it. "My cousins had an itinerary planned, it was exhausting. We attended everything—the performances and talks, reunions and parades, the museum, the cemetery. What didn't we do! How about you?"

"Mostly I took pictures, I didn't really feel like doing a lot. I did go to the Baron Hirsch Friday night."

Leah turns to Jess, surprised. "The synagogue? But surely you couldn't have taken very good photos at night, and it must have been awfully crowded."

"Yes it was crowded, but I didn't go to take photos."

"Really?" Leah says quietly. "I wouldn't have guessed you're religious," she adds, her voice verging on disappointment.

"I would never call myself religious." Jess is amused by the idea.

"Well, what was it like?"

"The synagogue?"

Leah nods.

"Wonderful. I even understood most of what was going on. The chanting wasn't much different from . . ."

"I've never been." Leah says.

"To the Baron Hirsch?"

"Oh I've been in, once with a girl friend, when we were very young. But I mean I've never been in when anything was going on."

"You're not serious?"

"I am. I told you that my grandfather was not a religious man. He didn't go into a synagogue any more than he had to."

Both Leah and Jess watch through the trees as two taxis pull up to one of the buses. The doors open, and the Lions Club group pours out, looking fresh and rested. Clearly they had just showered, and the women had their hair done. Obviously they knew the buses would not be leaving on time.

"I wonder how it is they always manage everything so much more smoothly then the rest of us." Leah says, perplexed. "I noticed on the trip out last Thursday, they were the first to be served at that little café we were stuck at. I saw the man with the wavy, white hair—the one who calls himself Judah—I saw him go up to the waiter before anyone even sat down, whisper something in his ear, and slip him some money."

"I'm not surprised."

"Then I saw them during the weekend," Leah continues, "when I was with my cousins. They were always working their way to the head of a line, somehow never having to stand and wait, like everyone else."

"Maybe it's because they have no real connection to Moisés Ville," Jess suggests. "They came for a good time, an excursion. They have no identification with this town."

"Perhaps you're right." Leah watches as Judah and his group load their suitcases into the bottom of the bus. "Is your family religious?"

"Not really," Jess says. "One of my grandmothers used to keep kosher, but my grandfather ignored her. You know what I mean?"

"I think so," Leah nods.

"In my home we observed the holidays, and my parents sent us to Hebrew school and Jewish summer camps, but it wasn't a big preoccupation." Jess nods toward the buses. "Maybe we should head over, people are starting to board."

"Wait . . ." Leah puts her hand on Jess's arm. "Did your parents fast on Yom Kippur?"

"Sure. We all did. At least we tried. If we kids didn't make it, it was O.K. too because there was always next year. My father was president of our congregation for a couple years." For the first time since Victor left, Jess thinks about her parents. They will not be happy with this turn of events. Her mother was hoping for a wedding.

"But Judaism was kept alive for you, and you aren't angry about it, are you, Jess?"

Jess smiles. "Why would I be angry?"

Leah shrugs. "I don't know. In this country, everyone is always angry about religion. For every generation, religion has been something from the past to rebel against. Until now, when we don't even remember or know what it was we rebelled against."

"Victor's family is like that. What about your husband?"

"Nojke?" Leah laughs. "I, at least, have some respect, I think. Mind you, Nojke's grandfather was a rabbi, or so I've heard." She glances over to the buses. "There are two Flechas de Santa Fe. I wonder which is ours?"

"Just follow the Lion's group. They always know!" Jess says, standing, reaching out her hand to help Leah up.

The boarding process takes forever. Bags are stacked into the luggage compartment, passengers are directed onto the right buses, and finally, heads are counted. Just as they are about to leave—and they are the last bus to pull out—a robust young man with curly brown hair jumps on, introduces himself as David, and says he will be traveling with them. Marisol, their original hostess, will accompany the other bus. As soon as they are under way, he adds, he will come around with refreshments.

"Victor would have been pleased that Marisol is out of the picture," Jess says, leaning back against the seat. She remains silent for a few moments. "Leah?"

Leah is still trying to settle in, turning in the seat, shifting her weight, busily refolding and adjusting her jacket she is attempting to use as a pillow. "It's always so difficult with my back," she apologizes softly.

"Leah," Jess reaches over to help her hold the jacket in place. "Leah, I keep wondering what he was like before I knew him. I'm sure there was a time when he was different. I always felt there was stuff I didn't know."

"Does he have family? Does anyone know him?"

Satisfied with her seating adjustments, Leah relaxes, breathes deeply, and momentarily closes her eyes.

"He has a sister, Masha. She's really wonderful, and she adores him. I don't know how much she knows. Neither of them talk very much." Jess watches as David begins passing out small paper cups of warm Coke. "I still can't believe it's over." Jess is silent for a few moments. "I got so tired of feeling on the outside, he never really let me in."

The bus leaves the village and starts out onto the highway. Leah looks longingly at the passing landscape. "I don't expect to get back to Moisés Ville."

"Perhaps you will."

"I doubt it, but it's all right. I'm almost seventy-three, and I've said my good-byes. It was wonderful to be back."

"Did you manage to get hold of your husband during the weekend?" Jess asks.

"No. You know it was impossible to get a line out of the village? Every time I tried, I was told to try again later. I'm a little concerned. I did tell him I'd call. It never occurred to me that I might not be able to. But surely Nojke realizes why he hasn't heard from me." Leah twists the corner of her scarf around her little finger. "Surely he isn't just sitting around going crazy?" Leah can't help wondering if he's picked up the phone and tried to get her. He knows where she was staying, he has her cousins' number.

"I tried calling Victor in Buenos Aires, just to see if he'd gotten back all right, but I didn't have any success either." Jess looks out the bus window. "By now he's probably back in his lab in New York, checking up on his shrimp. I wonder if he burned the toast before he went to work, and if he left the coffee perc on? I guess I could try calling his lab when I get back to Buenos Aires tomorrow." Jess shakes her head. "What am I saying? It's over." She closes her eyes, leans back against the seat.

David continues to come around with warm Coke. A few minutes later he appears with ice cubes in his cupped hands, dripping water onto the bus floor. Somehow the sight does not surprise Jess, but she wonders why they don't have a container for the ice.

"I got to the cemetery, did I tell you?" Leah asks.

"Did you find your grandparents?" Jess knows from their conversation on the ride up to Moisés Ville that finding their tombstones was a priority for Leah. Jess went to the cemetery too. In fact, she saw Leah there. The cemetery reminded Jess of Athens—the acropolis, the stones. The cypress swayed in the breeze. The light was crisp, clear. It struck Jess that only the sea was missing. At first, when she saw Leah approaching from a distance, she was going to call out to her, but something stopped her. She sensed this was a moment of privacy for Leah. Jess remained silent and unseen beside the cypress, while she watched Leah searching among the tombstones, intent on the inscriptions and old photographs.

"Yes, I found them."

Jess saw her finally pause at the right tombs, she even heard the sigh. Raising her arm, Leah rested her hand on the high flank of her grandfather's gravestone, as though it was the old man's shoulder. She stood silently for a few moments, her head leaning against her raised arm. Before turning to the adjoining grave, her grandmother's, Leah gently ran her flattened hand over the image of his face, a photograph, attached to the stone. Jess managed a few silent shots before Leah left the graves. After, she approached for several close-ups. The photograph was clearly from his middle years—still handsome, with energetic blue eyes and an unswerving presence.

She would send Leah photos once they were developed.

"Listening to you talk about your family has made me remember so many things," Leah says. She is finally comfortable in her seat. "People thought so highly of my grandfather. He was indeed wonderful—wise and intelligent, worldly. But there were rumors, you know." Leah turns to Jess, smiling.

"Rumors?"

"Yes. Some in the family said my grandfather had a life-long mistress in Buenos Aires, even while my grandmother was alive. My mother never spoke of it; naturally all the adults tried to keep it from the children, but we heard. My grandmother died the year I was born, so I never got to know her. I understand she was neither a happy nor healthy woman, and that she suffered from nerves and depression. From the time my mother was a young girl, she felt responsible for her. She looked after her, she humored her, while everyone else accused her of being old-fashioned because she kept the Sabbath and the holidays. Her sons reproached her, saying they were in a new land with new ways, and that she should get rid of the old customs that had kept them Jews, persecuted and in servitude in Russia. Here they were Argentineans, landowners. My grandmother said they had sacrificed too much in this new land. Only my mother was patient. But when she married my father and moved to Rosario with him, it was no longer possible to be so attentive, and she was racked with guilt.

"My mother used to tell me about her childhood, how she would help her mother prepare for the holidays. But by the end of her life, my grandmother had given up celebrating Rosh Hashanah and Succoth, Purim and Pesach. It was only Shabbat she observed until she died, lighting candles, alone, every Friday night. It feels so strange to name the holidays! I haven't thought about them in fifty years! I didn't know I remembered!" Leah says cheerfully, turning in her seat, adjusting her coat.

"I met his mistress once."

"Your grandfather's?" Jess asks, surprised.

"Yes, in 1939. I came to Moisés Ville with my mother to take part in the celebrations commemorating the village's fiftieth anniversary. My grandfather had been dead a year. It was at the Palacios train station—a hot, brilliant day. My female cousins and I were dressed in white. Uncles and aunts and cousins, we all drove to the station to meet her, the woman. Only my mother didn't go. She would have no part of it. I was twenty-three and very curious. Of course she wasn't introduced as his mistress, but we all knew. She was an old lady by then, but still very attractive, with white hair and bright, dark eyes. She limped. When she saw my back, she smiled at me." Leah becomes silent for a moment, remembering.

"I think your grandmother's inability to adjust was not such an uncommon story," Jess says sympathetically.

"Perhaps you're right. Jess?" Leah sits up. "Do you feel the bus is traveling slower, or is it my imagination?"

"I hope you're joking," Jess says looking out at the dark landscape. She has no idea how long they've been traveling. She yawns.

"I noticed that all the other tour buses passed us long ago, including the other Flecha bus," Leah says.

Jess watches as David hurries up and down the aisle passing out small sandwiches, wrapped in cellophane. The Lions tour group are all seated immediately across the aisle. Jess hears Judah kick up a fuss because the only available sandwiches are cheese. She listens while he asks David why the bus is traveling so slowly. David says he will check.

"I hope we're not going to have bus problems like we did on the trip up," Leah says.

"Is your husband expecting you at a certain time?"

"My God, I didn't even think of Nojke!" Leah covers her mouth. "Yes, of course, the brochure he has says the buses would leave in the afternoon and arrive back in the city by midnight. Look," she holds out her arm, "it's already 9:00, and we're nowhere near Rosario. We won't be in Buenos Aires until three in the morning."

Leah feels the bus carefully slow up and come to a full stop. The passengers sit up curiously. The door cranks open, and David, who's been talking to the driver in a low voice, peers out before climbing off.

"Now what?" It's Judah's voice again.

They wait for ten minutes. Finally David hurries back onto the bus, smiles, and says that everything is O.K. In a few minutes, the bus pulls off again.

People relax and settle back. David brings around coffee and small Danish. They are dry and hard, and Leah hears the usual complaints across the aisle. A short time later, the lights are turned out, and everyone tries to settle in.

Leah closes her eyes. The weekend events fill her mind as she tries to relax. Nojke would have been bored had he come. The one time she asked him to visit Moisés Ville was shortly after they were married.

But Nojke was too busy and really not interested. Even then she was not hurt; she understood that he was eager to get on with his life. He had sweat blood and tears to become a doctor, working day and night, clerking and odd jobs. Once a doctor, there were years of holding three and four jobs at once, just to support his wife and two children, not to mention his widowed mother and younger sister. And now, all the work was over. Two years ago there were changes in the hospital's administration, financial reversals, and he was asked to retire. He was so hurt, so wounded, he could not deal with the decision. In anger, he quit all his jobs at once, without a word. Leah had been indignant that he would not fight the hospital's decision. This last year of his paranoia and depression had left her drained.

An hour passes uneventfully, and then, abruptly, the bus jerks to a stop. Again David jumps off. This time they wait twenty minutes. Then he hurries on again, he picks up the microphone and asks for everyone's attention. He explains, in a low, somber voice, that the other Flecha bus is experiencing difficulty, and they are going to follow it, slowly, in case it runs into serious problems. It will, of course, delay their arrival into Buenos Aires and he certainly hopes this will not inconvenience anyone, but there is nothing else he can do.

A rumble begins across the aisle. The Lions become restless, fidgeting and complaining, especially their spokesman, Judah.

Jess hears his deep breathing; she sees his wife patting his hand, attempting to calm him. Finally the lights are dimmed again and within half an hour, people begin dozing. The conversations that continue are carried on in low, monotone voices. When it happens again, the jerking, stopping motion of the bus, the lights go on, and the driver curses.

"This time we're in for it, I know." Leah whispers, nodding to the other side of the bus and the Lions.

They wait. Passengers yawn and look at their watches. Cold air rushed in the bus when the door was opened. The woman in front of Jess pulls on her sweater.

David is back on. He stands beside the driver, scratching his head. "We have a major problem. The other bus has broken down completely, so we will be taking on its passengers."

A silence descends and the air feels suddenly still and close inside the bus.

"I know it will be a little crowded, but we've no choice. I hope you all understand." Just as David turns to descend the bus, Judah stands up at his seat.

"No!" His voice rings across the bus, defiant and loud.

All eyes turn to the Lions' spokesman. He looks exhausted, drained.

"What right do you have telling us we have to take on the other passengers! What right?!" The man is furious; he holds on to the back of the seat in front of him, straining forward toward David. "I will not permit it. We've had enough, absolutely enough. From the beginning, this trip has been a fiasco. We paid good money, and what have we gotten? Broken down buses and grief, only grief! I was told this would be a deluxe excursion. What kind of deluxe? A lousy hotel with bad service and terrible food! Free tickets to a pathetic theatrical performance! And you call that a museum? Boring speeches! Dried-out cheese sandwiches and no ice bucket? I tell you, no! We are sorry, but no! You will tell the driver to proceed on his way immediately, and we will get this trip over with!"

Impatience clouds David's face. "Do you, sir, speak as a representative of the passengers? Because if not, I think you would do well to hold your tongue."

"Yes, yes, yes! I represent the passengers. We will put up with no more, I swear! No more!" Judah is blue in the face and breathing heavily. His companion in the seat in front of him has also stood up and turned around, trying to calm him, patting his arm. "Judah," his voice is low, cajoling. "Judah, don't get yourself so worked up. Your heart Judah, your heart . . ."

Judah pulls away from his companion. "Ask! Ask the others if they want to take on more! If they come on, it will be impossibly crowded. Worse than a third-class bus! Many of us will have to give up our seats to old women. Why should we? We paid for these seats."

"We'll take a vote, it's the only fair way." David says, resolutely. All eyes turn to David. "Those who are in favor of taking on the other passengers, raise your hands." A deep silence falls over the bus.

Leah looks around, frightened. Most of the passengers seem stunned, dazed. Everything is happening so quickly. Feeling uncertain, unprepared, she turns to whisper something to Jess, when the next thing they know, David is asking for another show of hands. "Those who are for carrying on, for leaving the other bus and passengers to their own devices." After David officiously counts hands, he stands for a few moments in silence. "I will tell the other driver the decision."

"I didn't have time to vote," Leah says to Jess, shocked. "Wait!" Holding on to the seat in front of her, she pulls herself half up. "Wait! I haven't voted!"

But David is already off the bus. When he returns, he hurries directly to the back and comes forward carrying his knapsack. He is about to jump off again, but then hesitates and turns to the passengers. "I feel humiliated. I'm embarrassed that Jews have done this to Jews! I, for one, cannot abandon the other passengers. Good riddance!" He leaves the bus for the last time. The driver closes the door and starts the motor.

The next time the bus stops for refueling, Judah, the Lion, collapses at the small rest stop, where his wife is encouraging him to drink some milk. His companions manage to revive him enough to get him back on the bus. They stretch him out across two seats, flat, silent, and ashen. He is attended, in hushed tones, by his wife and friends for the duration of the trip.

The bus finally pulls in to Buenos Aires in the early dawn hours. Leah and Jess say good-bye to each other as they wait for cabs, shivering in the chill air, embracing and promising to keep in touch.

When Leah arrives home, Nojke is waiting for her in his bathrobe, absolutely beside himself with worry, just as she left him. He looks like a small child who was abandoned. There are shadows under his eyes, and the air in the house is stale. Leah knows that he hasn't opened a window in days because of thieves. She is tired, and not very sympathetic to his anxiety. As a matter of fact, after her brief explanation about her delay—to which he merely heaps on more outbursts about how lonely he was and how inattentive the children were—she tells him to stop complaining because she is going to bed.

Leah considers her Moisés Ville trip a success. But for a long time after her return to Buenos Aires, she worries about the events surrounding the other bus and the stranded passengers. Twice she calls the central Flecha office to make sure everything turned out all right. It did. Nevertheless, her preoccupation remains strong, and her feelings of guilt for not having voted, for cowering, continue.

She sees quite a bit of Jess in the months following. They often talk about the events on the bus, but they are unable to resolve anything. Leah tries to console herself. Everything happened so fast, she didn't have time to raise her hand, to show a sign of support for the stranded passengers. Leah knows it is only an excuse. She knows that the moment was a test, and she failed. She did not stand up for what she believed. Like her grandmother, she allowed herself to melt into the crowd; she allowed herself to be ground down. While her sense of failure never completely leaves her, with time, it is diminished. She learns to cope, as she copes with her hunchback, and her Nojke.

Eventually, Leah Uberman is able to wear her chrysanthemum dress again, enjoy her granddaughter, Letitia, and answer, as promised, Jess's many heartening letters.

The correspondence comes steadily, like little bunches of chrysanthemums, from a small town in Vermont, where Jess has married and given birth to a daughter she calls Leah.

THE RIFKE CHRONICLES

The year 1910 marks the 100th anniversary of Argentine independence. Anarchist violence associated with the labor movement has become a near daily occurrence. In 1905, an attempt was made on the life of the ex-president, and in 1908 another attempt failed to kill the president in office. In 1909 a bomb exploded on Corrientes Street, and the same day, an anarchist was arrested as he carried a second bomb into a church. In retaliation, police action against labor demonstrations was stepped up. In this year, 1910, perhaps as a foil to the violence, the Argentine women's movement becomes firmly established. In Buenos Aires, two separate women's conferences are held within months of each other. Rifke Schulman attends one.

From Volume Twelve.

November 15, 1909
Buenos Aires

Today is my thirty-eighth birthday, and yesterday afternoon, Peshke insisted on taking me to an outdoor café to celebrate. We sipped our coffees and ate the tiny pastries we both love, chatting lazily and admiring the beautiful day. How calm and peaceful everything seemed—the weather, the leafy plane trees lining the cobblestone street, shading the pedestrians hurrying to and fro. Children played and called out as they ran about on the street and under the shop awnings. A shopkeeper paused in his doorway, contemplating the weather and the clientele, before stepping out to rearrange his wares on the outdoor stand. Another merchant in an apron swept the sidewalk. It could not have been a more perfect afternoon.

Peshke and I had promised each other not to talk about the continuous unrest that had bathed Buenos Aires for the last six months. Last May 1st, Labor Day, police again attacked an anarchist demonstration. Eight people were left dead and many wounded. Not long after, 200,000 workers went on strike in protest. Yesterday, we successfully put aside thoughts of tension and conflict. Indeed, we were enjoying the day, until Peshke called to the waiter to order more coffee. The poor man came to us, distraught and diminished. Only minutes before he had heard the news. Visibly shaken, an empty tray dangling from his hand, he informed us that Ramon Falcon, the chief of police, and his secretary, had just been killed by a Jewish anarchist.

Seventeen-year-old Simon Radowitzky avenged his fellow workers by throwing a bomb at Falcon's carriage. With this violent act, Radowitzky put an end to Falcon's vicious repression of labor demonstrations.

Early this morning, as I was leaving for the factory, I found Peshke already at her wash tubs out on the walkway. She wished me a happy birthday and said she was glad we celebrated yesterday because we would never have done it today. She's probably right. The city is troubled and in mourning. Without question, Radowitzky's act will cause the deportation or imprisonment of thousands of workers. A shadow will be cast over all Jews.

May 15, 1910
Buenos Aires

In the six months since the assassination of Police Chief Falcon, there has been a dramatic increase in anti-Semitic, antiforeign sentiment. The newspapers deal with Jewish issues in the most constant, negative terms. In the last few days, there has been another terrible outbreak of violence. It makes me think it will never end. Last night, "patriotic," upper-class citizens and young nationalists, members of the Sociedad Sportiva Argentina, completely destroyed the offices of the anarchist and socialist newspapers. The police arrested many working-class leaders, including the head of the Socialist Party, Juan Justo. These "patriotic" mobs committed horrible acts right here in the eleventh district, my neighborhood. Only seven blocks from where I live, on the corner of Lavalle and Andes, they destroyed a Jewish grocery store and then raped several women.

But it didn't end there. This same mob continued on to the Russian Jewish Library. Yes, my library. I am devastated. They dragged the contents outside and set fire to everything. Peshke accompanied me this morning when I went over to inspect the site. All the books were lost. It is finished. For the third time I am left without a library. Once again I must pick up the pieces around me.

A few hours ago, I received a telegram from Henoch in Moisés Ville. He is desperate about the occurrences in the capital and anxious about my well-being. He asks that I write him immediately. I thank God for Henoch. He is a constant support in my life. I will write tomorrow. It is late, and I must get some sleep. My job at the factory is also a constant, and every morning I must get myself to work regardless of the realities of the night before.

June 30, 1910

More violence. A few days ago a bomb exploded in the Colón Theater, and the next day, the Law of Social Defense was passed by Congress. Anarchists and foreigners who've committed civil crimes will no longer be allowed to enter the country. Acts of violence against the government are prohibited, as are public meetings and demonstrations held by anarchists. The bomb, placed under the only unoccupied red velvet seat, exploded during a performance. There were minor injuries. The police arrested a Russian anarchist, though rumor is he was innocent of the crime.

Yesterday, after getting off work at the factory, I stopped to talk with Pincus, the cobbler, who still has his stand at the entrance to our building. I thought he might be willing to shed some light on the new law and the Colón bombing—given his anarchist connections—but he had nothing to say. If he knew anything, he certainly wasn't going to tell me. He's an odd fellow, Pincus, sometimes so talkative and other times he won't even give you the time of day. He did say I'm looking well, and glancing over his counter at my left shoe, he nodded approvingly. Then, sitting back, he asked when Rosenvitch was coming back to visit. He missed their chats, he said.

I've just returned from the Milekofskys. Peshke called me over to have a cup of tea with them because her brother-in-law, Aaron, had stopped by for a visit. His wife, Sonia, rarely accompanies him to Peshke's. Aaron expressed his condolences on the destruction of the library. He knows of my commitment and devotion to it. He is certain that within a few years a new library will be created, for he believes that Jews cannot be long without books. He told me the bakers' union had just formed, joining the anarchists. This association distresses him. Aaron is a genuine pacifist. He, like Henoch, like most of us, abhors violence. The Jewish tailors and carpenters have also formed a union, but they've joined ranks with the Socialists. They have more sense than the bakers, Aaron commented!

Aaron said he'd heard from Peshke that I'd attended the First International Feminist Conference in February. He asked if the conference really covered as many topics as the newspapers reported. I assured him it had, at least from what I saw during the few sessions I was able to attend. I explained that I only asked for one day off at the factory, and at that, it was on the pretense of illness. I dared not tell them I wanted to attend a feminist meeting! Not only was the conference well organized and efficiently run, I told the Milekofskys, but Argentine railway companies had discounted fares so women could attend from the interior of the country. Participants came from as far away as Chile, Peru, Italy, and the U.S. There were sessions on sociology, education, science, and arts and letters. Many topics were covered. There were calls to legalize divorce and pleas to eradicate prostitution, child abuse, truancy, and child labor. I told Aaron I was disappointed that the organizers chose not to focus on suffrage. I know that feminists in Europe and the U.S. are devoting enormous amounts of time and energy to this topic, and I feel that we in Argentina should be as well. Without the right to vote, the Argentine woman, like all women, will never be taken seriously or treated with equality. Peshke laughs at me when I talk like that. She says it will be decades before women are respected for their brains, and it will take more than the vote.

I asked Aaron after Sonia and her brother. He said they were well and that Sonia was expecting their first child. I congratulated him and told him not to be such a stranger!

July 1, 1910

Yesterday I stopped by Marcus Soltansky's tailor shop. I'd come on the excuse of needing a spool of thread, but in reality I needed to visit with the old man, who'd always reminded me so much of my father. As I stood warming my fingers and toes at his heater, Marcus told me that his son, Moses, will be going to London in a few months to attend an international meeting of the Jewish Association for the Protection of Girls and Women. The Argentine Association Against the White Slave trade is sending him. He will be Argentina's representative, Marcus said proudly.

"I'm making him a new suit! We can't have him go to London looking the way he usually does!" Marcus said, reaching for the half-finished garment. "Rifke, when that boy didn't want to become a tailor, breaking tradition with all the Soltanskys before him, I worried about him. What would he do? What would become of him? Who would have ever imagined that big, red-headed metal sheet worker could be so gentle, so involved in the protection of helpless women. Only one thing makes me sad," Marcus said quietly, hanging the suit back above his sewing machine., "He has no wife! In all the years of working so hard against the *tmeyim*, it seems unfair not to have a wife, a woman to support him. You know what I think, Rifke? I think that little Bela spoiled it for him. I don't think he's ever looked at a woman since."

I told him I thought he was right.

On the way home, while I was thinking about Big Moses in London, England, I ran into Peshke's daughter. Deborah is married now and has a fine baby boy. She and her husband have moved in with his people, a large Italian family. Besides the restaurant, they own a wine-importing business and farmland outside the city. Beautiful Deborah has become rather petulant since leaving home. Standing on the corner talking, she told me she can no longer deal with the religious issue. She does not care as much about her religion as they obviously care about theirs. She has agreed to raise her son, and any other children that come, as Catholics.

I know that Peshke has thrown up her hands. What can she do? She claims everyone must lead their own life. Not that Peshke ever held much stock in Judaism. It has always represented the past for her, and unfortunately, the most depressing aspects of the past: the poverty of her wooden ghetto in Poland, the hunger, the misery, all overridden by constant Russian anti-Semitism. It's not that she wants to dissociate herself, but what is there to hang onto? For what reason?

Peshke still prepares for Shabbat and Pesach, and probably always will. I believe that food traditions may be one of the only aspects of Judaism that continue to live on in this country. For people like Peshke, it's too hard to generate positive ideas from so much misery. It takes too much energy to think about the future, to think about the strengths that are inherent in cultural traditions, strengths that need nurturing and protection.

THE RIFKE CHRONICLES

When Sáenz Peña became president of Argentina in 1911, he extended voting privileges to the majority of the native male working class. Foreigners were still not allowed to vote. The first election under this law confirmed the strength of the Socialist Party. Both Socialist representatives, Palacios and Justo, were elected to the national parliament. Palacios was first elected to Congress in 1904.

BUENOS AIRES: In 1913, Enrique del Valle Iberlucea is elected the first Socialist senator in America.

PANAMA: The canal is almost completed.

MORELOS, MEXICO: Emiliano Zapata, the revolutionary leader of agrarian reform, puts forth a plan to divide the sugar plantations and restore land to the Indians.

From Volume Fifteen.

December 20, 1913
Villa Crespo, Buenos Aires

Peshke has finally convinced me to move! The Milekofskys have been out of number 1454 Lavalle for more than a year, and Peshke has been nagging me to join them for months. They have their own place in Villa Crespo, on Canning Street, near Calle Corrientes. They've opened a small grocery store with vats of olive oil, barrels of pickles and herring, and sacks of flour. The family has living space above the shop. It's small, but theirs! My quarters are two doors away, upstairs, above a carpenter's shop. I'm delighted with my new rooms! I have lots of sunlight and plenty of space. Despite the intense heat of these summer months, I've enjoyed my new home, especially the small balcony of red tiles and iron railing, where I grow a few flowers and keep my new friend, a very green parrot named Solomon. Solomon was given to me by a street vendor who became tired of feeding him. The vendor assured me the bird must be very wise because he rarely speaks. My balcony is within talking distance of Peshke's, and she worries that someday Solomon will begin to repeat what he hears.

Villa Crespo is rapidly becoming a new Jewish area, primarily for recent arrivals from eastern Europe. Tailors, carpenters, laborers of all professions are hurrying off the boats and into the ghettos. Some acclimatize to their new country by holding tightly to Judaism. Others, and it's seeming more and more the majority, adjust by leaving their religion behind. This phenomenon is precisely what some of the Argentine élite would like to see, total assimilation. This thinking is not exclusive to the upper class, for leaders of the Socialist Party feel the same.

This attitude has kept me away from the party. Not that I haven't come close to joining on more than one occasion. The Socialist Party has a progressive platform calling for universal suffrage, permanent electoral registration, supervisory committees to inspect factories and dwellings, and the eight-hour workday. These are only a few of their demands; the list is long and just. The party has become extremely popular. In 1909, even the chief of police of Buenos Aires suggested that a few Socialist deputies be allowed into parliament. Considering the volatile times, laws on strikes and working conditions would certainly be parliamentary topics.

To whom, in the working class, wouldn't these demands appeal? Most immigrant Jews fit into this category. But I am disappointed that such an important political movement insists on adhering to the notion that assimilation is the only way to be a true Argentine. I am discouraged that they are not more far-sighted. We recently read, in one of our Yiddish monthlies, the anti-Semitic comments make by Juan B. Justo, founder of the Socialist movement in this country. He remarked that if Jews are capable of circumcision, they could observe other blood rituals as well. This statement was made in reference to the sensational ritual murder trial of Mendel Beilis, a Jew living in Kiev. Accused in 1911, the poor man was not acquitted until this year, his name finally cleared of all charges.

It is beyond my comprehension how such a highly educated, highly respected man as Justo could hold such beliefs, could say such things. What right does he have implying such horrors? Are we back in the Middle Ages? Must we always be made to suffer under ignorance and inquisition? Dare I trust him? He has stated, "Religion is the drug of the people." I find that his preoccupation with this idea points to an innate lack of flexibility, an innate disregard for human freedom of belief. In dealing with immigrants arriving on this country's shores, why should we want and expect to take away their religious identity, as though it's baggage? I believe that homogeneity is neither necessary nor wise in the building and strengthening of a nation. I cannot help feeling Justo is a man to be watched carefully. He has the potential of being a destructive leader.

Peshke tells me I worry too much about society, and that I should try to be more practical, like she is. How can I not worry? I tell her the newspapers report that there are presently 300 registered brothels in Buenos Aires. And that's only one of our problems! Peshke shrugs and suggests I worry about buying a new dress for a change! As far as religion is concerned, she's never given it much thought. After all, she says, how important is it for her to teach her children old ideas, traditions that amount to nothing more than superstitions? Isn't the main thing to survive, make ends meet, and try to be happy? I understand what Peshke is saying, and in truth, I wish I could bring myself to worry about making ends meet and buying a dress. But I believe I am being practical and that these ideas—individual identity, freedom of religious expression, assimilation—could easily become serious social problems in this country. Yet very few people want to discuss such issues, and even fewer agree with me. Most people think like Peshke. They are in a new world. If they leave the old behind, forging a new way for themselves and their children, so be it.

The exciting news is that I no longer work at the *alpargata* factory! Last year when the Biblioteca Progreso formed, I was asked to join them. I am paid a modest salary, but I am so happy not to be at the factory, I do not complain. I do everything—work in the library, give Spanish lessons, organize talks, and sweep up! The Progreso began as a combination of the library from my old Union of Jewish Workers—before it became the Bikur Holim—and the books that we salvaged from the Russian Library, after its destruction three years ago.

So many new libraries and cultural centers are opening up all over the city, and they've become enormously important! The Jewish worker can come to them at the end of the workday, find an atmosphere where learning can be pursued, and at the same time maintain language and, to some extent, customs. Some come just to read the newspapers. The library now receives several of the American Yiddish daily journals, from Orthodox to Zionist publications. Naturally we don't receive every issue, but considering the distance, I believe we are kept relatively informed on Jewish life in the United States, even in other parts of the world! The most popular paper has been the *Jewish Daily Forward*. Through the *Forward* we learned about Mendel Beilis in Kiev, and in the same month, about the terrible fire at the Triangle Shirtwaist Co. in New York, where 146 women died. Besides recipes and advice, fiction, scandal and news, Socialist commentary flows from its pages, reaching the immigrant masses. The editor, David Cahan, is a strong supporter of the Jewish labor unions and their strikes. Henoch met Cahan in Vilna before they both emigrated. He remembers him fondly and says he was always in touch with the working class, even as a young man. Two men, Rosenvitch and Cahan, both driven by their ideas for social reform and justice, had to flee the persecution of their native soil before they could begin their life's work. Two countries, Argentina and the United States, received them and watch. I for one, am very grateful!

Between the libraries, cultural centers, and Yiddish theater, which has become abundant and popular, it is an exciting time in Buenos Aires! Aaron Milekofsky was quite right when he said Jews cannot be long without books!

Yesterday I went by number 1454 Lavalle to see if the cobbler Pincus would be willing to talk about Justo. I know I'm always baiting Pincus, but I genuinely would like to know how an anarchist interprets Justo's anti-Semitic remarks. Again he would not deal with the subject. Sometimes I feel Pincus thinks I'm a government spy! He did ask if I wasn't needing a new heel yet. Only when I showed him my shoe was he satisfied with my answer. He asked after Rosenvitch again, and if I've read about this place they've discovered in the Andean mountains of Peru, Machu-Picchu, the royal city of the Inca Indians. I told him I hadn't, so he bent down under his workbench and pulled out a worn magazine with the article. I thanked him and told him it would be returned.

VICTOR

Between planes—Buenos Aires / Miami, Miami / New York—Victor Levin called his sister and told her about Jess. It was a moment of acute fatigue and idleness, a deadly combination, resulting in the rash, unpremeditated act that could have as easily gone undone as done. In fact, if the phone booths hadn't been so close to his gate, Victor knew he probably would not have made the call. Afterwards, he was embarrassed.

While the news did not seem to surprise Masha, her voice became animated, nurturing.

"I'm always here for you, Vic, you know that." The words quivered long distance.

Three hours later Masha met his plane at Kennedy International. He saw her before she saw him, and he felt the familiar rush of irritation. She always seemed more anemic and her posture worse than the last time he'd seen her. She stood in the waiting section, alone and shy, predictably uncomfortable in her own skin. When their eyes met, her relieved smile appeared, the discomfort seemed to vanish, and Victor felt appropriately guilty. The truth was Masha was devoted to him, and she and her son, Nick, were the only family he had. So why was he always impatient with her? He supposed it was because he had wanted her to be so much more than he was—beautiful and talented, lively and charming.

Instead, she was intelligent and serious, and in her middle years she was looking too much like their Aunt Lou. Their mother's reclusive sister had an odd existence of stunted growth, strange habits, and that peculiar odor about her. The habits were unfortunate, their mother had always acquiesced quietly. But the odor was due to drugs, she'd insisted, strong drugs Lou had taken for her growth problems. Masha, thank God, only resembled Lou in looks.

After they located his luggage, she drove him straight to her East Side apartment through city traffic, school children, and October's falling leaves. She was a determined driver. Clinging to the wheel, she maneuvered the car in silence, except for the occasional spew of foul language directed exclusively at taxi drivers. It was the only time he heard his sister swear, and her language, after all these years, still offended him. Whenever he rode in the car with Masha, he felt as though he'd just been expelled from prep school. It was her silence and concentration. Masha was lonely; it had been five years since her divorce, five years since Nick left home for college, and five years of going to the same shrink.

Sitting in Masha's comfortable, warm apartment, Victor felt completely exhausted. He glanced out the window at the streets below, the East River in the distance. The thought of his own empty apartment was more than he could deal with. It was chilly for October, and he was still wearing his summer clothes from Argentina. God, he was glad to be back.

"I had just enough time to run across to the bakery before I left for the airport," Masha said, entering the dining room with a teapot and his favorite sweets. She placed the tray on the table and sat down. "Tea, Vic?"

"Please."

She poured, added a slice of lemon, and handed Victor the cup.

Victor knew that she prided herself on knowing everything important about her older brother—tea with lemon, coffee black. Once a wife, Barbara. Once a daughter, Robin. Numerous girl friends since. He ran every morning in Central Park. His research into the human nervous system was—what did she know? Victor didn't know what she knew. He never really talked to his sister about his work, except that one time a few years ago. It was an isolated incident, a strange aberration. Late one evening he had left his lab, and in the excitement and preoccupation of discovery, he had, without realizing, walked all the way to her apartment. While Masha prepared him something to eat—delighted with his unannounced visit—he told her of the activities at the lab. He had found one of his leeches to be a hermaphrodite. While he ate, he'd explained the significance, the probable consequences of the discovery. Afterwards, they had coffee and went on with their lives. Of course she never talked about her work either. He knew she edited fiction manuscripts at Farrar Straus & Giroux, but that was about it.

"So, *nu?*" Masha sipped her tea.

"I shouldn't have called you, Masha. I mean about it being over with Jess. At least not until I've dealt with this, you know what I mean?" Victor took off his glasses and began rubbing his eyes, massaging his forehead. "How's work? How's Nick?" His fingers worked his temples.

"Everything is fine here."

"The whole thing was awful." Victor shook his head, his eyes still closed. "I'm sure I shouldn't have gone. I would have been better off waiting for her to return. That country is something else." He didn't tell her about the horrible bus trip to Moisés Ville and how he hadn't completed the journey. He didn't tell her about Jess's crazy dream about renting a child.

Masha listened silently for a few moments. "Is she O.K.?"

"Jess?" Victor opened his eyes. "Sure, she's up to her gills in that Moisés Ville research. She tried to get me interested, but you know me. Since she's become involved with all that, she's convinced herself that most Jewish families who left Russia to escape the pogroms took the same route hers did." Victor laughed quietly. "I think she's spinning off into a different orbit. But she's tough! She eats nails for breakfast, that girl," he added self-consciously.

"Tough? What, because she won't come back to you, Victor?"

"I guess that's what I mean. I suppose that eating nails for break-fast has nothing to do with Russian Jews or Argentina."

"Right." Masha nodded. "She just wants a baby."

"Tell me about it!" Victor groaned. "No, never mind, don't. I've had it with that subject." He helped himself to an eclair and ate it slowly. He drank another cup of tea, staring out the window.

He looked miserable, Masha thought, watching her brother. "You didn't tell her, did you?" Her voice was quiet.

Victor removed his glasses, wiped them slowly, replaced them, and quickly glanced at his watch.

"Victor. Victor, you promised." Masha reached across the table for her brother's hand. "You promised," she whispered.

"I know, but I couldn't. I just can't talk about it. I've never been able to."

"All right, all right." Masha shook her head and straightened up. "But Victor, you know it can't get better unless you talk? You drive women away because you won't let them help where you hurt the most. You know that, don't you?"

"Yes, Masha." Victor's voice sounded tired, withdrawn. He

pushed away his tea cup.

"Victor, don't close me out! I'm trying to help you."

After several moments, Victor stood up quickly and smiled cheerfully. "You're such a fretful girl!" He walked around to the other side of the table. He had gathered his forces; he was matter-of-fact. "Look, I'm exhausted, I don't even know what crazy Argentine hour my body thinks it is, but I've got to get home. Tomorrow I have to go to the lab. God only knows what's happened in my absence. Maybe my assistant has mated with a shrimp." He leaned over and kissed his sister on the forehead.

"Victor, you did the same with the analyst. You wouldn't let him help."

"Masha, I've told you before, don't talk to me about shrinks."

"What do you know!" Masha said defensively. "You only went a couple times."

"And it was a couple times too many." Victor walked toward his bags. "Look, why do our conversations always have to end with shrinks? I know you think it works for you, and I'm happy. But I'm a different kettle of fish, Masha." He unzipped his bag and pulled out his trench coat. "I'm going to have to wear this, it's cold here. Isn't it a little early for this weather?" He asked, standing up and putting on his coat.

"Just remember, Victor, Jess might have her faults, but she's a good woman, and I believe she loved you. You should have told her. She deserved that. You know what I mean?" Masha looked at Victor. "It would have made everything easier to understand."

Victor's shoulders slumped. He stood silently for several minutes. Finally he looked up and walked over to Masha, still seated at the table. He bent over and once again kissed her tenderly on the forehead. "Thanks, for the airport, and tea, and everything."

Masha nodded. She could never stay mad at Victor.

"I just can't, Masha . . ." he uttered, his voice hoarse and thick.

Victor Levin left his sister's apartment house and walked up Second Avenue, then crossed over on 86th toward Lexington. Tomorrow he would run in the park, early, before he went up to his lab. He would give himself three days to get back into things. Days and weeks had been wasted. Everything would be back to normal in no time. He felt invigorated by the cool fall weather.

Masha certainly loved to worry. She always had. She was right that Jess was a good person and that she'd loved him. He knew that, and he'd loved her, and he would miss her. But life does go on. Victor understood he couldn't allow himself to sink because of Jess. He'd been through this before. There had been other women since his divorce, and he'd always survived and gone on. As long as he made it clear at the beginning of the relationship—the no marriage, no children bit—then things were cool. It had been all right with most of the women he became involved with. But this time, something had gone wrong. He was grieving, and he shouldn't be. After Robin, he swore he would never again allow himself to experience loss.

Masha always blamed his problems on his silence about Robin. Victor stopped at the corner to buy a newspaper. Robin was no one's business, he'd always insisted. Though he promised Masha he'd tell Jess in Argentina, he hadn't.

He'd never mentioned, even to Masha, that sometimes, in the early dawn hours, when he ran in the park, he stopped at the pond where he used to take Robin. She was a child then, and of course he and Barbara were still married. He could see her now, at the edge of the pond, a little kid in the sunlight, smiling, playing with a stick in the water. The way she'd lean over made his heart pound. He was always terrified she'd fall in. But he'd been a conscientious father, and he'd held himself back from calling out to her every time he was scared.

Later, when she was older, even thirteen and fourteen, whenever she wanted to talk, they went to that same spot. As a young teenager she used to sit in the grass beside the pond, still playing with a stick in the water, her long, red hair falling down her back. He missed her so much, he felt sick in his stomach when he thought about her. He missed her face and her eyes, full of questions, her mind, her wonderful, inquisitive mind. She'd wanted him to teach her everything he knew. He wished he could bring her back, just for a day, he would settle for a day, just to talk to her, to take her to his lab and explain how far his work had progressed, to watch her absorb, to hold her hand. He was in constant pain, and it was a pain worse than the moment he'd lost her. She'd been everything to him, everything no one had ever been.

"Hey, you all right?"

Victor looked at the newspaper vendor. He'd stopped at the stand to buy a paper.

"For a moment you looked like you were gonna pass out. You O.K., fella?"

"I'm fine, thanks." Victor bought the newspaper and continued up Lexington. Fatigue engulfed him. His bag felt heavy. He was too tired to even consider stopping to pick up juice and bread. He passed the florist, the gallery, and the jewelry store. He greeted the doorman, unloaded his mail box into his coat pockets, and walked toward the elevator.

His apartment smelled musty. Victor put down his bag. He turned on the answering machine and walked around opening windows but avoided the bedroom. He did not want to open the closet and find Jess's clothes. There were beeps and messages from his lab assistant, some garbled, angry words from his ex-wife, Barbara, and a welcome home jingle from Masha. Victor flipped off the machine, cutting out Masha's voice.

He sank into the armchair. He realized he hadn't even taken off his coat or turned on the lights. He reached into his pocket for the mail. He went through it, mechanically, but didn't open anything. If he rested for a few minutes, then he could get up and do things. He leaned his head back against the chair and closed his eyes.

He saw the hospital. He saw the room. He saw Robin lying on the bed, white, everything white. She was under an oxygen tent, but it wasn't doing any good. He and Barbara had rushed her there in the evening. Barbara was still wearing the navy blue sweat clothes she'd run in only hours before. They sat beside her bed the whole next day and night. She slipped into a coma at midnight and died at dawn. They had thought it was just flu, the fever and aches, vomiting, diarrhea. Three days of it, nothing more than that. Nothing. When she took a turn for the worse and her blood pressure dropped dramatically, they rushed her to the hospital. By then it was too late.

He still blamed himself. He, the scientist, who hadn't recognized the symptoms, who, in fact, had never paid much attention to the disease or the publicity about it. Masha wanted him to tell Jess, so she'd understand why he didn't want more children. She wanted him to tell Jess that his fifteen-year-old daughter had died of Toxic Shock Syndrome. Why the hell would it help Jess understand, if he didn't understand it himself?

Ringing pierced the silence. Victor twitched. He opened his eyes. It was dark. What time was it? He must have fallen asleep. He fumbled across the coffee table for the phone.

"Vic? Were you sleeping?"

It was Masha's voice.

"Are you all right?"

"Yeah, sure. I must have fallen asleep in the chair. What time is it?"

"It's about eight. Listen, I forgot to tell you something important, Vic."

"What?"

"Remember all that business about Dad's uncle living in Argentina?"

"What are you talking about Masha?" Vic was impatient. He reached to turn on the lamp behind his head, glancing at his watch.

"Before you left for Argentina, I told you I thought I remembered something about one of Dad's uncles going there from Poland?"

"No, Masha, you didn't tell me that."

"Really? Well maybe it was Jess I told—yes, I think it was. I told Jess before she left. Anyway, I looked through some of Dad's old papers and letters. I was right. His Uncle Chaim settled in some city called Mendoza. Don't ask me why we never heard much about it."

"Why the hell would we hear? It's not exactly important."

"Apparently," Masha continued, "there's a whole family down there. Did you get to Mendoza, by any chance?"

Victor burst into laughter.

"Vic? Vic, what's so funny?"

"Nothing, Masha. It's just that Jess had a dream about renting a child."

"Renting a child? What are you talking about, Vic?"

"She had this dream, and the rental agency was in Mendoza. For all we know, our family might be in the rental business. C. Levin Rentals—Recliners, TVs, Children."

There was dead silence from Masha's end. Then, "Victor, you need to get some sleep. I'll talk to you tomorrow."

So, maybe Jess knew what she was talking about after all, Victor thought, kicking off his shoes. Maybe that was why she was trying to get him interested in Moisés Ville, in Argentina. Too bad she wasn't here to enjoy the joke.

Victor Levin reached behind to turn off the lamp, but he didn't bother taking off his coat, as he settled back against the chair.

THE RIFKE CHRONICLES

SARAJEVO: On June 28, 1914, the Austrian archduke, Franz Ferdinand, is assassinated. This catastrophe signals the beginning of the Great War, 1914–1919.

The following entries are from Volumes Eighteen and Twenty.

March 15, 1916
Buenos Aires

While war continues in Europe, the Argentine Jewish community has formed a committee for the victims of war and has raised incredible amounts of money. In Santa Fe province, natural catastrophes continue to plague the colony of Moisés Ville, destroying harvest after harvest. First, the devastating drought of 1914, and then the same year, the flood. Last year, another flood ruined the alfalfa crop. Many settlers have become discouraged and have left. Those who remain expect this year's crop to be good. I don't know how in God's name they maintain their optimism, how they continue. But they do. They persevere, as though God put them on this earth to test them, as he did Job.

Henoch was in town two weeks ago, bringing the happy news that his daughter in Rosario has given birth to a baby girl with red hair. She has been named Leah. Unfortunately, the infant was born with a deformity of the back, so the parents have begun a course of medical evaluations. We are waiting to hear the results.

During Henoch's stay, his son, Julio, who studies medicine at the university, came to eat with us nearly every night. We enjoy having him with us. He is a bright, communicative young man. One evening as I prepared Henoch's favorite *lokshen kugel*, Julio entertained us with stories about anatomy class and his fellow students' amusing cadaver pranks. Julio has his father's wry sense of humor!

Henoch's recent Buenos Aires visit was spurred by the first Congress of Argentine Jewry, organized by various Zionist groups. Henoch was to represent Moisés Ville. There is much eagerness to unite Argentina's Jewish voice with that of world Jewry, pressing for peace and human rights and calling for an end to discrimination. One night, Henoch wanted to read us the speech that he was to deliver the next day, so Julio hurried next door to get the Milekofskys, including Aaron, who happened to be visiting his brother's family. Henoch's words were eloquent and direct, warning that we cannot remain optimistic in the face of so many attacks against Judaism in this country. He called for a central body to represent the entire Argentine Jewish community. As Peshke prepared her *maté* and I made tea, she said Henoch should be president of the country! Henoch seemed anxious, pressing us for our opinions. Was he succinct, to the point? I smiled. Henoch is always to the point.

The next day, I was one of the few women in attendance at the congress. Many of the delegates seemed disturbed by this fact, but I'm quite used to such nonsense, and I no longer let it bother me. It amazes me that six years have passed since the first feminist conference in Argentina. At times it feels as if the conference never happened, as if we've made virtually no progress. What will it take to make men feel comfortable with the presence of women outside the home? I plan to continue attending such events that interest me. I've seen no law saying this is not possible. My friend Moses Soltansky agrees, and more important, Henoch encourages me.

Henoch's speech was well received by the delegates, and there was much discussion on the topics of immigration, anti-Semitism, and education. One moment of excitement came when the Bundist group, Avangard, walked out of the conference, angry over the issue of Jewish autonomy, which was one of the points put forth on the platform. Except for the labor Zionists—the Paole Zionist, as they call themselves—so many leftist groups want nothing to do with a Jewish homeland. On this issue, they are in sharp conflict with the Zionists. So there is dissension everywhere.

I noticed that a special guest was Congressman Alfredo Palacios, the first Socialist to hold a seat in the nation's congress. Alfredo, brother of Pedro, on whose land Moisés Ville was founded, has long been a friend of the Jewish community. With regard to the Beilis case, in which Justo made anti-Semitic accusations, Palacios publicly defended the Jewish people by vehemently stating that Jews were incapable of carrying out blood rituals. He is such a sensitive, good-looking man, with his black mustache and his dark, serious eyes. Recently I read in a magazine that he is considered a bon vivant and is always engaging in duels.

During the third day of the conference, Henoch received the bad news that his wife had passed away, quite suddenly and unexpectedly. He and Julio returned to Moisés Ville immediately, cutting short Henoch's stay in the capital. Not long after, I received a short note from Leib Yosem, including few details. In deference to Henoch, Moisés Ville is in mourning. News of Mrs. Rosenvitch's death even reached *Der Tog*, Buenos Aires' Yiddish daily. That day, *Der Tog* also brought us news of the battle of Verdun and of the great losses of German lives.

November 1917
Buenos Aires

I try not to think of the problems in the world, they seem so overwhelming. With war still devastating Europe and the Russian Revolution at full force since March, we seem to be standing at the brink of disaster. The Bolsheviks have gained control in Russia, and the reaction to these events, here in Buenos Aires, has not been good. Jewish immigration is continually condemned by the press, and anti-Semitism has sprung out in textbooks throughout the nation. The government is nervous, convinced working-class violence will break out across the city. Perhaps they're right. Tensions run high.

The good news is the Balfour Declaration and the hopes of a Jewish homeland in Palestine. There is word that a Jewish Legion will be formed by the British. This will attract many Zionist Jews, and we are certain to see a large emigration from this country to Palestine. Henoch writes that a group of young men from Moisés Ville are already preparing to volunteer.

Enough of war and violence. Since I cannot write of companionship—Henoch has not been in town for months—I will deal with the next best thing, dance! In September, the great Russian dancer Nijinski returned to the Colón Theater on the occasion of his fourth wedding anniversary! I remember when he got married, in 1913. At that time, he opened the season with *Scheherazade*, by the Russian composer Rimsky-Korsakov. It was all over the papers, with a grand photograph of the wedding breakfast at the Majestic Hotel. On the women's page, an article described how Parisian high fashion had been influenced by *Scheherazade*. The "oriental look," the wild colors and patterns of designer Poiret's new line, made elegant Parisian women look like harem dwellers!

To mark his fourth anniversary, Nijinski danced Stravinski's *Petruska* for the first time, and I was present! A dream realized! I don't know why it is that the Colón has such an incredible hold over me. Perhaps it's simply that politics do not enter its doors—only music and dance and peace. My friends Peshke and Aaron and Moses carefully planned the event, surprising me with a ticket for my birthday. I could not believe their thoughtfulness. How they must have saved and scrimped! How did Aaron explain it to his wife, Sonia? What did Peshke do to save the money? And big Moses?

It was a wonderful performance, despite the reports that Nijinski did not dance well, and that he appeared to be "unbalanced." I thought he was superb. What a magnificent dancer! The leaps and twists! I swear he walks on air! Unfortunately the puppet booth was not securely fastened to the stage floor, and it collapsed while Nijinski was gesturing from the top of it, sending him into a dive across the stage! But what an exciting evening! I shall never forget it. There is talk that the performance I saw was to be his last appearance with the Ballets Russes. What must Nijinski and his companions think of the revolutionary events in their county, the deaths and endless suffering?

Work at the library continues, and we are moving ahead. More and more people make use of the facility. Books are lent, language classes given, and the lectures draw large crowds. Sadly, because of the war, we are not receiving the Yiddish periodicals from Europe. We rely on the New York *Jewish Daily Forward* to bring us news and commentary. Some of the other American publications have come and gone, but the *Forward* remains committed and steady.

THE RIFKE CHRONICLES

On January 7, 1919, after a month of labor disputes, workers finally strike at the Pedro Vasena and Sons Ltd. metal works factory in Buenos Aires. Police and strikebreakers clash with the workers. Five Vasena employees are killed and forty wounded. This event ushers in what becomes known as "Semana Trágica." At the end of this intensely violent week, 700 people are left dead and 4,000 injured.

From Volume Twenty-two.

January 8, 1919
Buenos Aires

It is late evening and I have just returned to my rooms after being with the Milekofskys. Tragedy has struck their family. Their eldest child, Abe, was one of those killed at the Vasena factory. Thank

God I happened to be at Peshke's when Moses Soltansky and the Milekofsky's second son, Jorge, brought the bad news. Moses was shot in the arm. I was able to stop the bleeding with bandages, and I convinced him to get to a doctor. The wound had to be treated, and I was afraid there might be a bullet lodged in the flesh. While I worked on Moses's arm, Jorge tried to soothe his parents. They were beside themselves with grief and bitterness. It seemed hours before we could finally quiet Peshke and convince her not to go out. She was half-crazed wanting revenge. I intended to accompany Moses to find a doctor, but neither Moses nor Jorge would hear of it. They insisted the streets were not safe. Moses left alone.

January 10, 1919

The Vasena factory deaths have triggered a citywide strike. This comes as no surprise. For more than a year Buenos Aires workers, from the Vasena factory to the port, have been fighting lowered wages. Ever since the Bolshevik revolution in Russia nearly two years ago, the Argentine labor movement has become inspired—more certain, more militant.

The government has called this strike a "proletariat uprising," and they've pulled in the militia. The January heat wave we've been experiencing has not helped the tension and turmoil of a shut-down Buenos Aires. Nothing functions; the city is virtually dead. All transportation has stopped, and the only vehicles on the streets are the large motor vans transporting armed marines. The men are delivered to the various "trouble" spots—the port, the Vasena factory, the president's residence, the Casa Rosada, the water and gasworks.

Because of the strike chaos, antiforeign sentiment has increased dramatically. Incredible as it seems, we Jews find ourselves in the midst of our first pogrom, here in Buenos Aires, here on this continent. It's hard to believe such things are possible. I remember worrying about this kind of catastrophe during the rent strike of 1907, and thinking that what occurred so easily in the Pale could never take hold here. Who would have ever thought that more than ten years later, it is indeed happening! A vigilante group calling themselves the "white guard," no doubt the same kind of "patriots" who burned the Russian Library in 1910, are assisting the police with the uprising.

The atrocities committed in the name of patriotism are despicable. Mobs of "white guard" sweep through the Jewish districts, claiming to search for revolutionaries. In reality, they're massacring the old, the young, the innocent. Dwellings are destroyed and household possessions are pulled into the streets and burned. Old men are victimized, children harassed, women and girls raped.

With this landscape, Jewish immigration continues to be publicly criticized. The government and élite Argentineans are terrified of the poor newcomers, especially the "Russians." They are convinced of a "Red Scare." To these people, all Jews are Russians, "Rusitos," and all "Rusitos" are Bolsheviks. Even the American ambassador, Mr. Stinson, is certain that Tragic Week and the Buenos Aires strike are part of an international Communist plot, instigated by outside forces.

We buried Abraham Milekofsky yesterday afternoon. The heat wave still hasn't broken. It has taken everything Moses and I possess to remain calm so that we can help the family through this ordeal. Moses's arm is bandaged and in a sling.

February 1, 1919

Order is being restored, but not before the strike spread to other provinces. In the capital, people are slowly returning to their normal lives. We are sleeping and eating better, and we are trying to carry on, but it is with trepidation. Jews have once again learned that we will be scapegoats even here, when crisis becomes severe enough.

A few days ago, I experienced the most peculiar encounter. I toy with the idea that I imagined it, but I know I didn't. I have relived it in my memory several times since then, yet it remains wonderfully dreamlike for me.

It's a beautiful afternoon, although unusually hot for that late in the day. I am crossing Plaza Lavalle with a small bag of oranges I purchased for Peshke. I'm thinking how wonderful it is to have the strike over, but what am I going to do about Peshke, still suffering terribly from her son's death? She hasn't been eating, and I know how much she loves oranges. I have my face down, not looking where I'm going, wondering about the unique bonding that happens between a mother and her first born, regardless of how many more equally wonderful children follow. Just as I think again about the oranges, hoping they will work, I collide with another stroller.

I glance up at an elegant lady in a beige linen suit and a sky blue blouse, and I feel the bag of oranges slip from my hand and fall to the ground. Our eyes meet for the few seconds before we both apologize, in our accented Spanish, before we both bend for the fruit. I know how odd it must sound—after all, we are complete strangers to each other—but we connect. I don't exactly know how to explain it. Perhaps the physical act of collision causes a form of fusion? I like the idea; it makes me think of astral bodies and shooting stars, the solar system, fate. In any case, it provides a good explanation for what follows.

I judge her to be approximately my age and clearly an American from her accent. She helps me collect the oranges and then straightens up, dabbing her forehead with a handkerchief she pulls from a small leather bag. She hesitates for a moment, turning to see where the nearest bench is, complaining politely of the heat. It's then that I notice her limp. One leg is shorter than the other. At the same moment, she notices mine. As naturally as if we've been life-long traveling mates, we walk the few feet to the bench and sit down, secure in our companionship.

The lady is indeed an American, a journalist visiting our country. Margaret Ellington, she says, extending her hand, asking, quite casually, that I call her Peg. She's come to Buenos Aires for a stay of a few months, on assignment from a Boston ladies' magazine. Peg is to write of her experiences and impressions of our capital. Naturally she's limited; her leg tends to slow her down, Peg says, but she tries hard not to let it interfere. Her light brown hair is bobbed short in the new style, and her eyes are the blue color of her blouse. Though she is not pretty, her jaw large and angular, her bones too prominent, she has an appealing broad smile and one of the most open, friendly faces I've ever encountered. At that moment, I suddenly realize I've never actually met an American, and I tell her so.

Peg throws back her head and laughs, saying something about Yankees not being so bad, and that very soon they are going to give American women the vote! We exchange a few words about suffrage, and I quickly learn the depth and seriousness of Peg's commitment. She spent many years actively campaigning in Boston. We must continue to work for women's rights in Argentina, she insists, especially suffrage and birth control. We must not give up the cause.

I am shocked, but excited. I listen as she speaks frankly and openly about Margaret Sanger and Emma Goldman, both of whom I've read about in the *Forward*. Of course we practice birth control in Argentina, but it is not treated as a woman's right, and it certainly isn't discussed. Peg tells me that for several years now, there have been birth control advice centers in the United States. I envy these American women.

Genteel and comfortable, Peg Ellington has obviously not

suffered hunger or cold. I've never met anyone who hasn't. But can I hold this against her? She seems genuinely compassionate and curious about our city's residents, and I'm impressed by how much she has seen of Buenos Aires and how knowledgeable she is. She has even accompanied one of our prominent female physicians on her rounds to the slums, the *conventillos*.

Her Spanish is not smooth, but she speaks eagerly. I'm impressed by her command of the language and how willingly she reveals things about herself and her life. She tells me she had just returned from a trip to India, where she'd gone to meet Gandhi. For several months she followed in his footsteps to peace, writing about him, sending home the articles to her magazine in Boston. She tells me that while she was there, she gave up Western dress and food and took to wearing a sari and eating a simple, meatless diet. She speaks at length about Gandhi's compassion—she calls him Bapu—about his nonviolence, his commitment to peace and self-rule for India. He will turn his country around, Peg says.

I am touched by how naturally we chat, as though we are old friends. She seems quite comfortable talking with me and asking me questions. Not once do I feel she is concerned about our obviously different backgrounds and life experiences. On the contrary, differences seem to excite her! This, I decide, must surely be an American trait, and I like it.

"So, when this unfortunate strike occurred," Peg continues, "it presented the unique opportunity to witness a genuine, working-class protest, an experience I've never had before." Peg straightens up and takes off her jacket. "I've already written home about it. I want Bostonian women to know everything! I've written about the workers' low wages and their miserable living conditions. I've written about your beautiful, downtown Buenos Aires, without its newspapers, its trams and taxis. How odd not seeing those large, shiny automobiles waiting outside the theaters! How odd to see the iron grill gates of restaurants tightly closed, and even the hotels in such chaos."

"Mind you, we are quite well off at the Palace," Peg assures me. "That is, compared to some of the other hotels. I understand that the Majestic, and even the Plaza have had to cut off all services to their guests! Of course, I'm not surprised. I stayed at the Majestic for the first few days I was in Buenos Aires, and I found it a very unpleasant atmosphere. The management was uncomfortable with the fact that I was a single lady traveling alone, and a crippled one at that!" Peg laughs. "If they cannot deal with that reality in 1919, I can well understand why a city strike would completely incapacitate them! At the Palace, we were still served our meals, though not in our rooms. Management asked us to go down to the dining room. Some of the guests grumbled. I've come to realize it doesn't matter where you go, there are always grumblers, and I'm sorry to say, in this case, most were my countrymen! Personally I don't consider it a hardship to go down to the dining room. I understand that the efficiency of our hotel was due to the amazing devotion of the staff. One should not take that kind of loyalty lightly, anywhere in the world. I was very grateful to them. But why am I talking about hotels? Such nonsense, Peg, shame on you."

"You must think me very silly to even mention my comfort, in the face of all the violence that accompanied those days. It was truly horrible, so many deaths, so much destruction. No doubt you've seen a great deal yourself, certainly far more than I. But I must tell you, I've never felt safer in the city than I did during the strike. Odd, isn't it?" Peg smiles.

"You look confused, and you're wondering how I could have possibly felt safe? Easily. I could go out for a walk in the evenings without fear of being molested. Cowards stayed home, and the other men were occupied!" Peg throws up her hands and laughs.

I can see I'm going to miss this Peg Ellington.

"Your city is so wonderful!"

Peg's voice is soft and deep. "The parks and boulevards, the vast range of trees. The eucalyptus beside the maple, the plane tree beside the bottle brush." She stops talking for a moment to look out across Plaza Lavalle. "I'm very fond of greenery in cities. Greenery anywhere, really! I was born in Boston, but I consider myself from our wonderful state of Maine. I spent every summer of my youth on an island off the coast of Maine. Rifke Schulman," Peg turns back and looks eagerly into my face. "I believe you would love my island! I believe you would love my pine trees, my granite, my ocean, as I love your Buenos Aires. Your city is so Parisian, isn't it? Have you been to Paris?"

I reply that I haven't.

"Well, you simply must go! There are no two ways about it."

She says this so easily, so naturally, I can almost believe her. Peg Ellington's eyes take in some children playing at the base of one of the large ombu trees, across from the Colón Theater. She turns back to me.

"Do you know that one evening, toward the end of the strike, I stepped out to my balcony for a breath of air. When I looked down, I spotted a chase taking place in the boulevard below. I'm sure it sounds strange, but I was very struck by the tranquility of the scene, despite its potential violence. It was the hour of dusk, and everything was still. There was no other activity on the street. White-clad marines were chasing strikers who had obviously resisted arrest. It was very exciting seeing the men moving through the bushes and trees, the strikers in their dark clothes and pulled-down caps, the marines' bared bayonets gleaming in the half light. Thank God, of course, that the strikers got away and nothing happened. The marines finally gave up quietly. Now, why would I have found that incident tranquil?" She asks, turning back to me, puzzled.

Before our visit on the park bench ends, we compare our specially made shoes, which we find not to be so different, and we exchange addresses. We promise to keep in touch. I watch as she walks slowly toward Cordoba Street, where I know she will stop to hail a cab. She turns back and waves.

February 14, 1919

I am in my forty-eighth year, and I feel restless and unhappy, as though I know less now than when I was eighteen. Of course, there weren't as many complications then, for I had the certainty of youth blowing in my sails. Events and happenings, people and ideas, life was either black or white. The older I get, the more gray I see; black and white rarely serve as a guide rule anymore. I often think about my conversation with the American Peg Ellington in Plaza Lavalle. Peg, with her curiosity and tolerance and her lack of anger, had an ability to appreciate everything around her, the way I never could. I am too jaded. This is not a new condition, but suddenly I am envious of those who aren't. I would like to blame it all on Peg Ellington, this malcontent I feel, but I know I cannot. It has nothing to do with her.

Lately, I can't seem to get things into perspective, and I'm suffering through an anxiety I have never experienced before, nor can I begin to explain. I miss Henoch, and I feel I need him more than ever. At times I am very happy, very optimistic, and then other days, life seems so bleak, and I feel so drained, so useless, I wonder what the point is. I see humor where there is none, and I weep for no reason. I think it must be related to "the change," as Peshke used to refer to it, some years ago, when she herself was in its grip. Poor Peshke. She has lost all spirit with the death of Abraham. She broods silently and has been unable to put aside her pain. She tells me she thinks of nothing else. I'm quite concerned, and I try to spend as much time with her as I can.

Some months after Henoch's wife died, he asked me to join him in Moisés Ville as his wife. Despite my terrible loneliness and my need for his support, I cannot do that. I cannot leave my work at the center, not now, now that I sense I am finally able to do some good. We are all needed, more than ever. Besides, I could never leave Peshke.

Lately, I've been seeing a lot of Henoch's youngest son, Julio. I'm very fond of the boy. His joy in life makes me laugh. He is the image of his father, Henoch—twenty odd years ago—when he first came to Moisés Ville. Sometimes Julio makes me wonder if I haven't wasted my life by not marrying and having a son of my own. Then I remember Abraham Milekofsky, and I remember how his short life gave his mother her greatest joy and her greatest pain. Julio comes to have tea with me on Sundays. He keeps me up to date on his studies at the university, and of course he always has bits of news of his family and of Moisés Ville. His niece, Leah, in Rosario, is doing well. She is already three years old and is a lovely, sweet girl, despite her hunchback. She basks in her parents' love. I do not know this child and will probably never have the pleasure of meeting her. Yet I feel for little Leah, and I think we could be kindred spirits.

Julio tells me things are going well for the colony, mostly due to its cattle industry. For the last few years, Europe's countries at war have been buying meat from South America, and thus prices have soared. This year Moisés Ville has found itself flooded with money, rather than water. The colony has been able to pay off its debts to the bank and the J.C.A. Julio has related stories of the colonists going crazy with their new money; they're buying cars and furniture and other luxury items. How ironical; good fortune has come to Moisés Ville, while here in the capital, we are in our darkest moment of anti-Semitism and violence.

THE RIFKE CHRONICLES

In June 1921, Jewish immigration to the U.S. virtually ceased. The open-door policy was over, and classification by racial origins was now in effect. In the following years, these strict laws had a great influence on the laws of immigration in other countries, including Argentina.

From Volume Twenty-five.

April 1923
Buenos Aires

For years now I have been very concerned with the government's attitude toward immigration. When Henoch is in town, it seems we talk of nothing else. Again, we must read of Justo's anti-Semitism! It wasn't enough that in 1919 at the International Socialist

Conference in Amsterdam, Justo declared he was opposed to the idea of a Jewish homeland in Palestine because it had nothing to do with the conference! As far as the "Jewish Problem" was concerned, Justo stated that if Jews had the same rights and the same education as others, they would assimilate. Since when have we become a Jewish problem? Where will this all lead?

A few days ago, we all read in *Vida Nuestra* Justo's article entitled "Why I Don't Like Writing for a Newspaper That Calls Itself Jewish." He lets us know that he admires some individual human beings who are Jews, but "together, instead, they become immediately suspicious and enigmatic to me."

Justo represents a common anti-Semitic voice in Argentina. As long as the Jew is willing to give up all ties to his culture and religion, as long as he is willing to melt into society, then he is acceptable. As long as he continues to teach his language and practices to his children, as long as he wishes to have Jewish neighbors, then he is simply unacceptable. So when and where can a Jew be a Jew? Now that the League of Nations has given the British the right to rule Palestine, we shall see what becomes of the idea of a self-ruled home-land. How long will it take?

Peg Ellington writes that the Americans have given women the vote. She is convinced that when women are allowed to be leaders, they will put an end to violence. I cheer her. Perhaps she is right.

In May of last year, Rabbi Halphon, from Congregation Israelita, established Soprotimis, the Society for Protection of Jewish Immigrants. Finally we have an official organization to receive and help newcomers. Representatives can board ships, give information on the availability of temporary lodgings, and even provide money for train tickets to the interior of the country. Soprotimis takes a special interest in looking out for single girls and women, providing them with work opportunities so they will not be prey to the white slavers. Bela Palatnik would have been deliriously happy. I wonder how this new organization would work with the J.C.A.? I can't help thinking there will be conflicts over who is to do what. Not that there isn't enough to do!

Last week, Julio came to tell me he is getting married to Miranda Ramirez, the girl he has been seeing for some time now. I am happy for him. She is beautiful and kind, and they love each other. Her Spanish family has invited me for dinner several times, and Julio has taken me. I admire them for their closeness and how they work. They are truly wonderful people. Yet I am saddened that Julio is following the same path of intermarriage as so many of our young people. I am not allowed to speak of this. Both Julio and Henoch accuse me of being old-fashioned and hypocritical.

To tell you the truth, I am very surprised at Henoch. I know that when I lived in Moisés Ville, Henoch took little interest in the shuls. He left that to the rabbi and to the more devout, while he concerned himself with the worldly problems of his people. But I would never have guessed that he'd take such an attitude. Henoch says I have no business judging Julio when I have been so steadfast about not going to shul. I tell him I am not religious, it's true, but I am a cultural Jew, and I don't want to see our traditions and values lost. Henoch only laughs, saying that Julio will always have his values, regardless of whom he marries.

Perhaps he is right. Nevertheless, I cannot help worrying about the future of our community. We came to these shores wrapped in our prayer shawls, carrying the Torah in one arm and our babies and matzos in the other. As we put down the babies, so too we have put down the Torah and shawls, so our children can assimilate to their new land. Will their children and their grandchildren know of our past and our arrival, of our future?

Manhattan Outreach

The people at the East Side Cleaning Agency call me Evalina la Argentina. It's because I'm small, more child than woman in size and shape, and because my black hair is straight and my skin brown, and my broad, flat features are like Papá's, the Indian from Jujuy. I must tell you, Reader, I've never known Papá. He walked in and out of my Cordobes mother's life, courting her with scented blossoms from the paradise tree. The agency people are ignorant and disrespectful. In fact, they're stupid. I don't waste my energy trying to make them understand about rights, about dignity. Trying to make them understand that small, brown people can be intelligent and speak English well, even though they have to clean houses to survive. Do I tell them that small, brown people also feel love and pain? Of course not, I just put up with them. Sometimes, even Juan Carlos Forsyth Botero calls me Evalina la Argentina. I put up with him too, because he is my husband, and because finally, I can no longer help him.

With Mr. and Mrs. Stern, it's different. They have reached their seventies in good health and good spirits, the Sterns, and they always call me Eva. They are kind and unassuming. Since they do not worry about their own importance, they have no need to make me feel lowly. At this moment, I hear their voices drifting out of the apartment kitchen. I close the library door behind myself, so I can be alone with the peaceful hum of the radiator, the rain, and the muffled street noises from Park Avenue. I like being alone. I often open the window to air the room while I clean. I fix the bright, silk cushions on the couch and arm chairs, I adjust the lampshades, the magazines on the end tables. Week after week I enter this room, pretending it's like any other; I will clean, with my usual efficiency, and leave, and nothing will happen. But it always does, and always when I climb onto my little step stool and begin dusting the bookshelves. The sudden dampness springs in the palm of my hands, the prickly sensation at the back of my neck, under my hair. My body becomes motionless, dust rag still, as my eyes move to the old photograph.

There are other pictures on the wall. New ones, more old ones, they are set among the books. The one of Mrs. Stern in her college days, smiling, holding a track trophy. The one of Mr. Stern, playing the clarinet. Photographs of children, weddings. But Reader, this is the one that draws me, that makes me save cleaning this small, quiet library for the end. This is the one that makes me remember things: Mamá as a beautiful, lonely young woman, the *abuelos*, my grandparents, the ancient stone house and windy village near Cordoba. I rarely think about my past anymore, yet in this room, it eagerly comes forward, merging with this sepia image. Together they give me peace and energy to go on into the next week. I reach to dust the ornate frame. An imposing-looking family has gathered around the patriarch, the matriarch. Single brothers flank the back row of dour spinster aunts. The mustachioed, cocky married son and his stunning wife in the striped, satin blouse stand directly behind the two old people. They sit in the center, the old ones; young grandchildren surround them, sitting and standing in the foreground.

It's just an old photograph, I tell myself, week after week. Typical, like the family images that Mamá stashed in hat boxes. But every time I stand before this photograph, the same thing happens. My palms sweat and the old man draws me in; his small, beady eyes riveted to mine, the long, white beard and dark clothes, like the *abuelo's*. The coat is ankle-length and double-breasted, of shiny, black fabric, like the small, tight-fitting cap. The old man's relaxed hand hangs from the chair's armrest—the very way Mr. Stern's does, when he watches TV—and every time I stand there, that hand beckons, and I follow.

I've learned it's not hard to enter a photograph. It's not hard leaving the present, with my doubts and frustrations, Juan Carlos, the children, the varicose veins and rough hands I've acquired cleaning these Manhattan apartments. It's a question of will. The old man beckons, and I follow. I travel the dark corridors of his small, wooden house, always calmly certain I've been here before, familiar with every slat of scrubbed floor, every doorway, every cluttered sill. I move silently past the women and children sitting around the dining room table, heads bent over consigned, piece-work sewing, elbows at a kerosene lamp. Behind them, on the modest mantelpiece, a pair of silver candlesticks. I move past the iron bedsteads with babies nesting, piles of clothing, the feather ticks and chamber pots. Finally, I come out on the other side of the water-stained, cardboard mat, where the inky handwriting is blurred, and the alphabet so foreign, I can read only the date, 1908. There I am, at the very edge of my own fugitive memories. Back, through tangled time, I land in the swept patio of youth, Mamá in the kitchen and the foothills of Cordoba in the distance. Everyday, I, the lonely child, entertain myself in that patio space, skipping around my cocoon-like *abuelos*, sitting in the sun. *Abuela* is tightly wrapped in dark woolens. Spots of old soup stain the lapels of *abuelo's* ancient, black coat. Still and silent, they never want to talk or play, but drift in and out of private dreamscapes, places unknown to me, the child. As the two old people feel the mantle of a shadow, their eyes open a slit, and they move to stand—more bent than straight—to drag their cane chairs across the ancient stones, in pursuit of the sun. I, the child, dance, and try to imagine them young and dressed in white, as in the summer photograph hanging in Mamá's bedroom, taken somewhere in Russia. They pose at a small table under trees, the pattern of leaves on their faces. With a white, lace cloth, a samovar, and two candlesticks, they await the future.

I refold the dust rag and gently wipe the glass. They are dead now, the *abuelos*. Mamá has been moved to a government housing project in the city of Cordoba, for the poor, the sick, the aged. How she must miss the patio, the sparse, stony landscape. Letters take so long. We've been in New York for nearly four years, and, Reader, I still haven't been able to save the airfare to send for my Mamá. In the library of this Manhattan apartment, in this photograph of matriarch and patriarch and clan, there are no feather ticks or chamber pots, or women and children sewing. So from where? Why am I so certain I've been and seen? The old man, with his beard and his satin cap, his eyes that will not close, not even blink, why does he insist he knows me?

A sudden, damp draft from the window makes me shiver. Stepping down from the stool, I turn away, finally, to finish dusting the book shelves, to damp mop the parquet floor. As I carry the bucket, mop, and my little stool past the French doors of the kitchen, I see Mr. Stern in his stocking feet, his tall figure leaning against the refrigerator. He is talking. Mrs. Stern works at the counter, still in her slicker and rain hat, still surrounded by groceries she hasn't put away. She's stepped out of her damp, flat shoes and stands in her nylons, her brown eyes deep in concentration as she unties the butcher wrap and examines the roast. Tall like her husband, and still with the athlete's grace she had as a star runner in college, Mrs. Stern is an attractive woman. She has a pleasing, angular face and thick, wavy, white hair, cropped at the nape of her neck. I know that under the yellow slicker, recently ordered through a catalog from the state of Maine, Mrs. Stern is wearing a denim skirt and turtleneck sweater. I watch Mr. Stern still leaning against the refrigerator, and I realize they've been engaged in conversation since I began cleaning the bedrooms. Something important must have happened. Usually on Saturdays, he's left the apartment by this time.

Today, for sure, I will ask Mrs. Stern about the photograph. I've put off asking for so long, not wanting to hear or know anything, not wanting to spoil whatever it is I share with that patriarch. But today I will ask, I resolve, lugging my cleaning supplies into the small bathroom.

"Mona, isn't the world feeling a little heavy on your shoulders?" Richard Stern asks, glancing at his wife. He straightens up, turns, and pulls open the refrigerator door. He takes out the pitcher of V-8 juice. "I thought we'd resolved this?"

Mona shrugs.

Disturbed, Richard pours himself a tall glass and drinks the juice quickly. "My darling, we're talking about one young man, for God's sake, one Jew! We're not dealing here with the whole past, present, and future of the Chosen People!"

Richard's words make Mona close her eyes and shake her head. She places the roast on a pan, feeling very long suffering.

"We've been through this already," Richard says patiently, lowering his voice. "I thought we'd agreed to be realistic? Our grandson, Nathan, is on the verge of marriage, and as far as Judaism is concerned, the odds don't look good." Richard rinses out the glass and leaves it in the sink. "As my old man would have said, 'This comes as a surprise?! We have a choice in the matter?!'" Richard smiles, remembering briefly, then pulls on his sweatshirt and smoothes his hair. "Listen, Mona, since when did Judaism play such a big role in Nathan's parents' 'blessed union'?" He chuckles softly.

Richard is entitled to his humor, Mona decides. Their son's marriage is on the brink of dissolution. It's nothing new. In fact, it's been a constantly recurring theme.

"For that matter, how about us? You know what I mean? O.K., so maybe religion didn't have to be a big deal because we're all Jews. Maybe that was enough. Who's to say? All I know is that with every generation, things change, it's natural law." Richard puts on his nylon jacket and zips up the front. "Aren't you going to take off your coat?"

She nods.

He opens the refrigerator again, looking for something to eat. "Your grandfather was a rabbi, my grandfather was a rabbi." He pops some grapes into his mouth and closes the door. "Would they have believed that in our house you could prepare a roast," he nods toward the meat on the pan, "to serve at the same table with cheese cake?" He pats the refrigerator. Not expecting an answer, Richard reaches for his athletic shoes and gym bag that are under the counter. "Is change for the better?" He shrugs, sitting down to pull on his shoes. "You know me. I don't worry about the 'A Problems,' the ones I can't do anything about. They're happy, aren't they? So O.K. They're gainfully employed attorneys, so O.K. Presumably they're old enough to know what they're doing, so O.K. He's a New York Jew, and she's an I-don't-know-what from Nebraska. So?"

"Born-again Christian," Mona says quietly, sticking slivers of garlic and sprigs of rosemary into the roast.

Richard looks up from his shoe laces.

"Judy's a born-again Christian."

"I heard the first time. You sure?" He asks cautiously.

"Positive."

"I see." Richard remains silent for a few seconds, elbows on his knees, arms dangling. "Didn't I tell you the odds weren't great?" He stands up. "What's left to say?"

Mona didn't ask him to say anything in the first place. It doesn't matter though, because her silence is usually good for two, three, maybe even four of his monologue statements, as long as he can guess which topic is bothering her, and he always can, because they've been married for almost fifty years.

"Well, maybe she's not a true believer."

"Wrong." Mona says ruthlessly. "Nathan had a long talk with me last week." She'd been choking on it, alone, ever since. But Richard is right. What's left to be said? She imagines there aren't any answers. So maybe she just feels like being sad and pouty. Doesn't the ripe old age of seventy-five entitle her to an occasional binge of self-indulgence? She'd agreed to be realistic. But she hadn't agreed to be upbeat about this, not so quickly, anyway. She isn't as accommodating as she used to be. Easy on the garlic, Mona reminds herself, looking down at the roast. By tonight, she'll shower and change into something nice, and she'll try to feel as close to 100 percent as possible. Richard's stomach has been kicking up lately. He blames it on her garlic.

"Mona, your coat!"

She hears the irritation in his voice. It isn't about her coat. She caught him off guard with the born-again Christian business. She reaches for her hat, shoving it into the large, patch pocket.

"Will you stop worrying, please?" Richard looks at her expectantly.

"I'll try," she struggles out of the yellow plastic.

He steps close, kisses her forehead, helps her with the coat.

"We're just Nathan's grandparents, let his parents worry about something, for a change. By the way, when do the unhappy yuppies get back from their vacation?"

"Next Monday," Mona smiles, amused. Richard has never called their son and daughter-in-law yuppies. The fast trip to London was another attempt to repair their failing marriage. "Nathan told me his parents are finding London very expensive." She drapes the coat over one arm and looks at it thoughtfully for a few seconds. In the catalog it seemed so nice and bright, reminding her of the sea and ships on a stormy day. In fact, it's the most uncomfortable thing she's ever worn, Mona decides.

"London, expensive? Surprise! Did I tell them, or did I tell them?!" Richard glances at the clock. "I'm out of here!"

Mona stands at the apartment door, watching as Richard heads down the hall toward the elevator, gym bag in hand. She can tell his back hurts, but he hasn't said a word. Not bad for an old guy approaching seventy-eight, Mona thinks, opening the coat closet. She hangs up the disappointing yellow plastic and returns to the kitchen. Maybe she shouldn't have told him about Judy. Has she ruined his afternoon? He returned from work, changed, and now he is off to the gym for a few hours. Even though he sold the business to his nephew three years ago, he still "gives the kid a hand," everyday, all day. Saturday afternoons are his. He exercises, has a steam, and maybe plays a game of cards with the guys. When he comes back for dinner, he'll be relaxed and talkative, hopefully, joking with Nathan and Judy, as though all is right with the world.

Mona adjusts the roast on the pan and slides it into the oven. She glances over the groceries spread across the counter. What's gotten into her? It's the first time in her life she's worried about this. Has it taken the reality of Nathan's marriage? Richard is so easy about everything. Does he truly believe all is right with the world? She's always envied his ability to take command and be upbeat, positive, certain that everything that happens is for the best. He's right. There are no surprises here. Nathan called last night, eagerly announcing that he and Judy had something important to tell them. For a moment Mona's heart sank, and then she bravely pulled herself together. In her most cheery, grandmotherly voice, she invited their only grandchild and his girlfriend for Saturday night dinner.

Mona bends down and puts the bags of potatoes and onions under the sink. The dark space has a musty, root cellar smell. Maybe she'll get Eva to clean it out. There are days when the poor girl looks so waiflike, so tired, Mona doesn't know where her energy comes from. On those occasions, it seems there is less of Eva than there was the week before. Sometimes, Mona dreams about her. Long, uncomfortable dreams about Eva gradually wearing herself away by her own hand, due to her diligent scrubbing and polishing. In every dream, Mona ends up carrying Eva in her arms because of her diminishing presence. And finally, in every dream, Mona hands Eva over to a waiting García Márquez, hoping he will better deal with the realities of the girl's life, hoping he will restore her and not keep her a cleaning woman for the rest of her life.

Has she taken on more cleaning commitments, and has her husband found a job? Mona has never met Juan Carlos, nor the children, but Eva once showed her some family snapshots taken at the beach. The kids played at the water; Eva and Juan Carlos sat on a driftwood log in the sand. It was nice to see Eva smiling, happy and relaxed. When she cleans, she's always so serious, so determined. But the beach photo caught her in a moment of ease and softness. She looked pretty with her long hair loosened around her face, and somehow she didn't seem quite as small wearing that long, gauzy dress instead of jeans. She certainly didn't appear to be a woman of thirty-five and the mother of two teenagers. Juan Carlos was lean and refined looking, almost languid, with fair skin and sandy hair. His arms were crossed over his chest, and his long, thin hands clung to his shoulders. He seemed painfully distant, disengaged. Mona remembers being struck by his eyes, pale and still. Even in the photo, she could feel the sadness of no obsessions, no passions. His family owned ranches near Cordoba, Eva once told her, and he has English ancestry. That probably explains his coloring, Mona decides, reaching for the edge of the sink, pulling herself up. As for Eva, Mona realizes she knows very little about her. Once, when she complimented the girl on her English, Eva told her she had taken lessons all her life because her mother wanted her to be educated, and because she herself wanted to be a doctor. There is something quite amazing about Eva.

So, Saturday night dinner for their grandson and his born-again Christian girlfriend. Mona scrubs the potatoes, peels the carrots, cries with the onions. The mezuzah on their apartment door has been painted over many times. They are New Yorkers; they've lived in the city all their lives. They have one child—who grew up playing in Central Park, when it was still safe—and they've never owned a car. Their one child, a physician, married a physician, and they too have one child, Nathan, an attorney, soon to be married to an attorney. Mona suspects that it would never occur to any of them that there is any other place to live, nor that there is anyone else to marry but a New York Jew.

Until now. One day, a few years ago, when Mona was still working at the 42nd Street library, one of her co-workers announced that he'd found Christ in the frozen food section of the grocery store. A tall, quiet man from Special Collections, he revealed how Christ's face and halo had appeared to him between the pizza and the orange juice. Shortly after, he became a born-again Christian.

I empty the bucket of water into the toilet and flush it. I put away the rags and cleaning supplies. As far as apartments go, it's not a bad one to clean, and the Sterns are good people. Reader, I, Eva, have never known any Jews before. I've never even known anyone who has. Only the nuns at my grammar school in Cordoba used to talk about how they killed Christ. I put away my step stool, the mop, and vacuum. I can hear noises from the kitchen as I wash my hands and run a dampened comb through my dark hair. It's the end of the day. Thank God. I can go home and prepare dinner. It's Saturday, so the children will be going out tonight. Now that they're teenagers, I worry about them constantly. Sometimes I feel I'm losing touch; I hear so many terrible things about drugs and gangs. The other day, my daughter and I were talking about clothes. After a minor disagreement, the poor child burst into tears and fled the room, crying that I don't know anything because I'm just a cleaning woman.

I'm tired. In the bathroom mirror, I stare at the dark circles under my eyes, at my bad color. I've become bitter, and I work too hard. I clean three, sometimes four apartments a day. The doctor at the clinic tells me that if I don't rest my legs, I'll end up needing surgery on my veins. Rest? Some joke. How can I rest when things have gotten so bad for Juan Carlos? He punishes me with silence—a stony, unyielding wall. Other times, he shouts in anger, furious because no one has ever understood him. I've come to realize that perhaps he is right.

Sometimes, when I'm cleaning apartments, I think about our lives, and I wonder if Juan Carlos feels he was forced into coming to the States. The plan was to study at Columbia, get his doctorate in engineering, and then return to Argentina and a job. His cousin in New York was the first to encourage Juan Carlos. He was certain, that because of Juan Carlos's command of English, he'd have no problem getting a teaching assistantship. Things moved quickly after that. Juan Carlos's mother, a demanding, dictatorial woman, insisted her son was destined to be more than a mere landowner in Cordoba. His quiet father, Don Botero, was reluctant—he enjoyed having Juan Carlos at his side—but a swift attack from his wife, and the man quickly acquiesced.

For the six months prior to our departure, every Sunday dinner at Estancia Forsyth, his mother's family ranch, became a three-ring circus. The entire, intrusive family, meddling aunts and uncles, doting grandparents, all wanted to be part of the act. They are a tall, fair tribe and consider themselves Anglo-Saxons, though resident Argentineans for generations. They hovered and planned. They advised and warned. Waiting for visas, they argued the pros and cons of this American phenomenon and that. None of them had ever been to the States.

During all the important decision making, I, of course, was not consulted. In fact, I was barely noticed. Juan Carlos did not marry well, his people have made that quite clear to me from the beginning. They are the kind who would call me Evalina la Argentina if they'd thought of it. Because of my size and Indian looks, and because only God and Mamá knew who Papá was and where he'd gone, everything about me was insignificant. My worries were of no concern to them. Only Don Botero, a thoughtful, gentle man, understood my anxiety about leaving Mamá behind. Only he understood my secret excitement about leaving Juan Carlos's family behind.

Juan Carlos did what his mother wanted because he always had. She'd protected, pampered, and given, and she'd always known what was best, so he believed. I did not marry him for his self-esteem or seriousness, nor his strength. I was pursuing medicine at the University of Cordoba. Yes, Reader, it's true. I had determined never to marry, but to practice among the Indians of Jujuy. But we fell in love, studying together under the beautiful shade trees in the Plaza San Martín, across from the ancient cathedral and the town hall. We brought each other freedom. I was certain that with time, he would mature, for he surely couldn't get younger.

Juan Carlos was almost as excellent a student as I was. He learned to work hard at the university, but ultimately he became bored. Later, the years helping his father manage ranches made him restless. In the meantime, I quit my studies to bear our children. While I nursed and cared for our babies, Juan Carlos and his family took little interest or pleasure, except for Don Botero, who truly loved his grandchildren. None of them seemed the slightest bit interested that in all probability I would not complete my medical career.

Here in New York, away from his family, I was certain things would be different. They were, in the beginning. Between his teaching stipend from Columbia and what his father sent us, we were in good financial shape, and I was hopeful about the rest. Juan Carlos studied and attended classes diligently. I kept my fingers crossed. He was conscientious about his teaching sessions, and even began research on his dissertation. I was impressed. He finished his course work in a little over a year. I wrote Mamá the good news. He had only his thesis left when the familiar discontent settled in, the need for something new.

During that time, the news from Argentina went from bad to worse, and slowly, Juan Carlos was drawn in. As the second year slipped into the third, he began spending more time pouring over letters, newspapers, and newscasts than he did with his work. He worried about his father's lands, though he never had while he was home. He spoke constantly about the nation's inflation and politics, though he'd never expressed interest before. The rumors were persistent; Argentina's economy was a disaster, and there were no jobs to go back to.

Juan Carlos became terribly dejected. One day, he simply refused to attend his teaching sessions, and he stopped all work on his dissertation.

Our friends stepped in, trying to be helpful, trying to convince Juan Carlos that he ought to be looking forward, not back. But it was no use. A few months later, his family suffered disastrous financial reversals, lost lands. When Don Botero could no longer send us money, Juan Carlos began applying for teaching jobs, without success. His cousin had been hired by a small college in New Jersey, and he hadn't finished his dissertation either, Juan Carlos complained bitterly. I tried to block out what I knew. How could his professors recommend him if he was not responsible, not dependable? Who was going to hire him if he didn't show up for classes?

I should have known Juan Carlos would be above finding an ordinary job. His mother is to blame. "I didn't go to school all those years to drive a cab!" he still insists, his long, thin hands pushing away reality. So, he neither studies nor works, but stays in, sulking, and growing more fragile, waiting until I come home at nights to listen to him, to prepare his dinner. I am a patient woman, but for how long? It's not easy being supportive. At first I humored him, encouraging him to apply for positions he heard about. But constant rejections only make him more vulnerable, more anxious. He is more exhausting than cleaning twenty apartments.

Yet despite everything, he is my husband. He has to know I trust him. I have to hang on and stand by him, especially now. It isn't easy. Slowly, our friends began staying away. Sometimes, if someone does drop by, Juan Carlos can still pull himself together and act almost normal, lucid, and talkative. So much so that the gauntness is politely ignored, the nervousness overlooked. But I know better. I know the constant frustration, the anger, the lashing out. He's always been self-involved, so that part isn't new. But the meanness is. I haven't told anyone, Reader. Only I know his black moods, and that he's recently tried to hurt me. I hit him back, hard, with my small, brown fists.

In all of this confusion, I went out to clean apartments. I never intended such work. I certainly never did this in Argentina. Even my poor Mamá always had a young girl who came in to sweep our house. When Don Botero could no longer support us, I listened to an industrious, young immigrant from Chile, who told me that cleaning houses was a good way to make fast money. Now what's next? I'm not prepared or trained for anything, and without that money, how will we manage? Juan Carlos's stipend was cut off long ago.

Mona checks the oven temperature. Nathan eagerly accepted the dinner invitation. He and Judy have been living together for almost two years, so everyone knows very well what the important news is. There are no surprises. Mona puts the vegetables in a pot of water and turns on the element. So, if there are no surprises, what is her problem? She breaks up the head of lettuce and places the leaves in the spinner. One grandfather might have been a rabbi, but her other grandfather read the Yiddish *Forward* everyday and refused to enter a synagogue, believing religion was the root of all social injustice. Her parents and most of their families were Socialists, if not Communists. So where does she get off having such doubts and hesitations, such sudden concern for Judaism? She, who's always considered herself so liberal, so accepting?

Here she is, concerned about another generation, a grandchild, when most of her friends' children haven't married Jews, and everyone around her seems to think it's best to erase any serious traces of ethnic and cultural differences. The norm has become intermarriage. Of course it's not that she disapproves; who is she to disapprove? But she allows herself to worry. It's become more than the norm, almost a movement. A movement "on a roll," the way "black is beautiful" blossomed during those early stages, and the way women ostentatiously burned their bras, and now all this business with gay rights. One might almost think a whole generation is waiting in the wings, waiting to be part of the "New Face" of Judaism that is sweeping the nation! It's true that her grandson is but one

Jew. Richard has no idea how much she thinks about this! No idea at all! If he knew, he'd probably shrug and say something like "at least he's getting married!"

Mona, bearer of burdens, has become silently preoccupied with the articles and editorials that fill the Jewish magazines. *Hadassah* comes to the apartment; she reads the others at the library. "Outreach programs" have become the latest obsession for Jewish America. Outreach for mixed marriages. For Jews by choice. For gay Jews by choice with non-Jewish partners. For Christians committed to raising their biological and/or adopted, occasionally Asian children as Jews, and so on, and so forth. A never-ending stream of outreach.

How about outreach for the Mona Sterns? The Mona Sterns, who, wittingly or unwittingly, have allowed workers in white overalls to paint over their mezuzahs, and now, in the same vein, they must accept, graciously, as though it hardly matters, the reality of probable non-Jewish descendants. Without a doubt, she, like many others, has taken her Judaism for granted. What now? Is there outreach for Jews who think their culture is on the point of dissolution because of assimilation? As she waits for the vegetables to parboil, Mona suddenly thinks of the Swede, Raoul Wallenberg. She imagines his famous trip to the train station of the frontier post of Hegyeshalom, Hungary, hurrying to save waiting Jews from the box cars and certain death. "Forgive me," he said, choosing from among them, "I want to save you all, but they will only let me take a few. So please forgive me, but I must save the young ones, because I want to save a nation." What would happen, Mona wonders, if the future of 5,000 years of this "nation" depended solely on her and Richard? She removes the pot of boiling vegetables from the stove and drains them in the sink. On one side of the scale, they had rabbi grandfathers. On the other, they will soon have a born-again Christian. Mother to future Sterns.

"Mrs. Stern?"

Mona looks up from the vegetables. "Eva. All done, dear? Ready for a drink?" The girl is clearly exhausted. She works too hard. Mona hates asking if her husband has found a job yet. She seems to ask that every week, and every week it's the same answer.

"First, can I ask you about a photograph?"

"A photograph?"

"The one of the old people, the family. It's hanging on the wall in the library."

Mona wipes her hands on the dish towel. "You mean Mr. Stern's family?"

"I think so."

"Why don't you show me." Mona puts down the dish towel and starts for the library, pleased with a break from the kitchen and her thoughts.

"That one."

Mona carefully reaches out to straighten the frame. "No one's taken any interest in this for years! Except me, of course. They're in my care now, Mr. Stern's family, his parents and siblings. It was taken in the old country, in Russia, before Mr. Stern was born. That was his mother," Mona points to the woman in the back row, in the striped, satin blouse. "She was very beautiful. Those two little boys in front are his older brothers."

"Who was the old man?"

"*Zaide* Stern, the grandfather. And she was the grandma, *Bubbie* Stern."

"They remind me of my *abuelos*, my grandparents."

"Really, Eva?"

Eva nods. "I feel I know them, as though I lived with them, the way I did with my *abuelos*. Did lots of old men wear little satin caps?"

"The yarmulke?" Mona smiles. "Sure, in the old days. Now they're mostly worn in the synagogue. Except for the orthodox, they wear them all the time."

"So did my *abuelo*, in Cordoba."

That evening, at the Stern dinner table, the roast is a tremendous success, and Nathan tells his grandmother that her cooking is delicious, as always. Then he asks her to tell Judy his favorite story of how she ran on the men's track team in college until a women's team was formed. Mona is delighted; she loves to tell the story. After Nathan and Judy make their announcement, Judy smiles a lot and eats little, nervously saying she is saving room for the cheesecake. Mona always makes cheesecake when Nathan comes. Richard tries very hard to act upbeat and relaxed. Mona is proud of him. She even feels pretty good herself. Good enough that she tells them all about Eva and her interest in the photograph of Richard's parents, taken in Russia. She doesn't tell them, however, about Eva's grandfather and his satin cap and their discussion about yarmulkes. Mona realizes she doesn't want Judy to feel uncomfortable, and she doesn't want to make herself feel sad.

Throughout dinner, I find Juan Carlos unusually calm. I'm so pleased with his mood that after the children leave and while we drink our coffee, I eagerly tell him about the photograph.

"Don't be ridiculous, Eva! White Russians despised Jews just as much as everyone else did in Russia, and your grandparents were White Russians. How can you have forgotten that?!"

"I haven't forgotten," I say softly, ignoring his tone. I'm happy that Juan Carlos wants to talk. "But how do I know that for sure?" I ask, playing with the napkin, the spoon. "Whenever I used to ask Mamá about the *abuelos*, and why they did the things they did, like light candles one night a week, her answer was always the same. 'They have their customs.'"

"Of course they had their customs, everyone has their customs!

So what?"

"Juan Carlos, I can't shake the feeling that I was somehow there, in Russia, that I belong in those traditions—"

"And I tell you, Eva, you're crazy! Crazy! And you think I'm nuts, for God's sake! Russian Jews?! How can you even think such a thing? Look at you! You're an Indian, and your father was an Indian. As for your mother, you know how religious she is. What would she think if she heard this?!"

I shrug.

"Listen to me, Eva. All those old people wore the same clothes. Do you understand? Clothes don't mean anything!"

Images of Estancia Forsyth and of Juan Carlos's tall, blond, maternal family jump before my eyes. "I don't remember seeing your mother's father in a satin cap."

"Enough of this nonsense!" Juan Carlos stands up. "I forbid you to speak of this, especially in front of the children! Understood? I suppose you told Mrs. Stern?"

I shake my head.

"Did she inquire again if I've gotten a job yet?" Juan Carlos asks suspiciously, leaning over the table toward me, a smirk forming on his mouth.

"Not this week, Juan Carlos."

"She must be getting tired of asking!" He laughs nervously.

"They're good people, Juan Carlos."

"Sure, they can afford to be. You know what it means to own a jewelry store?" He says bitterly.

"He doesn't own it anymore, he sold it to his nephew."

"You're so naive, Eva!" Juan Carlos turns and walks toward the kitchen counter for his cigarettes. He raises one to his mouth and lights it quickly, throwing back his head, inhaling slowly. "So naive!"

I see his long hands shake; I hear his heavy breathing. The calm did not last.

Juan Carlos stands staring at the darkness outside the kitchen window, his elbow on the sill. He smokes quickly, nervously, watching the rain. "Did you tell her I want you to enroll at the university, that I want you to continue your medical studies? Did you tell her that, Eva?"

"No."

"Of course not." He says loudly, sarcastically. "Because if you did, you would have to admit that I don't want you to be a cleaning woman all your life, and that would mean admitting I'm not such a bad person after all!"

"Juan Carlos!" I gasp.

"Juan Carlos!" He mimics, turning quickly toward me, his face anxious, pained. "You hate me, but you won't admit it." He aims for the ashtray with his cigarette, stubbing it out in short, angry taps. "You'd rather be a victim, Eva." He breathes deeply. "You've always been that. You enjoy the role. That's all you know!"

After a few seconds, I see his eyes pull back, retreat behind his abrupt silence. He says these things all the time now, so there's no point in contradicting him. This is not the moment to remind him about money. How we don't have any extra for tuition. How we don't have any extra to bring over Mamá, as he promised me. No extra for anything. How if it weren't for my cleaning jobs, we'd have nothing. To think, I had once thought I'd be a doctor.

"Evalina la Argentina!" Juan Carlos suddenly jumps into the third position of ballet, hands on his hips. "What am I going to do with you? Do you think I enjoy having a cleaning woman for a wife? Do you think the children like it? Do you realize how embarrassing it is for them?"

My husband is not well. I stand up, silently, and begin clearing the dishes.

After a few minutes, Juan Carlos announces he is going out. I plead with him not to go, to stay with me. I don't like it when he leaves me, angry. It makes me nervous, anxious. As he leaves the apartment, his only response is that I should not wait up for him.

I do wait up for the children. They come home together, happy and communicative for a change. They sit down beside me, laughing, snuggling up against me. I am happy and grateful for that. I do not know what the next step will be, but I remain calm, with my children beside me. After the children go to bed, I think about the photograph in the Stern's library, how the old man's small house looked so familiar, so comfortable. Then I think about Juan Carlos. The deepest pain comes from knowing I can no longer help him.

Where is he? The more I think about him, the more nervous I become. Is he in the subway? I hope he has the sense not to go down into the trains at this hour. Everyone knows it isn't safe—so if he isn't in the subway, where then? If he's out walking around on the street, out of our neighborhood, he could easily get mugged. And if he isn't on the street, he's probably in a bar, drinking. If he gets drunk enough, he could do anything.

I sit up waiting and worrying for another hour, and then finally, I fall asleep on the couch, my body succumbing to the familiar, aching rhythm of exhaustion. Reader, I am half asleep when I hear the knocks, when I pull myself upright on the couch. Juan Carlos? It can't be, he has his own key. Who then? The police? More knocks. They're coming to tell me something has happened to Juan Carlos—that he's dead! I stumbled toward the door.

I put my hand on the knob, hesitating. There will be two officers, they always send two, they'll be young, nervous. Their voices will shake as they tell me that his body has been retrieved from the East River. I pull open the door.

"Juan Carlos?!"

"Who'd you expect?" He asks morosely, stepping into the apartment. "The president of the United States?"

I stare at him.

"What are you staring at?!" He turns toward me. His movements are slow, ponderous. "For God's sake, I might be drunk, but I'm not dead!" He breathes deeply. "You look like hell, like you've seen a ghost! What's wrong with you?"

I shake my head. He's O.K., I realize. He's pale, and his eyes are bloodshot, and he's had too much to drink, but he's O.K.

"I forgot my keys, that's all," he says, looking at me again, curiously. "Did you think I wasn't coming home?" He grins through slurred speech. "You thought I wasn't coming home!"

I nod, forcing a smile.

"Don't worry." Juan Carlos waves his hands dismissively, as he walks over to the couch and throws himself down. "Don't worry, my Evalina la Argentina, I'll never abandon you," he says sleepily.

I watch as his body settles into the couch, his head against the cushions. I watch as his eyes withdraw, and the lids slowly close over the stupor and stillness.

THE RIFKE CHRONICLES

The year is 1925.

ITALY: Mussolini's Fascist government is in power.

INDIA: Gandhi continues his peaceful protest against the British.

CHINA: Sun Yat-Sen, frustrated because he cannot unite his country and successfully govern it as a whole nation, turns to Russia, declaring that the Chinese and Russian revolutions are part of the same global liberation movement. He dies shortly after.

EGYPT: Archaeologist Howard Carter is in his third year of clearing King Tut-ankh-amen's tomb.

BUENOS AIRES: fifty-four-year-old Rifke Schulman has been asked to join Soprotimis, the Society for Protection of Jewish Immigrants.

From Volume Twenty-seven.

February 21, 1925
Buenos Aires

Rabbi Halfon has asked me to join Soprotimis. It is a privilege, and I am honored. He told me he knows of my work at the library, and he said my name is highly recommended. Peshke hasn't stopped talking about it for days. She says this is my big moment! I don't see that it's such a big moment. I'm embarrassed that in all these years, I've never stepped foot in the rabbi's synagogue, the Congregation Israelita, on Libertad Street. Yet I feel genuine affection for the building, no doubt because it was inaugurated in 1897, the same year I arrived in Buenos Aires. Henoch says one thing has nothing to do with the other, the fact that I've never entered the synagogue, and that the rabbi has asked me to join Soprotimis. Besides, he says, the rabbi understands these things.

Moses Soltansky dropped by for a visit the other day, and he agrees with Henoch. There is no question that I must do it. I am needed, Moses says. I thought about it for a day, and then I said yes. It means giving up my work at the Progreso Library. There isn't enough time for both; I believe I can be more helpful to Soprotimis. Dr. Halfon wants me to begin as soon as possible; he tells me they are kept incredibly busy. In 1923 alone, more than 13,000 Jews, most from Poland, entered Argentina.

The committee that was set up to aid war victims has joined Soprotimis. Together, they are a stronger presence and can accomplish more. The committee will still be in charge of fund-raising for overseas relief, and Soprotimis will handle immigration. While my main role will be handling visa applications, I look forward to occasionally helping out at the docks, informing new arrivals and looking out for single girls and women. We have been given special permission to board the ships and warn the passengers about white slavery. This remains a terrible problem in our city. It will be like the old days, with Bela Palatnik.

Julio and his wife, Miranda, have had a child, a beautiful baby boy. Henoch is beside himself with pride, and so am I. They have named him Pablo. Miranda agreed to his circumcision, but she did not want the *Pidyon ha-ben*. She felt she could not handle yet another custom so foreign to her traditions. Her mother, Estelle Ramirez, kept clear away from this decision. I have great respect for Estelle. We all love Miranda, and I know we all want this to pass smoothly. Henoch assures me he is not bothered by this. I do not believe him for a moment.

Now that the baby has arrived, Henoch finds more excuses for prolonging his stay in the city. I am delighted with his constant presence in my little apartment, and I do believe we are more in love now than ever before.

February 23, 1925

Once again, tragedy has struck the Milekofsky family. My old friend Aaron has drowned, along with Sonia's niece and her entire family, except one child. A few days ago Aaron rented a small boat and traveled to Salta, Uruguay. He refused to allow Sonia's brother to accompany him, insisting he must stay with Sonia, who is well advanced in her fourth pregnancy. In Salta, he was to pick up Sonia's niece and her family and bring them into Argentina. They had journeyed from Vilna and had been unable to obtain visas to enter the country legally because one of the children, a boy of eight, was deaf and dumb. He had sustained an injury to the temple as an infant in Lithuania, lost his hearing, and never learned to speak. Once out at sea, a storm broke, and the boat capsized. They were not far from Concordia, Entre Ríos, when the accident happened.

It is a typical, final Aaron Milekofsky story. He was always help-ing others. Always. He labored as a baker from the day he stepped foot in this country, often working through the night, day after day. I know of no other man who paid the passage for so many relatives to this country. He had saved for years to send Sonia's niece and her family their tickets. Last night, Peshke wept as she told me that they still don't know which child survived the accident. They know only that it is a boy.

I will have to go and visit Sonia. She must be beside herself with grief, and I am grateful that she has her brother here to help her. Aaron will be missed by everyone. Poor Aaron. He always seemed such a tragic figure to me. I hope that Sonia will keep his trumpet. Perhaps someday one of his sons will play it.

Peg E. and I have kept up a lively correspondence. The last letter came from her family home in Maine, where she is spending the winter. She tells of snow and wood stoves, of skating on the frozen river with her nieces. She is writing a book about her travels in the last five years, and her 1919 Buenos Aires visit will figure as a separate chapter. The work goes well, and she hopes to have the first draft done by spring. She is looking forward to returning to Argentina soon for another visit.

April 25, 1925

A month ago, the scientist Albert Einstein came to speak at the University of Buenos Aires. He was sponsored by the university and the Hebraica Society of Argentina. He spoke on his scientific theories as well as the current situation of the Jews. I attended the lecture with Julio. Although Julio's medical practice keeps him very busy, he insisted on hearing the great scientist. The discussion of

Einstein's scientific work left me absolutely baffled. I walked away feeling thoroughly confused about this whole business of time and space and the speed of light! Julio tried to explain it to me, but eventually he gave up. I enjoyed being present however, and I was impressed with the caliber of questions from the student population.

I have visited with Sonia Milekofsky several times. The situation is truly sad. Sonia has given birth to her fourth child, a boy, and she has named him Aaron. With her brother's devoted attention, Sonia and the children are managing, but it is not easy. Her niece's child, who survived the boat accident, is the deaf mute. The poor boy. From what I see, Sonia bears him no ill will. In fact, she has accepted him as some sort of sign. While she nursed her baby, she told me she will have to find some line of work, for she certainly can't expect her poor brother to support them all. If her brother hadn't completely devoted his life to her before, he certainly has now.

Seeing Sonia in her cotton housedress, appearing so tired and worn out, I could not help remembering the night I first met her. How beautiful she looked in her wonderful velvet dress! The years have passed and things have changed for all of us. Sonia told me how very kind Peshke has been to her. She said she drops by almost everyday and always brings something to eat. I was glad to hear this. They do, after all, share both Milekofsky joy and Milekofsky grief. Peshke has not told me of her visits. She probably doesn't want me to think she is going soft.

December 1927
Paris, France

Today I sent Peg E. a postcard from Paris! Yes, I have gotten to this incredible city! I was asked to go to Europe as one of the representatives from Soprotimis. Today we were in the J.C.A. headquarters, and tomorrow we are to meet with HICEM, a new international commission that has combined several immigration organizations. It has offices in Lithuania, Turkey, Holland, Argentina, and England, to name only some. We believe they want to discuss the possibility of sponsoring a South American congress on Jewish immigration to be held in Buenos Aires. Many people are still looking to South America as the hope and solution for Europe's displaced and homeless.

In the meantime, I am in Paris! We are here for two days, then on to London and Berlin. I walked from our pension to the Louvre this afternoon, and while the weather is nasty and cold, I find this city as beautiful as I've always read. Before I left Buenos Aires, Peshke made me buy a new outfit, a wool traveling suit with a fox collar, and one of those new felt hats, worn pulled down over the head. I've never felt as elegant as I do here, walking around in my new suit, pretending I visit Paris at least once a year! I must admit, now that the skirt styles are shorter, I am very aware of my left shoe, always quite obvious with its large heel. However, I am not so self-conscious that I will allow it to stop me.

Last night when we took the taxi from the station to the pension, I noticed that the street lamps on the bridges and the fine mist from the Seine combined to form a remarkably soft, hazy light. If Henoch were here now, I must admit, I might say yes. Only last week, Henoch again asked me to marry him. I told him I would think about it during my trip. I can't believe my own words. Peshke told me as I was packing my bag that I was no "spring chick," and perhaps the time has come for a "yes." I think she was trying to tell me I don't have to worry about her anymore. Ever since her brother-in-law Aaron drowned, Peshke has put aside her own grief over her son Abraham's death and her own ill feelings for Sonia and has become totally involved helping her with the family, no small feat.

The Musée du Louvre is remarkable! Of course I went looking for the pieces I know from books, the *Winged Victory*, the *Mona Lisa*, the rooms and rooms of Greek pots.

But I also saw things I had never heard about—beautiful, breathtaking painting and sculpture. I thought of my friend David Kaminski, the painter, and wished he were with me to tell me about everything. David, who more than twenty years ago talked to me about the Moorish motifs on the elephants' house in the Palermo zoo. David, who wanted me to go with him to the mountains of Cordoba, and I wouldn't because he did not care to understand my commitment to that first, small workers' union. I guess some things never change! I can't believe so many years have passed. I understand he still lives in Cordoba and has become a well-respected modern painter. Peshke tells me his paintings command big prices and that he has had exhibitions in Cordoba, Mendoza, and even the capital. I don't know how it is that Peshke always knows so much about everyone, especially someone like David, whom she never liked and always called "the dreamer"!

Before I returned to the pension, I wandered around the Left Bank for a while. It's a wonderful area, with the small shops and cafes, the galleries and bookstores. I stopped to buy a book of French fairy tales for Julio and Miranda's son, Pablo, who is almost two. I've never seen so many bookstores, so many artists and writers! I passed one bookstore called Shakespeare and Co., and there was an announcement of a reading by the American writer Ernest Hemingway. I remembered that Peg E. told me about him and said I should watch for his name because someday he would make the literary world spin. There was a photograph of him in the window. He is a handsome young man, with dark, brooding eyes. I am sorry not to understand English well enough to read his novels, and I am sorry I will be far from Paris when he is scheduled to read.

David Kaminski would have loved Paris when he was young! It

has its own atmosphere, its own life. I can easily imagine myself staying on in Paris, living here. Looking around my pension room, I can see making it more comfortable, making it mine. I decide I would have no trouble adjusting to France and the French. Of course, I would have to learn their language and find a job. I am pleased to think I have the capacity to be adaptable, that I could live away from what I consider home. Of course I would miss Henoch and Julio, Peshke, Miranda, and the baby. But at the moment, my realities of Jewish immigration seem very far away.

THE RIFKE CHRONICLES

The 1929 crash of the American stock market triggers the Great Depression, worldwide. In Argentina, as in other countries, prices of agricultural produce fall, and repercussions are felt in urban centers. The financial scare causes a cutback in construction. Factories close and unemployment becomes rampant. On September 6, 1930, the radical government of Yrigoyen is deposed by an military coup, the first in seventy-seven years of Argentine political history.

From Volume Thirty-three.

December 1930
Buenos Aires

Due to the economic crisis, the drop in the price of wheat, bad crops, and unemployment, Soprotimis has had to slow down its activities. This was a direct request from the Yrigoyen government. Shortly after, Argentina underwent a change of administration; we moved from a democracy to the first military rule this country has seen since the signing of the constitution!

On September 6th, Peshke and I were out together and we saw the junior officer cadets marching toward the Casa Rosada. We had no idea what was going on. Peshke was disgusted to think they were in a parade mood, given the depressed economy. Peshke hates the military. I know she still associates it with Russia and the Cossacks and the pogroms. It wasn't until later in the day when I was at the Soprotimis offices that I heard the army had taken over the government, and there was little resistance. I wondered if Peshke had heard. I did not look forward to telling her. I consider this a disastrous event. When the military has the power to drive out a democratic government, this does not bode well for the political future of a country.

One of the new government's first decisions was to increase the visa fees from three gold pesos to thirty-three. Things have become extremely difficult for the poor, struggling to make their way across the ocean, and Soprotimis is having trouble providing them with aid. Our organization has ended its language and vocational training. Most of the new arrivals have relatives in this county, so there is no longer need for these programs. But we continue to push. Despite all of these problems and the financial depression worldwide, this year, 7,805 Jews managed to reach Argentina. Now we are seeing even further tightening of immigration.

Every day the Soprotimis offices are crowded with the unemployed. I feel for these people. They are extremely disillusioned, and many want the Jewish institutions to send them back to Russia. Some are returning on their own. They say that next year, for the first time, more people will be leaving Argentina than entering it.

In all of this gloom, there is good news. The white slave trade has finally fallen. Thanks to R. Lieberman, an art dealer who had been enslaved for four years upon her arrival in Argentina, the police were able to infiltrate their main offices and make arrests. I know that Moses Soltansky was an important figure in their downfall. Shortly after the Semana Trágica events, when his friend Abe Milekofsky was killed, Moses quit his job at the sheet metal factory. For ten years he has been working as a detective. On several occasions he has told me how much he loves his work, how gratified and useful he feels.

It was to Moses that R. Lieberman turned when she was ready to denounce her husband, S. J. Korn, the infamous Polish dealer. The organization of white slave dealers took the name *Zvi Migdal* just in the last year of its operation. They called themselves the Warsaw Society until the Polish Ministry complained. They operated under the pretense of being a mutual aid society, while in reality, records prove this organization had been buying and selling girls and women for fifty years. Many arrests were made after the May 21 bust of the *Zvi Migdal* headquarters. The newspaper coverage was outstanding, accompanied by endless photographs. One image became quite familiar; it was reproduced many times in the press. Moses S., with his now graying hair, is pictured seated at the police chief's desk, R. Lieberman beside him.

It made me think of that rainy day on the dock, and how Moses, with his wild red hair, had picked up Bela Palatnik's body so effortlessly and with such tenderness. I have often thought about that old man who gave us the shawl off his back, who recited the prayer for Bela. I've thought about him, but I know there would be no way of locating one old man in the maze of Buenos Aires' Jewish immigrants.

While all this is happening in the capital, in Moisés Ville things are very bad. In September and October there were droughts, and it is predicted that in January, floods. The crop was ruined, the farmers had no seeds, and the banks restricted credit. In 1928 when Louis Oungre, director of the J.C.A., visited the colonies, he reported that the entire J.C.A. program was in danger. A large number of colonists were leaving the system and starting out on their own. He felt there was general stagnation in the colonies. Henoch is very discouraged by these events. His letters sound low. I know that he is concerned about his shortness of breath, although he does not want to worry me.

June 1933
Buenos Aires

The depression continues with incredible intensity, and in Buenos Aires there are many out of work. Argentina is suffering along with the rest of the world.

In March Soprotimis received a hasty telegram (from HICEM in Europe) asking permission to send Jewish refugees from Germany. This Adolf Hitler, who came to power a few months ago in Germany, will prove to be very dangerous. His continual persecution of German Jews should be enough for anyone in doubt! We submitted HICEM's request for entry to the government immigration authorities, but it was rejected because the refugees had no relatives in Argentina, and because they had not been hired in advance of their emigration, and because they were not farmers. The J.C.A. could still bring in farmers for the colonies.

We scrambled to suggest a new agricultural colony near Buenos Aires, which could become a haven for refugees rushing to flee

Hitler's Germany. It could focus on vegetables and fruit farming, as a foil to the established colonies' work with grains. But the J.C.A. office in Paris felt the land was too expensive; they preferred seeing German families settled in existing colonies. That idea didn't work because many felt that new families would put an undue burden on the financially troubled communities.

In the case of waiting German Jews, bribery was next. There were officials in the department of immigration willing to do this, look the other way, but the J.C.A. would not.

I'm very worried about Henoch. He sounds terribly stressed in his letters, and I know this cannot be good. The colony has been subjected to more drought and locust attacks. Because of the bad crops and bad harvest, the Banco Comercial Israelita has closed its doors. Wouldn't it be wonderful if I could take Henoch away, far away from all our worries, perhaps to Paris? Just the two of us. I would make him sleep and eat well, and rest. I would make the energy return to his blue eyes. Lately they have seemed dull, almost listless. Is taking him away so far-fetched? When I next see Peshke I will ask her. When I next see Henoch, I will suggest it. Yes.

I've received a sad letter from Peg E. She has recently undergone surgery for breast cancer and is recuperating at her home in Maine. She reports that she is doing well and fully intends another visit to Buenos Aires once this horrible depression is over. She says that in the U.S., the cities have been badly struck by the depression. Unemployment and bread lines are so depressing in Boston, she intends to remain on the island for the summer.

THE RIFKE CHRONICLES

In July 1936, civil war erupts in Spain. Forces loyal to the Second Republic—Republicans, Socialists, Communists—have united as the left.

The military, the clergy, the landed aristocracy form the right, or the nationalists. The democratic world has vowed to remain neutral, leaving Spain to resolve her internal conflicts alone.

From Volume Thirty-eight.

August 1936
Buenos Aires

Brigades are already forming to go help the Loyalist Republican forces in Spain. Miranda's youngest brother, Carlos, has joined up, and he left last week. Julio came by a few nights ago, and he told me

223

the whole family was at the pier, bidding Carlos and his friends fare-well. It was raining fiercely on the docks, so they all gathered for a drink in a port bar. While everyone toasted the Loyalists, Doña Ramírez sat alone, weeping and knitting quietly. In that hour, she managed to finish off the last stitches of a navy blue turtleneck that Carlos pulled over his head as he walked up the gangplank, smiling and waving. Julio told me that his mother-in-law had filled Carlos's suit case with extra sweaters and socks, just in case some of the boys didn't have enough.

Yesterday I went to visit Estelle Ramírez. I've become very fond of her in the more than thirteen years we've known each other. She has lived alone since her husband died five years ago. Her children are devoted to her, and they want her to come and live with them, any one of them. But she insists on their privacy, and hers. I admire her independence, her total devotion to her family, and her unswer-ving sense of right and wrong. We have shared some good times, Estelle and I, and of course we share Pablo, Julio and Miranda's son, who is now eleven. He is a delight, and I don't know which of us old women is prouder. Estelle still lives in the house her husband built in the countryside. Years ago, when the children were small, he had purchased a piece of property west of Buenos Aires, just beyond Villa Devoto on the new subway line. It's no longer country, really more suburb. But she still has her large garden, her goat, and the few chickens. She spends her days quietly gardening, preserving peppers and eggplant in seasoned olive oil, and preparing food for her extensive family and for those who are ill or in need.

While we ate the special lunch she had prepared, she spoke at length about Carlos, her youngest, and about poor Spain, still in her heart her country. She told me about Carlos when he was little, about the things he did, about the things he said. I let her cry. I tried to assure her he would be all right, that this Spanish war would not last long, that he would be home soon. We both knew I was probably wrong on all counts.

Finally, in the late afternoon, before I took the train back to the city, Estelle and I went out for a walk. We shared new stories about Pablo. He was often the center of our conversations, and nothing thrilled us more than the summer afternoons we spent together with him, here in Estelle's house. After eating and laughing and singing to the gramophone, we would retire to the garden. Estelle and I would sit in the sun, satiated and sleepy, while Pablo entertained us with more stories, more jokes, more tricks, reaching for grapes from his grandmother's arbor, as he continued to charm us.

I climbed onto the subway, loaded with the products of Estelle's kitchen. Sauce for Miranda and Julio. Desserts for my sweet tooth and Peshke's. Bread for Henoch, whom she adores. Henoch, what am I going to do about Henoch? During the subway ride back to the city, I racked my brain for a solution to his relentless pushing and working. He's always so tired, and he doesn't look after himself. But he won't listen. He refuses to delegate work if he can do it. He says there is no time for rest, that he still has much to do. In his last letter, his spirits seemed better. He wrote that after the great devastation of the last few years, there have finally been some good harvests in Moisés Ville. Prices are rising for agricultural products, especially linen. The bank is stable again, and in general there is a more optimistic outlook. He says he is looking forward to his next Buenos Aires visit. He wants to spend some long months with me. Peshke says it is high time for a vacation. When he is next in town, once again I will try to convince him.

This morning I read of more violence and bloodshed in Spain. It is no wonder that Doña Ramírez weeps.

Soprotimis is trying to help the illegal immigrants who enter the country, but the situation is risky and dangerous. We can assist if they leave the capital and settle far away, especially in the north, along the Rio Paraná. In Rio Negro, a colony for the cultivation of fruit trees has been established for Jewish German youths, another attempt to get as many Jews out of that country as soon as possible. But last year when a Mr. Oronstein visited the colonies on behalf of the J.C.A. office in Paris, he reported that they were in a slump, a view Louis Oungre offered years earlier on a similar visit. This has dampened the hope that the colonies could become a serious possibility for immigrants. The word is that immigration will be further tightened to keep out the Communists, a direct result of the outbreak of civil war in Spain.

I've received a postcard from Peg. She has been sent as a correspondent to cover the war there. She writes that she met the American writer John Dos Passos, and that the heroic E. Hemingway will be returning soon. She can't wait to meet him. She claims to have been in love with him since she first read his work and saw his picture. It matters not that he has a wife. She would run away with him anyway!

How I enjoy Peg! I don't know this Hemingway; I still haven't read any of his work, but whoever he is, he would do well to run away with Peg Ellington!

December 10, 1938
Buenos Aires

My oldest and dearest friend, Henoch Rosenvitch, is dead. A month has passed since the funeral, and this is the first time I've been able to sit down and write about it. Henoch died here, with me. One evening, we were reading the papers with the horrible accounts of Kristallnacht. I attributed Henoch's unusual agitation to the bad news from Germany. When I stood up to get more boiling water for the tea, I saw him suddenly go pale and begin to perspire.

Earlier, standing at the balcony, he had complained of the closeness, the lack of air. I had found it a little odd because usually I am the one affected by Buenos Aires' climate. While sitting with his tea in front of him, he wiped his forehead with his handkerchief and gingerly touched his chest. Before I realized what was happening, he stood up, violently pushing away the small table as though it was pressing in on him. Slightly bent forward, he glanced over at me where I still stood near the stove and quietly fell over.

I ran to get Peshke; she got hold of Julio and Miranda. I remember nothing after that. Peshke tried to get me to eat, doctors came. It was dark. Arrangements were made. I was in a haze for several days. Peshke stayed with me. Moses Soltansky came around to see me. The doctors said it was a massive heart attack.

I did not travel to Moisés Ville for the funeral. I did not want to be present when they lowered Henoch into the ground beside his wife. Julio understood.

I miss him terribly, and I am sorry I was not able to convince him to go away, to take a vacation. Perhaps if he had gotten some rest, the attack would not have happened. I feel guilty that I didn't marry him after his wife passed away. The truth is, a part of me died with Henoch. I would never say that to anyone, not even to Peshke, but it's a fact. It doesn't mean I don't want to continue, or that I won't do it to the best of my ability, but inside I feel an emptiness, and I know it will always be.

Poor Julio. I've talked his ear off this last month. He is a busy doctor, but he always finds the time to come to me. He assures me that by staying in Buenos Aires, I did what I had to do, just as Henoch did what he had to by returning to Moisés Ville. Where would I be without Julio and Peshke? And Pablo? He comes to visit me every day after school. He's almost thirteen, almost a young man, and the image of his grandfather, Henoch Rosenvitch.

February 1939
Buenos Aires

The Spanish civil war continues. The cruelty and violence is overwhelming. After Guernica was bombed by the Germans in April of 1937, I believe that between the Spanish Fascists and the German Nazis, anything is possible.

Carlos Ramírez has returned. He lost an arm in the fighting, but he is home. Estelle came to see me after Henoch's death. We consoled each other.

I think about Henoch all the time. When I am at the Soprotimis office dealing with the red tape of visa applications, I find myself daydreaming about him. Lately I've been having these fantasies that we were married and had a child, a daughter. In my daydreams, she looks like Bela Palatnik.

October 1939
Moisés Ville

I am writing this entry from the Rosenvitch farm in Moisés Ville. Henoch's eldest son has been managing the land for many years now, and he has done a wonderful job. His second son has been in charge at the Moisés Ville creamery. I know how proud Henoch was of his children. I know too how difficult it was for him to tell them. But I feel they understand. I have returned to Moisés Ville with Julio and Pablo, on the occasion of the fiftieth anniversary of this village. Peshke said that if I didn't go, she would never speak to me again!

We took the train up to Palacios, just as I traveled from Palacios to Buenos Aires forty-two years ago. I can hardly believe so many years have passed. Does it sound ridiculous if I write that I feel unchanged, no different than that young woman who helped set up those first tents? Julio's brothers and their families met us at the Palacios train station, but they came in cars, not a surrey.

I took a moment to look around the station. It was a bright, sunny day, similar to the day I had left. The hitching post was still there. I pointed it out to Pablo and his cousins, pretty girls in starched, white dresses. They hardly believed me when I told them that was where their Grandfather Henoch had tied his horse when he came to bid me farewell! The girls smiled sweetly; Pablo nodded seriously.

Then I saw her, Leah. I saw the burden of her hunched back, I saw the small waist in the linen dress, the reddish hair gleaming in the sun. She is truly lovely, just as her Uncle Julio has always said of her. I never forgot his words: "she basks in her parents' love." Now she is a young lady, perhaps twenty? Have so many years passed, so quickly? This pretty girl, with the calm face and curious blue eyes, has grown and matured with her parents' devotion. Was her shyness due to our deformities, hers and mine, or did she know about me, about Henoch? Indeed, I wonder what all those young people know of me, what they know of their grandfather? Perhaps it suffices that I am a family friend.

I have been here only a few days, and the entire family is already saying I must come back to retire. Of course the village is completely changed, but I feel as though I know it! Henoch used to write me in such detail about every new construction, and sometimes he sent me photographs. The four synagogues, the Kadima Theater, the library, his beloved co-op. His descriptions were so precise, I've impressed all his sons by knowing exactly where the buildings are and what they look like before I even see them. But it's the landscape of the country that moves me so, still as I remember it! There are more trees and more farms, real houses with verandahs and patios. Yet the feeling of open space is the same, the color of the fields and sky, the dry smell of earth and grain ready for harvesting.

After the anniversary celebrations, the parade, the speeches and lunch, Julio took me out to the cemetery to visit Henoch's grave. It is on a high spot, where the wind blows through the cypress and eucalyptus, and there is a fine view of the fields of Moisés Ville. Henoch would approve.

Perhaps I will come back to retire. My days of helping immigrants are numbered. While it is still possible for a few "legitimate" farmers to get into the country, Jewish immigration is rapidly ending. Now that war has broken out in Europe, immigration to Argentina has virtually ceased. Argentina, like many of the Latin American countries, has declared itself neutral. In December 1938, at the Eighth Pan-American Congress in Peru, the government of Argentina was an outspoken opponent of aid to Jews.

THE RIFKE CHRONICLES

PEARL HARBOR: December 1941. The Japanese attack the American fleet. The United States enters the war.

From Volume Forty-five.

Buenos Aires
October 1943

On two occasions last year German submarines sank Argentine merchant ships, and we've been informed of a Nazi spy network that has been operating in this country. Yet we remain neutral. I'm glad Henoch is not alive to see this. I've often wondered what he would have thought of all that is happening.

The anti-Jewish activity has been overwhelming. At this

moment, Jewish newspapers and publications have been closed, and no printing house remains open anywhere in the country. In August, the government banned kosher meat processing in Buenos Aires stockyards. That move is really hard to believe. Violence accompanies the government bans. Anti-Jewish slogans appear on the streets, anti-Semitic gangs attack Jews, and synagogues are continually vandalized.

As for my work with Soprotimis, I feel I have ultimately failed in my last and final mission. There have been many botched attempts to get Jewish children out of Europe, and I was responsible for Soprotimis's negotiations in the most recent case, the 5,000 children trapped in Marseilles. What a painful story. As the Vichy government began to deport Jews, Americans working in the south of France sent out an appeal to the United States and to Latin American countries, Argentina included, in the case of the Jewish orphans. As soon as the Argentine Jewish organizations were contacted, delegates met with the president of the country. I represented Soprotimis. The government agreed to allow 1,000 of the children into Argentina, much to the outrage of the anti-Semitic press, which screamed that the children would grow up to endanger true Argentineans!

In early November, after much negotiating, the Vichy government granted departure permission for 1,000 of the 5,000 children. As caretakers left the United States to meet the children and escort them to safety, the Allied forces invaded North Africa, and Germany took over southern France. The U.S. could no longer help with the children; all travel arrangements were canceled. Because of its neutrality, Argentina still had the power to help.

By this time, and in the midst of this drama of the orphans, news of the Nazi's systematic extermination of European Jewry had reached the world. Disbelief and fury spread quickly. On December 2, 1942, Buenos Aires' Jews demonstrated against Nazi atrocities. I went with Moses Soltansky, Peshke, Julio, and Pablo, who is now a very tall and handsome seventeen year old. I thought about Henoch, and how proud he would have been of his son and grandson. Peshke can hardly walk now because of her rheumatism, but she insisted on going. Wild horses wouldn't keep her away, she said. She gets about with two canes, and she refuses to allow anyone to help her. She told me she has finally caught up with me. Now we both limp! My crazy Peshke.

It was a huge and moving demonstration, thousands and thousands of Jews filled the streets—young and old, shop keepers and laborers, professors and professionals, and pregnant women well into their last trimester. I wondered whether their babies would grow up to be as outspokenly Jewish as their mamas. Big Moses kept his eyes peeled for problems; he is never truly away from his detective duties.

Peshke wept with emotion, and I was never so happy to be part of a public demonstration. Of course, there are always those who stay away from such things because it is better not to get involved, better not to put oneself in danger. Peshke's sister-in-law, Sonia Milekofsky, and all her boys were of that mind. Sonia and her family have become very affluent—they run a mail-order business—and when Peshke had asked Sonia to join us in the demonstration, she refused, along with her sons. Pity they didn't inherit their father Aaron's sense of social justice.

Following this mass protest, the public was made aware of Soprotimis's plan to rescue the French orphans, and of course the overall impression was that it would proceed quickly, smoothly. This was not to be.

There were complications. Exactly where were the children? Argentine entry permits were pointless unless the Germans would let the children go. There were delays, and although the president supported the plan, instructing his consuls in Europe to arrange for passage for these children as well as others in concentration camps, the foreign ministry failed to carry out his plans. Then, our president was overthrown, and we had a new military junta. More delays. There was talk that the Nazis were willing to bargain, the children's lives in exchange for certain conditions. But Argentina procrastinated, did not intervene. Finally, the military junta told the Argentine ambassador in Vichy to drop the issue of exit permits for the children. No more would be done. My role was finished. I was devastated by my failure.

Given Argentina's neutrality during the war, I grieve that it has done so little toward the rescue of German Jews. But the government's position is firm. Argentina will no longer take in anyone who is immigrating because of persecution. I cannot be of much further help to Soprotimis. With so many restrictions, there is not a lot the organization can do at the moment, except of course, plan for immigration after the war.

I am seventy-two, too old and too disillusioned for that. I will leave that work to the next generation. Soprotimis wants me to stay on; they want me to become its director, saying I have the vision and wisdom it takes. How Peshke loved hearing that! She said she was sorry Henoch wasn't here to enjoy the moment. Well, perhaps I have wisdom, but I certainly don't have the energy. And my God, do you need energy! Besides, I don't like the idea of having to deal with this Juan Perón, who is slowly rising in the ranks of this country's government. In my opinion, he will prove to be a dictator. I'm embarrassed to say that there are Argentine Jews who actually believe that when Perón becomes leader, he will be a friend to the Argentine Jewish community. I think they will have to eat their words.

LOSERS AND KEEPERS

When my favorite cousin, Vincent Hernán, married Lily, none of us knew much about her. We knew she was Dutch, from Leiden, and that she'd come to Buenos Aires because she'd heard of our extensive artisan community. We knew that in her past, there had been an accident. Even Vincent didn't know much about it. A car collision in Amsterdam, he once told us briefly, someone had died. After the accident, everything changed for Lily. She abandoned Holland, her bourgeois family and life style—Vincent delighted in this part of the story, hippie that he was—and she went off to India. In India, she found a guru, and in India, she found herself. So Vincent told us.

I first met Lily ten years ago, just before their Buenos Aires wedding. She was a tall, willowy girl, easy and sensuous, with large, dark eyes and white skin. There was a relaxed self-knowledge about her. She often went barefoot or, at the very most, in a pair of thin huaraches. She adorned her long, black hair with blossoms. She wore the most unusual gauzy garments—tie-dyed purples, mauves, pinks, with fringes and beads and uneven hems.

Lily was quite a hit in our male-dominated family. We boys had no sisters or female cousins, and for generations we'd been chemists and engineers, except for Vincent, of course. Lily especially delighted my uncles, who were accustomed to my short aunts in English tweeds. Vincent was enormously proud of her. I'd never seen my cousin look as good as he did before their wedding—happy and handsome, his long, horsy face animated, the tall body lean and strong. They had met in the artisans' market in San Telmo, where Vincent had a stall. That was the period in his work when he was making bracelets out of bent spoons and forks.

I never learned the nature of Lily's artisan work. Shortly after their wedding, my wife left me—after a long time of anger and pain—and I left Argentina. I asked for a leave of absence from the engineering faculty at the University in Buenos Aires, where I was teaching several classes, and the request was granted. They were neither surprised nor especially saddened to see me leave. I traveled in Europe for half a year, visiting museums and libraries, doing research for my book dealing with the treatment of flowing water in the history of art. It was a very lonely time.

When I finally returned to Buenos Aires, Vincent and Lily had taken off for Mendoza. None of us knew why Mendoza. We assumed it was for the Andes and the air. Our family's only connection to the city was several generations back. Our paternal great-grandparents, the Hernáns, had settled there, having originally come from the province of Santa Fe. Once back in Buenos Aires, I re-established myself at the university and continued work on my book. Despite Buenos Aires' hot and humid January weather, I was even feeling glad to be home.

It was mostly Lily who wrote to us. She had mastered Spanish to perfection, and her letters were long and leisurely, meticulously detailing their life. The old, abandoned schoolhouse they had acquired was slowly being pulled into shape. Vincent was doing well with his jewelry, selling everything he could make, and word was out in the countryside that Lily was a fine herbalist. On the piece of land that came with the schoolhouse, they kept a goat and some chickens, and they grew a plentiful garden of vegetables and the plants that Lily needed for her work. They now had three children, all named after stars: Aries, Leo, and Lera.

I'd always admired Vincent. While quiet and an introvert, he seemed the happiest and most independent of all of us Hernán cousins—as boys, and now as men. He had always done what he wanted, pursuing his interests, while the rest of us never seemed to know what our interests were. Like our fathers and even grandfathers, we took the path of least resistance—chemistry, or engineering. Our family is not known for its adventuresome spirit or spunk. Hernán men tend to marry conventional women, live in conventional houses, lead conventional lives. After six months of being back, I became suddenly restless again. The old anxiety about my conventional existence was reasserting itself. Toward the end of July, I decided the time had come for a pilgrimage to Mendoza to visit Vincent and Lily.

Vincent was expecting my call. From a phone booth in the Mendoza train station, I received instructions for the final leg of my journey. I was to take the #16 bus up into the mountains and get off at the last stop. From there, it was a mile walk to their home. The bus took an hour climbing the mountain. It twisted and turned and occasionally stopped to let someone off in what appeared to be the middle of nowhere. I noticed that after we left the train station in Mendoza, no one got on the bus, people only got off. It was an unseasonably warm day, and I was sorry not to have come equipped with a bottle of drinking water. Finally, we pulled into a one-street-village, passed a small *tienda* with a Coca-Cola sign and a gas tank. The bus parked in a field under some shade trees, where the road ended. I had arrived at the last stop.

As I descended the bus, I asked the driver directions to the #7 Schoolhouse. He pointed out a small dirt road that twisted to the left, behind the little store.

"That's where the hippies live," he said.

I stopped for a drink in the *tienda* and then followed the road down and around and up again. Finally the schoolhouse came into view. It was a low stone structure, slung out on a clearing. They truly lived in the foothills of the Andes, and the view from the clearing was phenomenal, snow-capped mountains in every direction. The air was clean, and there was a cooling breeze. It was not hard to see what had attracted them to Mendoza and the mountains.

The children ran to greet me. The boys were healthy, blond, and friendly, reminding me of Vincent as a child. The little girl, Lera, was dark and shy, with black eyes. We talked for a few minutes, then Aries, the older boy, took my bag and hurried toward the house. When I looked up from my conversation with Leo, I saw Lily in the doorway.

She was still as I remembered her. Tall and lovely, the same gauzy stuff for clothes, the same sandals. As we kissed and greeted each other, Vincent appeared out of another door, wiping his hands on a rag, smiling broadly. He too was the same—perhaps more serious looking and with somewhat less hair, but obviously thriving on marriage and fatherhood. We clasped hands and embraced warmly, excited and heartened to see each other again.

After a plentiful lunch of steamed vegetables, bread, and fresh figs, I was taken on a grand tour. The children showed me their rooms and their toys, the pet rabbits and chicks. Lily took me first to the kitchen and then to the herb shed, where bunches of odd plants hung drying. She had a small, round table and two wooden chairs for her consultations, she explained. Vincent's workshop was crammed with the metals and stones and tools of his trade. Shelves and shelves of jewelry lined the walls—completed work, work in progress.

By early evening I found myself exhausted from the fresh air. Not long after the children went to bed, I apologized to Vincent and Lily, explaining I could barely keep my eyes open. They understood, assuring me it was normal in the mountains. They warned me, cheerfully, that I would take a few days to adjust. I excused myself and went off to find my bed.

My room was simply furnished but very comfortable. A fine, bamboo mat separated my mattress from the immaculate tile floor. I had noticed earlier in the day that there were no beds in the house. I was too exhausted to think about this fact. I unpacked my bag. A few moments later, there was a gentle knock at the door.

Lily stood in the doorway, holding a glass with a steaming, green beverage.

"My famous sleep tea," she handed me the glass. "Not that I think you'll need it tonight!" She laughed lightly.

I took the glass and thanked her.

"There is something else," she stepped into the room. "Please, your mattress, it should face east." She glanced quickly at the mattress, then turned back, apparently satisfied that everything was in order. "It's very important that we all face the same direction, to be on the same night waves. This ensures a sound, restful sleep and harmony in the house." She smiled confidently.

"Sounds good to me," I said.

She was about to leave the room when I asked her why it had to be east.

"For Jerusalem, of course." Lily closed the door behind herself.

Jerusalem? I drank the tea, quickly. It was pleasant enough, and I was too exhausted for another thought.

The next morning, I lay in bed, wondering why a mattress on an Argentine mountain had to face Jerusalem. I was baffled. Israeli events had certainly been dominating the news lately, especially the endless conflicts over the issue of a Palestinian homeland. But clearly the mattresses in this house faced east despite these current events. What was the connection? Vincent and I were indeed descendants of a Jewish family. But that was the past, and long ago. Like so many Argentine family histories, time and the natural process of assimilation had eroded away our differences, our memories. As for Lily, I remembered Vincent telling us years ago that she'd come from a long line of Dutch Calvinists. On a visit to Holland, she had taken him to a church in Leiden and shown him her family's history—the births, the deaths recorded in a large, somber book. I decided the mattresses facing east might have more to do with Lily's holistic interests rather than with religion.

When I finally got out of bed, Lily and the children were cheerful and alert and had been up for hours. The boys were happily building a sand house under the fig tree, while Lera played with a rabbit beside the kitchen door. Lily made me breakfast and apologized for running off, but said she must tend to a patient who was waiting in the herb shed. I poked about the kitchen while I drank my coffee. Lily was organized in her storage system, and the cupboards were neat and tidy. Canned goods, spices and herbs, teas, pastas, flours. On the very top shelf, among the displayed plates, cow bells, and antique metal platters, I noticed a brass candelabra. It had eight branches and a higher, central holder. I thought I recognized the Jewish star perched in the middle, between the branches, but I wasn't certain.

Finishing my coffee, I wandered off to find Vincent, who was in his workshop. I soon learned that my cousin, while almost always cheerful and in good humor, was no more of a conversationalist than he'd ever been. In fact, in response to some of my questions about their daily life, their plans and goals, he said he wasn't sure, but that I should ask Lily because she remembered and knew everything.

Over the next few days, while taking part in family life—helping Lily tend the garden and animals, playing with the children, and making the occasional trip into the village for necessities—I noticed that Lily had many peculiar "rules," like the one about the mattresses facing east. Certain foods should never be mixed, certain beverages never consumed after sundown. With every meal, more and more herbs crept into the food. I could not help feeling she had restrained herself in the beginning of my visit, but as the days passed, she reverted to the pull of her strong, eccentric nature with respect to food and other things.

One afternoon, as I passed her herb shed while she was tending to a patient, I heard Lily reciting incantations in a low, monotone voice. I listened for a few moments, then cautiously peered into the small window. Lily stood at her table, leaning over a steaming cup and a single lit candle. She held back her long hair with one hand, while the other made circular motions toward her face, over the cup and flame. She stopped, straightened up, covered her eyes with her hands for a moment, and then continued the circular motions toward her face, her eyes closed. The patient sat on the other side of the table. She was a very plump, middle-aged woman, wide eyed and perspiring. She kept one hand pressed into the side of her belly.

Later, with some hesitation, I asked Lily about the woman. To my surprise, Lily was not at all upset that I'd heard and seen what she was doing, nor that I asked. In fact, she quite willingly told me about the patient. After all, it was her work, she said. The poor lady suffered from gall bladder attacks, and Lily was treating her for nerves.

"The tea," she said, "had three grains of wheat, two of barley, one sprig of mint, and a bit of thread from an article of clothing the woman was wearing."

"Did she drink it all?" I asked.

Lily threw back her head and laughed. "It was not to drink," she said, "but to read. When I read the tea, the tiny air currents created by my words help align the grains and the thread. Once properly aligned, her nervous condition will abate."

"So, Lily, tell me why alignment, in all things, is so necessary?"

"Now you're teasing me." She looked serious.

"No, I'm quite earnest. Please, an explanation."

"Perhaps someday. Now I must prepare our dinner."

That evening, I asked Lily and Vincent if they didn't miss talking to people, or hearing news, or reading newspapers. I knew that occasionally they went down to Mendoza to sell the jewelry and herbs, but the trips were not frequent. I was beginning to feel constrained by this life style. I longed for entertainment—television, a movie, perhaps a restaurant or even a bar.

"Why would we? We are content with our own company," Lily said confidently, smiling graciously. "Why would we want to hear news, if all the news is so depressing and violent?"

"But don't you want to keep abreast? Don't you feel this kind of life is a form of escapism?"

Lily frowned, and I saw a nervousness pass over Vincent's face.

"Did I ask the wrong thing?"

"Of course not!" Vincent laughed out. "Lily, let's have some tea," he suggested.

Lily nodded silently and quickly left for the kitchen.

I had asked the wrong thing.

"You know," Vincent said, casually changing the subject as he leaned across the low table for a handful of almonds, "you still haven't told us about the family in Buenos Aires. We don't often get news, and I'd like to hear how everyone is doing."

And so I told him.

That night, I turned my mattress around. I don't really know why, but I did.

The next morning, Lily would not look at me. She was troubled and nervous and finally went out and sat under an almond tree to sip one of her teas, silently. She remained there for hours, alone. She did not go out to the herb shed; she did not tend to the house or make meals. Even the children were not themselves. They fought and argued all morning. This was most unusual. I helped them prepare lunch, and that seemed to help a bit. I didn't see Vincent all day. I decided he was hiding.

Finally, in the late afternoon, I approached Lily and offered my apology. "Whatever I've said or done, Lily, please forgive me. I meant no harm."

She looked up at me, her dark eyes angry and hot. "Your family is all the same!" She shot out.

"My family?" I asked, surprised.

"Yes, your family! All you Hernáns. You stand in judgment of us, all of you. Parents, uncles, aunts, cousins! You criticize because we have chosen to live on a mountain. You suggest we are not facing reality, that we hide. You're great ones to talk! In three generations you have managed to erase your roots and deny your heritage!"

"What are you talking about, Lily? What roots, what heritage?"

"See, you need to ask! You don't even know or understand what brought Vincent to Mendoza in the first place, do you? Has your family ever thought about that or discussed it? Have they ever wondered, why Mendoza?"

"I don't know, Lily. I guess I've never heard any talk about that."

"Right. Well, let me tell you! His heritage, that's what!"

"Lily, I honestly don't know what you're talking about."

"Come with me!" Lily stood up, grabbed me by the hand and pulled me toward the house, like a child.

I followed, speechless.

In the kitchen, she stood on a ladder, reached carefully for the brass candelabra on the top shelf, and brought it down.

"Do you know what this is?" Lily asked, placing it on the table. I shook my head.

"For shame!" Lily said sadly. "This is Malke Silberman's Chanukah menorah. She took it from her family home in Moisés Ville, when she ran off with your great-grandfather. You do know that Malke Silberman was your great-grandmother?"

Although I nodded quickly, I would not have remembered her name had Lily not mentioned it. "How did you get it?" I asked, quietly.

"Vincent came to Mendoza to find the spirit of his great-grandmother. He could not find it in Buenos Aires. No one would help him. Your father and uncles seem determined to remember nothing. Here, he was able to track down your grand-uncle, David, Malke's eldest son, and the only member of the family who did not leave Mendoza for the capital. You do know you had a grand-uncle living in Mendoza until three years ago?" Lily stared at me.

"I know that my great-grandparents had four sons." I volunteered. "When I was younger, I used to hear my father occasionally speak about the older people, but that was years ago. I don't remember anything about this uncle, and I don't know if anyone in Buenos Aires kept in touch with him." I hoped Lily was satisfied.

"I can tell you that your Grand-uncle David was very lonely. He never married and cared for his parents until they died. Before he died three years ago, he gave Vincent the menorah and told him he was now the keeper of the faith and thus, the keeper of the family. We became very close." Lily said quietly.

"Are you practicing Jews?" I asked, bewildered.

"How can we be practicing Jews on an Andean mountain?" Lily finally smiled.

I smiled back.

"No. What we learned from Uncle David, we are blending into our lives, our ways." Lily said humbly. "We follow the laws of ancient

Judaism, inasmuch as they fit our system. We do not observe the holidays, but we bring their depth of meaning to our own celebrations. I do not keep the Sabbath, or light Sabbath candles, but I recite prayers over my teas to help my family and my patients."

Anger and impatience rushed me. I don't know why. I had no stake in any of this. I decided that the weeds drying in Lily's shed must be choking her brain. Lily was a charming girl, but I'd never heard such a pile of nonsense. It was hard for me to believe that what she was doing to and for Judaism was better than our neglect.

Herbalist and soothsayer, Lily sensed my thoughts. Like a child, she became pouty and silent, then mean and taunting.

"Do you know that your own father once denied to me that there is, or ever was, anti-Semitism in this country?" Lily looked at me, waiting.

"How would I know that?" I asked impatiently. "I've never discussed the topic with him. I don't get hung up on these things, Lily. This is a progressive, assimilated country."

"Right." She said sarcastically, turning away from me for a second to glance out the window. When her eyes found the children, still playing, she turned back.

"And I suppose you're going to tell me," her voice quavered, "there is no Argentine prejudice, no hatred, no anti-Semitism because everyone has assimilated!" Lily's face was anxious. Her fingers nervously twisted the gauzy material at the hem of her loose blouse. She continued.

"Jews ought to be hung up on these things! Why should a Dutch Protestant have to make a Jew understand that? In that same discussion, your father insisted that Tragic Week had nothing to do with anti-Semitism. That's a pretty tough one to swallow, don't you think?"

"Lily, I am neither a Jew nor a student of Argentine Jewish history. I don't even know what Tragic Week was, or when it was."

"Well, you should be a Jew, and you should know about Tragic Week!" She had worked herself into a state. Her face was flushed and her words fired out with a clip.

"You should because it was the only pogrom that ever took place in all the Americas, and it occurred in Buenos Aires, in 1919! Buenos Aires, the *Paris of South America!*" Lily said smartly.

"All right, Lily, all right! Peace." I held up my hands. "Peace?"

She said nothing.

"Tell me, Lily, when did Vincent become interested in Judaism?"

For a few moments there was silence.

"When he met me." Lily's voice was calm now, her face cool. When she spoke again, her words were poignant, slow, and certain. "Someone has to learn and remember!" She pleaded, with dignity. "There have to be some keepers, among the losers."

Perhaps she was right.

A few days later, I left Vincent and Lily and the children. We all knew the time had come. I parted on good terms, and Vincent embraced me warmly, saying I was always welcome in their home. Lily agreed. When we kissed good-bye, she whispered that I should never have turned my mattress around.

I reached the Mendoza train station in good time and found I had an hour before my train departed for Buenos Aires. I hurried to the bar for a drink. I sat at the crowded counter, relishing the noise and the smoke, and the sound of the television above my head. I drank half my beer before I glanced up at the television screen, and the Buenos Aires news. The death toll had climbed to ninety-two from the bombing.

"What bombing?" I asked, shocked.

"At the Jewish community center, the AMIA building downtown." The man beside me said, shaking his head and watching the television.

The camera was focused on the rubble of the seven-story

building. It was a bright, sunny day. The reporter stood with his microphone beside relief workers, stretcher bearers. It might be days, he said, before the debris would be cleared away, days before they could come up with a final count of the dead and missing. The reporter reminded his television audience of the terrorist attack on the Israeli embassy in Buenos Aires two years before. Explosives, a planted truck, twenty-nine dead. A mourner with a bandage wrapped around his head walked in front of the camera and paused, disoriented, beside the reporter. The reporter held out his microphone. "Why us?" the mourner asked. "What did we do?"

A Lebanese Islamic radical group, Ansarallah—a branch of Hezbollah—had already claimed responsibility. They had issued a statement saying that they would continue until the Zionists were wiped out and justice prevailed in the world.

"When did it happen?" I asked.

"Two days ago." The voice beside me answered. Then the man turned to me, annoyed. "The whole world knows. Where have you been?"

"In the mountains," I answered. "Learning about keepers."

THE RIFKE CHRONICLES

From the final volume.

December 1946
Moisés Ville

I'm delighted to report that I've been back in Moisés Ville for two years now! I followed the advice of the Rosenvitch family, and I've retired here. They have been extremely kind and insist I am to participate in all family celebrations. I do not argue, it is my pleasure! I celebrated my seventy-fifth birthday last month. I've purchased a house with a small garden. I have a eucalyptus in the front and a paradise tree in the back. This is the first property I've ever owned. Papa would have been proud. He always wanted to own land. My house is near the teachers' seminary, which was established three years ago and has already become enormously important in the education of Hebrew teachers. From here, they go to all corners of the country. I have more room than I need in my house, so I generally have one of the two spare bedrooms occupied by a student teacher studying at the seminary. I feel good about this, as though I still have a finger in the pie!

I was saddened to hear last month of Estelle Ramírez's death. She died peacefully in her sleep, in her garden. She had gone out to sit in her arbor after lunch, and they found her in her wicker chair, smiling, a cluster of grapes in her hands. Shortly after, Pablo, still grieving over the loss of his grandmother, came up to visit me for my birthday. He brought Peshke with him. He is kind to do this, for he realizes that there is no one else who will take the time with Peshke, except for Moses Soltansky. Moses has promised to visit next month. Now that he has retired from his detective work, and never having married, he has all the time in the world, he tells me. Peshke loves it here; she says the dry heat does wonders for her rheumatism. She comes for long stays and we thoroughly enjoy ourselves. She does not mind leaving her husband for these spells because she knows he is well looked after. The children have truly been devoted and loving to their parents.

When the war ended last year, Peshke was here, and we went to the Kadima Theater to celebrate the Allied victory. All of Moisés Ville crowded into the theater for speeches and singing and food. With the relative prosperity and stability of the last few years, Moisés Ville has been transformed from an Old World religious town to a modern society. While there are still four synagogues that function formally, basically people only attend them at the High Holidays. Indeed, at other times, it's hard to get a *minyan*. There are religious schools and government schools. The libraries and theater are extremely active. In the last eight years or so, there has been an influx of German Jewish refugees, and they've become well established in the functioning of the colony. There has also been a tremendous effort made to bring back colonists' children who've gone off to the cities, usually for higher education. Julio is one of these, but he only returns for visits.

Pablo, on the other hand, comes up frequently, and I am very grateful for our closeness. Since his Grandmother Estelle's death, he seems to have a special need to be with me. I am the bridge to his past, to his grandfather and to his father as a young man. Pablo attends the School of Fine Arts in Buenos Aires and has become quite serious about his painting. He tells me his father, Julio, worries about him because he feels he may never be able to make a living as an artist. Pablo does not believe me when I tell him David Kaminski, from Cordoba, is an old friend of mine. He would believe me even less if I told him that I did not marry Kaminski because of his Grandfather Henoch!

One day, for fun, I pulled out Henoch's old drawing for my special shoe. Pablo was fascinated by it, studying it carefully, turning it upside down and every which way.

He said his grandfather had been quite a draftsman, and he wondered if he'd ever made drawings for anything else. I told him I remembered sketches for farm machinery, and that perhaps they still existed among his belongings at the farm. I gave him the shoe drawing. I don't need it anymore. I don't know why I've kept it all these years; by now I can explain the design with my eyes closed!

I do not lack for things to do. My days are full and content. I help Henoch's sons in any way I can, and two afternoons a week I help at the Baron Hirsch Library. So I have come full circle. I started my adult life in Moisés Ville working in the library, and I will end my days doing the same!

Probably the most exciting news of all is a letter I received last week. It is a long and complicated story, with many twists and turns, but my brother, Chaim, is alive, and has been living in Palestine for the last forty-five years! He writes that he is well, that he's been a printer all his life, and his wife a teacher. Sadly, they never had a family. He says that everyone is hoping and waiting for the day that Israel is declared a state. He feels it is not long off. The July bombing at the King David Hotel in Jerusalem, killing ninety-one people, made it very clear that Jews will stop at nothing. When Israel has been declared a state, he will gladly leave his country and travel to Argentina for a visit, so that we might be reunited. I wouldn't be at all surprised to hear Chaim had been active in the underground against the British.

Chaim sent me a photograph of a short, squat man—I'd forgotten I was taller than all my siblings—and an even shorter woman, standing outside their home in Jerusalem. The light in the photograph is a brilliant white, no doubt from the sun and the sea. Chaim is wearing dark trousers, a short-sleeved white shirt, open at the neck, sunglasses, and a hat. I try and try, but I cannot recognize him. Nothing. I wish the photo had been just of his face.

He also sent me a very old photograph of a pretty young woman with black hair and intense, dark eyes. The backdrop is a velvet curtain, and her left foot is raised onto a cushion. The bottom of the mat has the photography studio's imprint, *Michal Greim*. On the back, I recognize "Kamenets Podolsk, July 1889," in my own handwriting, and something about Papa's cart and a heat wave.

November 30, 1947
Moisés Ville

Yesterday the U.N. voted on the resolution for an independent Israel. The vote passed thirty-three to thirteen, with ten abstentions. Peshke and I were glued to the radio! We here in Moisés Ville understand that last night Jews in Palestine danced in the streets for joy!

This afternoon we will all go to the plaza to celebrate. There will be speeches and a band, a picnic and a dance! Peshke and I are thrilled to be part of this momentous event. The only remaining thing will be for the British to leave Palestine and for Israel to be declared a state. Then I can look forward to a visit from my brother, Chaim.

Tomorrow, I will write of how the festivities went!

January 1948
Buenos Aires

On the morning of December 1, 1947, in the colony of Moisés Ville, Santa Fe, Peshke Milekofsky was unable to awaken her long-time friend, Rifke Schulman. Death at the age of seventy-seven was attributed to heart failure.

Except for a few personal items left to her friend, Peshke, Pablo Rosenvitch was the inheritor of Rifke Schulman's estate.

Obituaries in the Moisesviler Tribune, as well as in the Colonist-cooperator, and Di Idishe Tzeitung from Buenos Aires, all paid tribute to the "immigrant's angel," as she had come to be known. It was stated that her work and perseverance will be missed not only by the colony of Moisés Ville, but by the entire Jewish community of Argentina—the many who came within the sphere of her assistance, understanding, and steadfast devotion.

Author's Note

Events occurred, places exist, but Rifke Schulman and her chronicles are invented, not discovered. The stories, interspersed with the journal entries, are also works of fiction.